This is a wonderful book.
Yeah it was Tom-rrific

Good Night,
Mr. Tom

Good Night, Mr. Tom

Michelle Magorian

HARPER & ROW, PUBLISHERS

NEW YORK

Cambridge
Hagerstown
Philadelphia
San Francisco

1817

London
Mexico City
São Paulo
Sydney

Good Night, Mr. Tom

Copyright © 1981 by Michelle Magorian

First published in England by Kestrel Books, Penguin Books Ltd.
All rights reserved.
Printed in
the United States of America. For information address
Harper & Row, Publishers, Inc., 10 East 53rd Street,
New York, N.Y. 10022.

Library of Congress Cataloging in Publication Data
Magorian, Michelle.
    Good night, Mr. Tom

    Summary: A battered child learns to embrace life
when he is adopted by an old man in the English country-
side during the second World War.
    [1. World War, 1939-1945—England—Fiction.   2. Coun-
try life—Fiction.   3. Child abuse—Fiction.   4. England
—Fiction]   I. Title.
PZ7.M275Go 1982   [Fic]   80-8444
ISBN 0-06-024078-4   AACR2
ISBN 0-06-024079-2 (lib. bdg.)

To My Father

Contents
—— ※ ※ ——

Meeting   1
Little Weirwold   15
Saturday Morning   30
Equipped   44
Chamberlain Announces   59
Zach   72
An Encounter over Blackberries   84
School   96
Birthday Boy   106
The Case   116
Friday   134
The Show Must Go On   147
Carol Singing   160
New Beginnings   165
Home   178
The Search   199
Rescue   213
Recovery   236
The Sea, the Sea, the Sea!   255
Spooky Cott   271
Back to School   285
Grieving   293
Postscript   308

Good Night, Mr. Tom

Meeting

"Yes," said Tom bluntly, on opening the front door. "What d'you want?"

A harassed middle-aged woman in a green coat and felt hat stood on his step. He glanced at the armband on her sleeve. She gave him an awkward smile.

"I'm the Billeting Officer for this area," she began.

"Oh yes, and what's that got to do wi' me?"

She flushed slightly. "Well, Mr., Mr. . . . ."

"Oakley. Thomas Oakley."

"Ah, thank you, Mr. Oakley." She paused and took a deep breath. "Mr. Oakley, with the declaration of war imminent . . ."

Tom waved his hand. "I knows all that. Git to the point. What d'you want?" He noticed a small boy at her side.

"It's him I've come about," she said. "I'm on my way to your village hall with the others."

"What others?"

She stepped to one side. Behind the large iron gate that stood at the end of the graveyard was a small group of children. Many of them were filthy and very poorly clad. Only a handful had a blazer or coat. They all looked bewildered and exhausted.

The woman touched the boy at her side and pushed him forward.

"There's no need to tell me," said Tom. "It's obligatory and it's for the war effort."

"You are entitled to choose your child, I know," began the woman apologetically.

Tom gave a snort.

"But," she continued, "his mother wants him to be with someone who's religious or near a church. She was quite adamant. Said she would only let him be evacuated if he was."

"Was what?" asked Tom impatiently.

"Near a church."

Tom took a second look at the child. The boy was thin and sickly looking, pale with limp sandy hair and dull gray eyes.

"His name's Willie," said the woman.

Willie, who had been staring at the ground, looked up. Round his neck, hanging from a piece of string, was a cardboard label. It read "William Beech."

Tom was well into his sixties, a healthy, robust, stockily built man with a head of thick white hair. Although he was of average height, in Willie's eyes he was a towering giant with skin like coarse, wrinkled brown paper and a voice like thunder.

He glared at Willie. "You'd best come in," he said abruptly.

The woman gave a relieved smile. "Thank you so much," she said, and she backed quickly away and hurried down the tiny path towards the other children. Willie watched her go.

"Come on in," repeated Tom harshly. "I ent got all day."

Nervously, Willie followed him into a dark hallway. It took a few seconds for his eyes to adjust from the brilliant sunshine he had left to the comparative darkness of the cottage. He could just make out the shapes of a few coats hanging on some wooden pegs and two pairs of boots standing below.

"S'pose you'd best know where to put yer things," muttered Tom, looking up at the coat rack and then down at Willie. He scratched his head. "Bit 'igh fer you. I'd best put in a low peg."

He opened a door on his left and walked into the front room, leaving Willie in the hallway still clutching his brown carrier bag. Through the half-open door he could see a large black cooking stove with a fire in it and an old threadbare armchair nearby. He shivered. Presently Tom came out with a pencil.

"You can put that ole bag down," he said gruffly. "You ent goin' no place else."

Tom handed him the pencil. He stared blankly up at him.

"Go on," said Tom. "I told you before, I ent got all day. Now make a mark so's I know where to put a peg, see." Willie made a faint dot on the wall beside the hem of one of the large coats. "Make a nice big un so's I can see it clear, like." Willie drew a small circle and filled it in. Tom leaned down and peered at it. "Neat little chap, ent you? Gimme yer mackintosh and I'll put it on top o' mine fer now."

With shaking fingers Willie undid his belt and buttons, peeled off the mackintosh and held it in his arms. Tom took it from him and hung it on top of his greatcoat. He walked back into the front room "Come on," he said. Willie followed him in.

It was a small, comfortable room with two windows. The front one looked out onto the graveyard, the other onto a little garden at the side. The large black stove stood solidly in an alcove in the back wall, a thick dark pipe curving its way upward through the ceiling. Stretched out beneath the side window were a few shelves filled with books, old newspapers and odds and ends, and by the front window stood a heavy wooden table and two chairs. The flagstoned floor was covered with a faded crimson, green and brown rug. Willie glanced at the armchair by the stove and the objects that lay on top of the small wooden table beside it: a pipe, a book and a tobacco jar.

"Pull that stool up by the fire and I'll give you somethin' to eat." Willie made no movement. "Go on, sit down, boy," he repeated. "You got wax in your ears?"

Willie pulled a small wooden stool from a corner and sat down in front of the fire.

Tom cooked two rashers of bacon and placed a slab of bread, with the fresh bacon drippings beside it, on a plate. He put it on the table with a mug of hot tea. Willie watched him silently, his bony elbows and knees jutting out angularly beneath his thin gray jersey and shorts. He tugged nervously at the tops of his woolen socks and a faint smell of warm rubber drifted upwards from his white sneakers.

"Eat that up," said Tom.

Willie dragged himself reluctantly from the warmth of the fire and sat at the table. "You can put yer own sugar in," Tom grunted.

Willie politely took a spoonful, dunked it into the large white mug of tea and stirred it. He bit into the bread, but a large lump in his throat made swallowing difficult. He didn't feel at all hungry, but remembered apprehensively what his mum had said about doing as he was told. He stared out at the graveyard. The sun shone brilliantly, yet he felt cold. He gazed at the few trees around the graves. Their leaves were all different colors—pale greens, amber, yellow . . .

"Ent you 'ungry?" asked Tom from his armchair.

Willie looked up startled. "Yes, mister," he whispered.

"Jest a slow chewer, that it?"

He nodded timidly and stared miserably at the plate. Bacon was a luxury. Only lodgers or visitors had bacon, and here he was not eating it.

"Mebbe you can chew it more easy later." Tom beckoned him over to the stool. "Put another spoon of that sugar in, boy, and bring that tea over 'ere."

Willie did so and returned to the stool. He held the warm mug tightly in his icy hands and shivered. Tom leaned towards him.

"What you got in yer bag, then?"

"I dunno," mumbled Willie. "Mum packed it. She said I weren't to look in." One of his socks slid halfway down his leg, revealing a large multicolored bruise on his shin and a swollen red sore beside.

"That's a nasty ole thing," Tom said, pointing to it. "What give you that?" Willie pulled the sock up quickly.

"Best drink that afore it gits cold," said Tom, sensing that the subject needed to be changed. Willie looked intently at the fire and slowly drank the tea.

Tom stood up. "I gotta go out for a spell. Then I'll fix your room, see. Up there," he pointed to the ceiling. "You ent afraid of heights, are you?" Willie shook his head. "That's good, or you'd have had to sleep under the table." He bent over the stove and shoveled some fresh coke into the fire.

" 'Ere's an ole scarf of mine," he muttered, and he threw a khaki object over Willie's knees. He noticed another bruise on the boy's thigh, but said nothing. " 'Ave a wander round the graveyard. Don't be scared of the dead. Least they can't drop an ole bomb on yer head."

"No, mister," agreed Willie politely.

"And close the front door behind you, else Sammy'll be eatin' yer bacon."

"Yes, mister."

Willie heard him slam the front door and listened to the sound of his footsteps gradually fading. He hugged himself tightly and rocked backwards and forwards on the stool. "I must be good," he whispered urgently, "I must be good," and he rubbed a sore spot on his arm. He was such a bad boy. Mum said she was kinder to him than most mothers. She only gave him soft beatings. He shuddered. He was dreading the moment when Mr. Oakley would discover how wicked he was. He was stronger-looking than Mum.

The flames in the stove flickered and danced before his eyes. He turned to look for something that was missing. He stood up and moved towards the shelves under the side window. There, he was being bad again, putting his nose in where it didn't belong. He looked up quickly to make sure Mr. Oakley wasn't spying at him through the window.

Mum said war was a punishment from God for people's sins, so he'd better watch out. She didn't tell him what to watch out for, though. It could be in this room, he thought, or maybe the graveyard. He knelt on one of the chairs at the front window and peered out. Graves didn't look so scary as she had made out, even though he knew that he was surrounded by dead bodies. But what was it that was missing? A bird chirruped in the garden. Of course, that was it. He couldn't hear traffic and banging and shouting. He looked around at the room again. He eyes rested on the stool where the woolen scarf lay. He'd go outside. He picked it up, and wrapping it around his neck, he went into the hall and closed the front door carefully behind him.

Between him and the graveyard lay a small flat garden. Along the edge of it were little clusters of flowers. Willie stepped forward to the edge where the garden ended and the graveyard began. He plunged his hands deep into his pockets and stood still for a moment.

The graveyard and cottage with its garden were surrounded by a rough stone wall, except for where the back of the church stood. Green moss and wild flowers sprang through the gray stonework. Between the graves lay a small, neat flagstoned pathway down the center. It broke off in two directions—one towards a large gate on the left where the other children had waited, and one leading to the back entrance of a small church to his right. A poplar tree stood in the far corner of the graveyard near the wall with the gate, and another near Mr. Oakley's cottage by the edge of the front garden. A third grew by the exit of the church; but the tree that caught Willie's attention was a large oak tree. It stood in the center of the graveyard by the path, its large, well-clad branches curving and hanging over part of it.

He glanced down at a small stone angel near his feet and began to walk round the gravestones. Some were so faded that he could barely see the shapes of the letters. Each grave had a character of its own. Some were well tended, with little vases of flowers; some were covered with large stone slabs, while others had weeds growing higgledy-piggledy over them. The ones Willie liked best were the gentle mounds covered with grass, with the odd surviving summer flower peeping through the colored leaves. As he walked around, he noticed that some of the very old ones were tiny. Children's graves, probably.

He was sitting on one Elizabeth Thatcher when he heard voices. A young man and woman were passing by. They were talking and laughing. They stopped and the young woman leaned over the wall. Her long fair hair hung in a single plait scraped back from a round, pink-cheeked face. Pretty, he thought.

"You're from London, ent you?" she said.

He stood up and removed his hands from his pockets. "Yes, miss."

"You're a regular wild bunch, so I've heard," and she smiled.

The young man was in uniform. He stood with his arm around her shoulder.

"How old are you, then?" she asked.

"Eight, miss."

"Polite little lad, ent you? What's your name?"

"William Beech, miss."

"You can stop calling me miss. I'm Mrs.—Mrs. Hartridge." The young man beamed. "I'll see you on Monday at school. I expect you'll be in my class. Good-bye, William."

" 'Bye, miss, Mrs.," he whispered.

He watched them walk away. When they were out of sight he sat back down on Elizabeth Thatcher, tugged at a handful of grass and pulled it from the earth. He'd forgotten all about school. He thought of Mr. Barrett, his form master in London. He spent all day yelling and shouting at everyone and rapping knuckles. He dreaded school normally. Mrs. Hartridge didn't seem like him at all. He gave a sigh of relief and rubbed his chest. That was one ordeal he didn't think would be too terrifying to face. He glanced at the oak tree. It seemed a sheltered, secluded sort of place. He'd go and sit beneath its branches.

As he walked towards it he tripped over a hard object. It was a tiny gravestone hidden by a clump of grass. He knelt down and pushed the grass to one side to look at it. He pulled away at the grass, plucking it out in great handfuls from the soil. He wanted to make it so that people could see the stone again. It looked forgotten and lost. It wasn't fair that it should be hidden. He became quite absorbed in this task until he heard a scrabbling noise. He turned. Sniffing and scratching among the leaves at the foot of the tree was a squirrel. Willie recognized its shape from pictures he had seen, but he wasn't prepared for one that moved. He froze, terrified. The squirrel seemed quite unperturbed and went on scuffling about in the leaves, picking up nuts and titbits in its tiny paws. Willie stayed motionless, hardly breathing. The squirrel's black eyes darted in a lively manner from place to place. It was tiny, light gray in color, with a bushy tail that stuck wildly in the air as it poked its paws and head into the russet and gold leaves.

After a while Willie's shoulders relaxed. He wriggled his toes gingerly inside his sneakers. It seemed as though he had been crouching for hours, although it couldn't have been more than ten minutes.

The little gray fellow didn't seem to scare him as much, and he began to enjoy watching the squirrel. A loud sharp barking suddenly disturbed the silence. The squirrel leaped and disappeared. Willie sprang to his feet, hopping on one leg and gasping at the mixture of numbness and pins and needles in the other. A small black-and-white collie ran around the tree and into the leaves. It stopped in front of him and jumped up into the air. Willie was more petrified of the dog than he had been of the squirrel.

"Them poisonous dogs," he heard his mother's voice saying inside him. "One bite from them mutts and you're dead. They got 'orrible diseases in 'em." He remembered the tiny children's graves and quickly picked up a thick branch from the ground.

"You go away," he said, feebly, gripping it firmly in his hand. "You go away."

The dog sprang into the air again and barked and yapped at him, tossing leaves by his legs. Willie let out a shriek and drew back. The dog came nearer.

"I'll kill you."

"I wouldn't do that," said a deep voice behind him. He turned to find Tom standing by the outer branches. "He ent goin' to do you no 'arm, so I should jes' drop that if I was you."

Willie froze with the branch still held high in his hand. Sweat broke out under his armpits and across his forehead. Now he was in for it. He was bound to get a beating now. Tom came towards him, took the branch firmly from his hand and lifted it up. Willie automatically flung his arm across his face and gave a cry, but the blow he was expecting never came. Tom had merely thrown the branch to the other end of the graveyard, and the dog had gone dashing after it.

"You can take yer arm down now, boy," he said quietly. "I think you and I 'ad better go inside and sort a few things out. Come on." And with that he stepped aside for Willie to go in front of him along the path.

Willie walked shakily towards the cottage, his head lowered. Through blurred eyes he saw the tufts of grass spilling up between the small flat stones. The sweat trickled down the sides of his face and chest. His armpits stung savagely and a sharp pain stabbed at his stomach. He went through the front door and stood in the hallway, feeling the perspiration turn cold and clammy. Tom walked into the front room and stood waiting for him to enter.

"Don't dither out there," he said. "Come on in."

Willie did so, but his body felt as if it no longer belonged to him. It seemed to move of its own accord. Tom's voice grew more distant. It reverberated as if it was being thrown back at him from the walls of a cave. He sat down on the stool feeling numb.

Tom picked up a poker and walked across to the fire. Now I'm going to get it, Willie thought, and he clutched the seat of the stool tightly. Tom looked down at him.

"About Sammy," Willie heard him say. He watched him poke the fire and then he didn't hear any more. He knew that Tom was speaking to him, but he couldn't take his eyes off the poker. It sent the hot coke tumbling in all directions. He saw Tom's brown, wrinkled hand lift it out of the fire. The tip was red, almost white in places. He was certain that he was going to be branded with it. The room seemed to swim and he heard Tom's voice echoing. He watched the tip of the poker spin and come closer to him and then the floor came towards him and it went dark. He felt two large hands grip him from behind and push his head in between his knees until the carpet came into focus and he heard himself gasping.

Tom opened the front window and lifted him out through it.

"Breathe in deep," Willie heard him say. "Take in a good sniff."

He took in a gulp of air. "I'll be sick," he mumbled. "That's right, go on, I'm holding you. Take in a good sniff. Let yer throat open."

Willie drank in some more air. A wave of nausea swept through him and he vomited.

"Go on," he heard Tom say, "breathe in some more," and he was sick again and again until there was no more left inside him and he hung limply in Tom's arms.

Tom wiped his mouth and face with the scarf. The pain in Willie's stomach had gone, but he felt drained like a rag doll. Tom lifted him back into the cottage and placed him in his armchair. His small body sank comfortably into the old soft expanse of chair. His feet barely reached the edge of the seat. Tom tucked a blanket round him, drew up a chair by the fire and watched Willie fall asleep.

The tales he had heard about evacuees didn't seem to fit Willie. "Ungrateful" and "wild" were the adjectives he had heard used, or just plain "homesick." He was quite unprepared for this timid, sickly little specimen. He looked at the poker leaning against the stove.

" 'E never thought . . . No . . . surely not!" he murmured. "Oh, Thomas Oakley, where 'ave you landed yerself?" There was a sound of scratching at the front door. "More trouble," he muttered. He crept quietly out through the hallway and opened the door. Sammy bounded in and jumped around his legs, panting and yelping.

"Now you jes' shut that ole mouth," Tom whispered firmly. "There's someone asleep." He knelt down and Sammy leaped into his arms lathering his face with his tongue. "I don't need to 'ave a bath when you're around, do I?" Sammy continued to lick him until he was satisfied just to pant and allow his tail to flop from side to side.

Tom lifted him up and carried him into the front room. As soon as the dog saw Willie asleep in the chair, he began barking again. Tom put his finger firmly on his nose and looked directly into his eyes.

"Now you jes' take a rest and stop that." He picked up his pipe and tobacco jar from the little table and sat by the stove again. Sammy flopped down beside him and rested his head on one of Tom's feet.

"Well, Sam," Tom whispered, "I don't know nothin' about children, but I do know enough not to beat 'em and make 'em that scared." And he grunted and puffed at his pipe. Sammy stood up, wriggled in between Tom's legs and placed his paws on his stomach.

"You understand every blimmin' word I say, don't you? Least he ent goin' to bury bones in my sweet peas," he remarked, ruffling Sammy's fur. "That's one thing to be thankful about." He sighed, "S'pose I'd best see what's what." He rose and went into the hallway with Sammy padding after him. He took some steps and placed them under a small square trapdoor above him. He climbed up, pushed the trapdoor open and pulled down a long wooden ladder.

The ladder was of thick pine wood. It was a little over forty years old, but since his young wife, Rachel, had died soon after it was made, it had hardly been used. A thick cloud of dust enveloped his head as he blew on one of the wide wooden rungs. He coughed and sneezed.

"Like taking snuff," he muttered. "S'pose we'd best keep that ole ladder down fer a bit, eh, Sammy?"

He climbed down and opened the door opposite the front room. It led into his bedroom. Inside, a small chest of drawers with a mirror stood by the corner of the front window. Leaning up against the back wall was a four-poster bed covered with a thick quilt. At the foot of the bed, on the floor, lay a round basket with an old blanket inside. It was Sammy's bed, when he used it, which was seldom. A blue threadbare carpet was spread across the floor with bits of matting added by the window and bed.

Beside the bed was a fitted cupboard. Tom opened it. On the top two shelves, neatly stacked, were blankets and sheets, and on the third various belongings of Rachel's that he had decided to keep. He glanced swiftly at them. A black wooden paint box, brushes, a christening robe she had embroidered, some old photographs, letters and recipes. The christening robe had never been worn by his baby son, for he had died soon after his mother.

He picked up some blankets and sheets and carried them into the hall. "I'll be down for you in a minute, Sammy," he said as he climbed up the ladder. "You jes' hang on there a bit," and with that Sammy was left to watch his master slowly disappear through the strange new hole in the ceiling.

Little Weirwold

🌿 🌿

Willie gave a short start and opened his eyes. In a chair opposite sat Tom, who was drinking tea and looking at a book. Sammy, who had been watching Willie sleep, now stood up.

Tom looked up. "You feelin' better?" he asked. "You's lookin' better." He poured a mug of hot, sweet tea and handed it to him. " 'Ere, you git that down you."

Willie looked apprehensively at Sammy, who was sniffing his feet.

" 'E won't harm you," said Tom. " 'E's a spry ole thing, but he's as soft as butter, ent you, ole boy?" And he knelt down and ruffled his fur. Sammy snuggled up between his knees and licked his face. "See," said Tom, " 'e's very friendly." Willie tried to smile. "You want to learn somethin' wot'll make him happy?" Willie nodded. "Hold one of yer hands out, palm up, like that." Willie copied him. "That's so he knows you ent going to harm him, see. Now, hold it out towards him and tickle his chest." Willie leaned nervously forward and touched Sammy's fur. "That's the idea. You jes' keep doin' that."

Willie stroked him. His fur felt silky and soft. Sammy gave his fingers a long lick.

" 'E likes you, see. When he licks you, that's his way of sayin', 'I likes you and you makes me happy.' "

"Why does he sniff?" he asked, as Sammy crawled under the blanket to get to his legs.

" 'E likes to know what everythin' smells like so's he knows who to say hello to and who not."

"Stop it!" said Willie as Sammy put his nose into his crotch. "Naughty dog." Immediately Tom dragged him from under the blanket, and he began barking and chasing his tail. "You'm gettin' overexcited, Sam. 'E needs a good romp in the fields"—and he looked at Willie—and I reckon you do an' all, he thought.

Willie pushed the blanket to one side and slid onto the floor.

"Smells like rain," said Tom, leaning out of the front window. "You got boots?"

Willie shook his head. "No, mister."

"Best put yer mackintosh on, anyways."

The three of them trooped out into the hallway. Willie stared at the ladder.

"That's your room up there. Sort of attic."

"Mine?" He didn't understand. Did Mr. Oakley mean he was going to have a room to himself? Tom nodded. Sammy leaped up excitedly.

"Hang on a minute, Sam. We's jes' goin'."

Tom looked at Willie's mac on the way out and noticed how thin it was.

They walked down the pathway and out the gate, Sammy leading, Tom striding after him and Willie running to keep up with them. It was late afternoon now. The sun hung in a fiery ball above the trees. A mild breeze shook the leaves and a few dark clouds scudded across the sky. Sammy ran backwards and forwards barking ecstatically.

"That dog's half mad," Tom said to Willie, but found that he was talking to the air, for Willie was several yards behind, still trying to keep up, his cheeks flushed with the effort.

"You're a quiet 'un. Why didn't you tell me I was goin' too fast?" But Willie could not answer and only gasped incoherently.

Tom slowed down and Willie walked beside him. He stared up at the gruff old man who was so kind to him. It was all very bewildering. He looked down at Tom's heavy brown ankle boots, his thick navy overcoat and the green corduroy cap with the tufts of white hair sticking out at either side. A small empty haversack dangled over his shoulder.

"Mister," he panted. "Mister!" Tom looked down. "Can I carry your bag, mister?"

Tom mumbled something to himself and handed it to him. Willie hung on to it tightly with both hands.

The narrow road sloped gently upwards. Willie could just make out, in all the speed of their walking, the wild hedgerows flashing in low green lines beside him. It felt very unreal, like a muddled dream. When they reached the top of the hill Willie saw a row of small thatched cottages standing on either side of the road ahead. He tugged at Tom's sleeve.

"Mister," he gasped, "they got straw roofs."

"That's thatch," said Tom.

"Wot's . . ." But he bit his lip and kept silent.

Tom glanced down. "I got some pictures of them at home. We'll have a look at them tonight."

Across the road a plump, middle-aged woman with graying auburn hair was peering out of a window. She disappeared for an instant and opened her front door.

" 'Ello, Tom," she said, looking with curiosity at Willie.

He grunted. "Evening, Mrs. Fletcher. How are the boys, then?"

"Boys are doin' nicely."

"William," said Tom, "go and keep an eye on Sam. I'll be with you in a minute."

Willie nodded shyly and went after Sammy.

"Skinny ole scrap, ent he?" said the woman.

Tom gave another grunt.

"I didn't believe it was true when I heard," she continued. "I ent got room meself, but Mrs. Butcher got two to contend with. Girls, mind you, but they're regular tearaways, and Mrs. Henley, she had three last week and they keep runnin' away. Homesick, like."

"How's the knittin' coming on?" said Tom, changing the subject.

"What you talkin' about?" she said, leaning back and looking at him. "Since when have you been interested in my knittin'?"

"Since now," he replied shortly. He pushed his hands into his pockets and scraped one of his boots against a piece of stone. "Busy, are you?" he asked.

"No more 'n usual."

"Could do with a thick jersey. Not fer me, mind," and he looked at Willie trundling on ahead.

"You ent gotta clothe 'em, you know. They shoulda brought that with them."

"Well, he haven't," said Tom gruffly. "Can you knit me a jersey or can you not, that's what I'm askin'?"

"If that's what you want."

"And," he continued, "you don't know where I can get some good stout boots, small-like, and I don't want no commentary, jes' want to know."

"I'll ask around."

He mumbled his thanks and strode on up the road.

Mrs. Fletcher stood quite motionless and stared after him, until she was sure he was out of earshot. "Madge," she cried, running into the next cottage, "Madge, you'll die when I tell you. . . ."

The road leading through the row of cottages extended into a long stretch of open country with lanes leading off it. Inside the last cottage at the corner there was a small shop.

"Won't be long," said Tom, and he took the haversack from Willie and left him and Sammy sitting on the stone steps. Willie stared in amazement at the fields, his thin woolen socks heaped around his ankles. As Tom came out he became conscious of them again and quickly pulled them up. Sammy sniffed at the food in the bag and Tom tapped him tenderly on the nose.

"If I start gettin' me stride up agin," he said to Willie, "you jes' call out."

It was a long, quiet road, the silence broken only by the whirring of a tractor in the distance. They turned to the right and walked down a tiny lane.

Willie's attention was drawn to a small brown bird in one of the hedgerows. Tom stopped and put his finger to his lips and they stood and watched it hopping in and out among the changing leaves.

"That's a hedge sparrow," he whispered. "See its beak? Very dainty." The bird looked up and flew away. "And shy."

They continued down the lane towards a farm. Sammy was already sitting waiting for them, his tail thumping the ground impatiently from side to side. They pushed open the long wooden gate where he sat. It squeaked and jingled on its hinges as they swung it behind them. Tom led Willie round the back of a large, cream-colored stone house towards a wooden shed. A middle-aged man with corn-colored hair and the bluest eyes Willie had ever seen was sitting on a stool milking one of several cows. Willie gazed at the gentle way he fingered the teats and at the warm white liquid spurting down into a bucket underneath.

"Mister," he said, tugging at Tom's coat sleeve. "Mister, what's that?"

Tom was astounded. "Ent you never seen a cow?" But Willie didn't answer. He was too absorbed in watching the swollen udder decrease in size.

"I'll be wantin' extra milk from now on, Ivor," he said. Ivor nodded and glanced at Willie.

"One of them London lot?" he asked. Tom grunted. "You'd best take a jug with you. Roe's inside."

Tom tramped across the yard to the back of the house. He carried Sammy in his arms, as he had a habit of yapping at cows. Willie stayed to watch the milking.

A fresh-faced brunette woman in her thirties, wearing a flowery apron, opened the back door.

"Come in," she said. "You'll be wantin' extra milk."

"How d'you know?" said Tom.

"Lucy saw you comin' up the yard with him."

A chubby six-year-old with brown curly hair, earth smudged over two enormous pink cheeks, was standing at her side holding on to her skirt.

"Don't be so daft, girl," she said. "Go on, say hello to him. I got things to do."

She clomped down the steps and stood shyly beside Willie, twisting the hem of her dress in her hand till her knickers came into view.

"There ent much difference in size between them two," said Tom, observing them together. "I dunno what they do with little 'uns in that ole city." And he disappeared into the warmth of the kitchen.

———

After calling Willie several times and getting no response, he eventually gave up and tapped him on the shoulder.

" 'Ere, dreamer, you carry that," he said handing him a tin jug. "You can take a look if you've a mind."

Willie lifted the lid and peered in. Fresh milk. Lucy stared at him. She'd never seen a boy so thin and pale-looking. She still hadn't spoken and had only just, so she thought, heard his name.

" 'Bye, Dreema," she said suddenly, and turned and fled into the house.

"Where's that ole thing?" said Tom, looking round for Sammy. He caught sight of his black-and-white fur at the gate. He was sitting waiting for them with a bone in his mouth.

Willie looked at the front of the house. The woman called Roe was putting up some black material inside the front window.

"What's she doin'?" Willie asked.

"Puttin' her blackouts up, boy. We all got to do it from tonight."

Willie was about to ask why—but he knew that was rude, so he kept silent.

"It's so planes don't see where to bomb," continued Tom, as if he had read his thoughts. "Waste of time if you asks me. Reckon it'll all be over by Christmas, and anyways who'd want to bomb Li'l Weirwold. That's the name of this village," he added. "Little Weirwold." He looked up at the sky. It had suddenly become darker. "Best be movin'," he said, and set off at a jaunty pace back up the lane towards the main road. They had walked past the cottages and were halfway down the hill when the first drop of rain fell. As they neared the foot of the hill, the sky opened and a heavy torrent fell mercilessly down. It blinded Willie and trickled down inside the collar of his mackintosh. Tom buttoned his overcoat up to his neck and raised his collar. He looked down at the drenched figures of the boy and dog. Willie had to run to keep up with them. His sneakers were now caked with heavy clods of wet earth, and his jersey was already wet from his soaked mackintosh.

Willie and Tom ran up the pathway towards the cottage, through the graves and under the oak tree. They ran into the hall, Tom's boots clattering on the tiles. He shook the rain from his overcoat and cap and proceeded to undo his boots. Sammy stood on the mat shaking his fur by the open door. Willie struggled with his mackintosh. His fingers were mauve with the cold.

"You're soaked through," said Tom. He pointed to Willie's bespattered sneakers. "Take them ole canvas things off. Stay here while I put some newspapers down."

Willie pulled off the sneakers and stood in the dark hallway shivering helplessly, his teeth rattling inside his clamped jaw. After much shuffling from the living room Tom opened the door. He had laid newspaper in front of the range and was putting up blackouts at the windows. But for the glow of embers in the fire, there was almost total darkness. He lit a gas lamp that hung from the ceiling, and an oil lamp on the table.

"Stay on them newspapers. You too," he said to Sammy, who was sending out a constant spray of water with his tail.

He added some coke to the fire and left the room. Willie hopped on one leg and then on the other in front of it. Steam began to rise from his jersey and shorts. He heard the front door being closed, and Tom returned with his brown carrier bag. He placed it on the table and took out the contents.

There was one small towel, a piece of soap, a toothbrush, an old Bible and an envelope with "To whom it may concern" written on it. He looked under the towel for some nightclothes but there were none. He opened the envelope. Willie heard the paper being torn and turned to watch him. He knew the letter was from his mum. He checked that his wet socks were pulled up and stood very still.

"Dear Sir or Madam," the note read, "I asked if Willie could go and stay with God-fearing people so I hope he is. Like most boys he's full of sin but he's promised to be good. I can't visit him. I'm a widow and I haven't got the money. The war and that. I've put the belt in for when he's bad and I've sewn him in for the winter. I usually keep him in when I wash his clothes and I got them special for the cold weather so he should be alright. Tell him his Mum said he'd better be good. Mrs. Beech."

Tom folded the letter and put it into his pocket. He found the belt at the bottom of the bag. It was a brown leather one with a steel buckle. He put it back in the bag and took out the towel, soap and toothbrush. Willie stood with his back to the fire and stared uneasily up at him.

Tom was angry.

"While you're in my house," he said in a choked voice, "you'll live by my rules. I ent ever hit a child and if I ever do it'll be with the skin of me hand. You got that?"

Willie nodded.

"So we can forget the ole belt." And he lifted the bag from the table and took it out of the room. Willie turned to face the fire, his head bowed over the stove.

His shoulders felt tense, and the top of the stove hissed as a tear fell from his eye. He heard the door close behind him and hurriedly wiped his cheeks.

Tom put a bundle on the armchair. "Best get out of them wet things," he said, kneeling down beside Willie, "so's I can dry them for tomorrow."

Willie sniffed. Tom peeled off his wet jersey and shorts.

"And them socks," he said as Willie clung to the tops of them. He pulled them off. Tom said nothing. There was no need. Willie's arms and legs were covered with bruises, weals and sores. Tom went to pull off his undershirt. Willie flinched and touched the top of his arm.

"New one, eh?" he asked quietly.

Willie nodded and blushed.

"Best be careful then," and Tom tugged gently at the undershirt.

"It won't come off, mister," said Willie, and then Tom understood what his mother had written in the letter. His undershirt had been sewn to the waist of his undershorts.

"Soon settle that," said Tom, picking up a pair of scissors from the bookcase. Willie shrank backwards.

"I'll sew them back when you goes home. I promise." Still Willie didn't move. "I promise," he repeated.

Willie stepped forward and allowed him to snip away at the stitching.

He dried Willie's thin, bruised body, wrapped him up in a towel and sat him in the armchair. Taking an old flannel nightshirt from the bundle, he cut the bottom halves off the body and sleeves. He stood Willie on the armchair, took the towel away and placed the nightshirt over his head, cutting more until Willie's toes and hands came into view. He handed him a thick pair of woolen socks. The heels almost reached the back of Willie's knees. Willie gave a small, tense smile and watched Tom hang his clothes over a horse near the fire.

"You can dry Sammy with that ole towel," said Tom, indicating one lying on the armchair. Willie knelt down on the newspapers and began to dry him. Sammy stuck his nose in the air, delighted at such attention.

Tom unpacked the haversack and wandered round the room putting the groceries away. He put on potatoes, and after a while he cracked some eggs into a saucepan, adding milk and butter. Slicing a few large pieces of bread, he put one on the end of a long fork.

"You toasted bread afore?" he asked. Willie looked up at him and shook his head. " 'Ere, have a go," said Tom, handing him the fork.

Willie sat on the stool holding the fork in front of the fire, his long socks trailing across the floor. Beside his feet Tom placed a bowl filled with scraps of meat and biscuits for Sammy, who had already started chewing the end of one of the socks.

Willie placed the toasted bread on plates while Tom spooned a large quantity of steaming scrambled eggs onto them. A bowl of hot, buttered boiled potatoes stood in the middle of the table.

"You can sit down now," said Tom.

Willie picked up a potato in his hands, gasped and dropped it onto his plate. Feverishly he attacked the meal. His small elbows stuck out at the sides as he cut and ate food in a frenzy. When the meal was eaten, Tom unwrapped a small brown package that contained four pieces of dark, homemade ginger cake.

"One fer tonight; one fer tomorrow," said Tom, handing him a piece.

Willie had never eaten cake before. When he had finished it, he leaned back in his chair and, resting his hands on his stomach, he watched Sammy eat.

Tom heated some water on the stove for the dirty dishes.

"You can look through them books if you like," he said, indicating the shelves under the side window.

Willie got up from the table excitedly and moved towards them. Then he stopped and frowned. "I got to read the Bible," he said miserably.

Tom gave a grunt. "I'll tell you a Bible story meself. In me own way. That do you?"

"Yeh, thanks, mister."

"Pull out that pouffe to sit on."

"Pouffe?" said Willie.

Tom pointed to a low, round, cushiony type of seat next to the armchair.

Willie squatted down in front of the shelves and chose three books. He pulled out the pouffe and sat on it with them propped on his knees.

"Ent you goin' to open one then?" asked Tom.

"After me Bible."

Tom sat down in the armchair, and lit his pipe. He leaned back puffing at it, wondering which one to tell. Willie watched him and pulled his strange sacklike garment over his feet.

" 'Noah's Ark,' " exclaimed Tom. "That's a good un." He looked at the books Willie had chosen and picked some others from the bookcase with animal pictures in them. "Once, long ago," began Tom, and Willie leaned forwards to listen until finally he stood up and leaned on the arm of the armchair to get a closer look at the pictures. Tom mumbled on in his own way, a little flattered at the rapt attention he was receiving. The gas lamp hissed gently above them and the coke stirred softly in the stove. Even the rain outside seemed to cease falling so heavily.

When Tom had finished, he found Willie gazing at him with adoration. Feeling a little embarrassed, he quickly cleared his throat and glanced up at the clock.

He made Willie cocoa and left him with Sammy to look at the "straw roofs" while he went upstairs to put up more blackouts. Willie sat back on the pouffe and traced his finger over the pictures. He blew over his cocoa and gave Sammy some of the skin. Tom appeared at the door with a lamp and Sammy began to crawl between his legs.

"Thought you was being too good for it to last," Tom said as Sammy tugged at his trouser leg. "Give me the cocoa, William, and you carry the book."

Willie climbed up the ladder, but the enormous socks kept making him slip. After much balancing and juggling with cocoa, book and dog, they all three eventually reached the attic.

It was a tiny room, shaped rather like a ridge tent. The ceiling sloped downwards at both sides with a straight piece in the center. The wooden floor was covered by two mats. A small bed lay under one of the rafters, and blackouts were pinned on the slanting window beside it. Tom had swept the room clean and had fixed a lamp to a hook on the white plaster ceiling.

Beside the bed was a low wooden table. "For yer books and such," said Tom. He pointed to a china chamber pot on the floor at the end of the bed. "That's so's you don't have to go outside if you wants to go to the toilet," he explained.

The heat from the front room rose up through the floorboards, so that the room was warm. Willie crawled under the bed and curled up into a ball.

"What you doin'?" asked Tom. "You gets into it, not under it."

"Wot, right inside?" exclaimed Willie.

Tom drew back the sheets and Willie climbed in between them. He stroked the blankets with his hands.

Sammy, meanwhile, was standing impatiently at Tom's side, wagging his tail in lunatic fashion. "Go on, you daft dog," said Tom, and Sammy leaped onto the bed between Willie's arms and licked his face. Slowly Willie put his arms around him, gave a small cry and burst into tears.

"Sorry, mister," he blurted out, and he buried his head in the dog's fur.

Tom sat on the edge of the bed until the crying had subsided a little.

" 'Ere," he said, handing him a large white handkerchief. " 'Ave a blow in that."

Willie looked up shamefacedly. "I ain't ungrateful, mister, honest. I'm happy." And with that he gave another sob.

Tom nodded and Sammy licked his face.

"You can have the lamp lit fer ten minutes," he said, patting the dog, "but mind you behave yerself, Samuel."

He made his way downstairs to the front room and turned Willie's damp clothes around. His pipe was on the table. He picked it up and tapped the old tobacco out onto the stove.

"Best not get fond of the boy, Thomas," he muttered to himself. He sat back in the armchair and watched the smoke drifting upwards from his pipe towards the gas lamp. He glanced at Willie's thin gray clothes. S'pose another pair of socks and one of them balaclava hat things wouldn't come amiss, he thought. There were sounds of scrabbling from upstairs.

He climbed up the steps, pipe in mouth, grunted out a few words as he entered the attic and blew the lamp out, plunging them all into total darkness.

"Take them blacks down now," he mumbled, removing them from the window. "You warm enough?"

Willie raised his head. "Yeh," he answered, and he sank happily back into the soft white pillow. Tom stared out of the window and chewed the end of his pipe. He gave a little tap on the floor with his foot and then moved towards the bed and gently ruffled Willie's hair.

He was halfway down the hatch with Sammy in his arms when he remembered something. "Don't forget them ole prayers."

"No, mister," said Willie.

Tom paused for an instant. "And you'd best call me Tom. Good night and God bless." And with that he descended from view, closing the trapdoor behind him.

"Good night, Mister Tom," Willie whispered. He listened to the door downstairs close and slipped out of bed to look through the window. A crack of lightning lit up the whole sky.

"Not much use, these blackouts," Tom had said earlier in the evening. Still, it was fine, thought Willie, standing in the moonlight. He could just make out the two rows of cottages and the fields beyond them. A dog howled in the distance.

Underneath the attic, Tom sat in his armchair with Sammy collapsed across his feet. He held a large black wooden paint box on his lap. He raised the lid, gazed for an instant at the contents and quietly blew away the dust from the tops of the brightly colored pots.

Saturday Morning

When Willie awoke it was still very dark. The pain that had brought him sharply back to consciousness seared through his stomach. He held his breath and pushed his hand down the bed to touch his nightgown. It was soaking. It was then that he became aware that he was lying in between sheets. That's what they did to people after they had died, they laid them out in a bed. He sat up quickly and hit his head on the rafter. Crawling out of bed, doubled over with the pain in his gut, he hobbled over to the window and let out a frightened cry. He was in a graveyard. He was going to be buried alive! The pain grew in intensity. He gave a loud moan and vomited all over the floor.

In the morning Tom found him huddled under the bed. The sheets were drenched in urine. He stripped them off the mattress and carried Willie down to the living room.

It was a hot, sultry day. The windows were wide open but no breeze entered the cottage. Willie stood in front of the stove. Through the side window he could see his gray garments and underwear hanging on a small washing line outside. Tom pulled the voluminous nightshirt over his head and threw it into a copper tub with the sheets. He sluiced Willie's body tenderly with cold water and soap. The weals stuck out mauve against his protruding ribs and swollen stomach. He could hardly stand.

"Sorry, mister," he kept repeating, fearfully, "sorry, Mister Tom."

Tom just grunted in his usual manner.

He pulled Willie's clothes off the line and handed them to him. "Too hot for socks," he muttered. "Leave them off."

"I can't go aht wivout me socks," cried Willie in alarm. "Please, Mister Tom, I can't."

"Why?" Tom snorted.

"Me legs," he whispered. He didn't want everyone to see the marks of his sins. Tom sighed and threw the socks on the table. They had breakfast by the open window. Tom sat with his shirt sleeves rolled up, the beads of sweat trickling down the sides of his ruddy face, while Willie continued to shiver, managing to drink only half a cup of tea and eat a small piece of bread.

"Blimmin' blue," muttered Tom to himself as he observed Willie's face. He cleared the breakfast things and left him with the small addressed postcard that he had been provided with to write a message on for his mother. Willie sat dejectedly at the table and watched Tom drag his small mattress past the window. He could hear him scrubbing away at it. He lowered his head. He was so ashamed. Everyone who came near the church would see it and realize how wicked he had been. He hadn't meant to wet himself. He didn't even remember doing it.

He stared at the small postcard in front of him. Clasping a pencil between his fingers, he clenched his free hand into a fist and dug his knuckles into the table so that he wouldn't cry.

"How you gettin' on?" asked Tom.

Willie jumped and flushed hotly. "Can't think of what

to say, that it?" He took the pencil from Willie's hand and turned the postcard towards himself. "Not much room, eh?"

Willie tugged at his hair in embarrassment.

"Lost yer voice?"

"No, Mister Tom," he answered quietly.

"What d'you want to say, then?"

He shrugged his shoulders and looked dumbly at the grain on the wooden table.

"Are you happy here?"

He looked up quickly and nodded. "Yeh."

"Arrived safely, is happy and . . ."

"Mister, Mister Tom," said Willie, interrupting him. "You goin' to tell her I was bad?"

"No," Tom said, and went on writing. "Here, listen to this. 'Dear Mrs. Beech, William . . .' "

"She don't call me that. She calls me Willie."

He altered the word. " 'Willie,' " he continued, " 'has arrived safely, is happy and good. Yours sincerely, Mr. Thomas Oakley.' There." He handed the postcard and pencil back to him. "Now write yer name."

Willie paled. "I can't."

"Didn't they have school in London?"

"Yeh, but . . ." and he trailed off.

"How about readin'?" asked Tom. "You can read, can't you?"

"No."

"But you was lookin' at them books last night."

"I was lookin' at the pitchers."

Tom scratched his head. The village children were reading at least some words by the time they were six. This boy was eight, so he said. He glanced down at the label on the table to check. "William Beech. Born Sept. 7th, 1930."

"Nine on Thursdee," he remarked. "Your birthday's in five days' time." Willie didn't understand what was so particularly special about that.

"You're nine on Thursdee," Tom repeated, but Willie couldn't think of anything to say. "Anyways," he continued, "about this here schoolin', didn't yer teacher help you?"

"Yeh, but . . ." he hesitated. " 'E didn't like me. The others all called me Sillie Sissie Willie."

"What others?"

"At school."

"What about yer friends?"

He whispered something.

"I can't hear you, boy."

Willie cleared his throat. "I ain't got no friends."

Tom gave a snort. He noticed Willie looking at the black box on the stool.

"Blimmin' heat," he grumbled, wiping his forehead with a handkerchief. "Pick up that box, William, and bring it over here."

Willie did so and placed it carefully on the table. "Lift the lid, then." Willie stared at it. "Go on, cloth ears, open it."

He raised the lid and gazed at the brightly colored pots. "Paints?" he inquired.

Tom grunted in the affirmative. "Bit old, but the pots'll do. You paint?" Willie's face fell. He longed to paint. "Nah, 'cos I can't read. . . ."

"The ones that can read and write gits the paint, that it?"

"Yeh." Willie touched one of the pots gently with his hand and then hastily took it away. "I done drawin' with bits of chalk and crayon, on me own."

Tom straightened himself. "We'd best post yer letter.

Mustn't worry yer mum. Climb out. Where's that ole thing?" he mumbled. "Sammy," he shouted, "Sammy."

Willie shaded his eyes and looked around for him. He caught sight of a mound of black-and-white fur slumped under the oak tree.

"Mister Tom," he said, pointing to the dog, "look." Sammy lifted his head. Heaving his body up to his feet, he left his cool sanctuary and ambled over towards them.

They walked round to the back garden of the cottage, past the little wooden outhouse that was the toilet. On top of its roof lay Willie's mattress.

"Don't worry, boy," said Tom, "it'll be dry by to-night."

They went on to the end of the garden, where there was a small neat wooden gate with a hedgerow on either side.

They turned left down a road, and after a few paces Tom opened a gate into the field next to the graveyard. A large cart horse stood drowsily eating grass. Willie hung back.

"Come on," said Tom impatiently.

Sammy bounded on ahead and gave a loud bark at the nag. She lifted her eyes for an instant, shook her head and resumed eating.

"She won't hurt you," said Tom. "You walk alongside of me," and he gave him a gentle push into the field and swung the gate behind him. Willie hung on to Tom's left trouser leg and peered gingerly round at the mare as they walked past her.

"She won't hurt you," Tom repeated, but he could feel Willie trembling so he decided not to pursue the matter.

To Willie's relief, they eventually reached the safety of the gate at the other end of the field. Tom unhitched it and Willie darted through into a small lane.

"Sam," called Tom. "Here, boy." Sammy had been flopped over on one of Dobbs's hooves, enjoying the shade of her large head. He rose obediently and lolloped towards them.

"Let's see you shut it now, William. You must always remember to shut every gate." Willie hurriedly closed it with a crash. "Put the bolt through." He did so. "Good." Willie stood stunned for a moment, for he had never been praised by anyone ever.

The lane they were standing in was bordered by two rows of trees. Their overhanging branches formed a tunnel and, although their leaves were already falling, there was still enough clothed archway to cool them. Willie had never walked through so many leaves. They clustered around his ankles, hiding his sneakers entirely from view.

They walked by a large gate and an enormous, neatly kept garden. A middle-aged man was bending over one of the beds, sadly digging up clusters of gold and russet dahlias.

Sammy had already bounded on ahead and was now sitting lazily by an old wooden gate, waiting for them.

"Blimmin' mind reader," exclaimed Tom to himself.

He pushed at the gate, and after a struggle it creaked and groaned open on its one rusty hinge. The tangled hedgerows that grew on either side had almost strangled it into being permanently closed. Willie closed it carefully behind them and they walked into a wild and unkempt garden. The grass reached Willie's knees.

Tom knocked at the front door but there was no reply.

He could hear the sound of a wireless, so he knew someone must be in. After several attempts at attracting attention with the knocker, he walked round the side of the
cottage to the back garden.

Leaning back in a wicker chair sat Dr. Oswald Little,
a plump, red-faced man who was attempting vainly to
wipe the steam from his spectacles. His wife, Nancy, a
tall, thin, freckled woman with closely cropped iron-gray
hair, was digging a trench in the garden. A cigarette
dangled in her mouth. The wireless was blaring out light
organ music through the kitchen window.

"Dr. Little!" said Tom. The doctor looked up and
put on his spectacles, which immediately slid down his
nose.

"Hello, Tom. This is a surprise. You can't be ill."

"No."

He glanced briefly down at Willie, who was now re-
treating rapidly on hearing the tubby man being called
"Doctor." Nancy, noticing how scared he was, sat down
at the side of the trench and took the cigarette out of
her mouth.

"I'm Mrs. Little," she said hoarsely. "I expect you'd
like an orange juice while Mr. Oakley and the doctor
have a chat. Yes?"

Willie nodded and followed her through the back door
into the kitchen.

Tom sat down.

"What's the problem?" asked the doctor. "The boy,
is it?"

"Been sick twice already. He had a good tuck in last
night but brung it up."

"Malnutrition," the doctor remarked. "Probably used
to chips. All that good food might have been too much
of an assault on his stomach. Clear broth, rest, exercise

and milk to begin with, and maybe a tonic. Try some Virol and cod-liver oil. I expect he's bed-wetting too," he added.

Tom looked surprised.

"It's quite common," the doctor continued. "Especially if they're small. Give him a month or two to settle. How old is he? Five, six?"

"Eight, goin' on nine."

It was the doctor's turn to look surprised.

"Like a frightened rabbit he is," said Tom.

"Yes," said Dr. Little thoughtfully. "He's obviously been brought up to look on the doctor as the bogey man."

"There's somethin' else. The boy's had a bit of a whippin', like. He got bruises and sores all over him. Done with a belt buckle mostly. He's too ashamed to let folks see. If you could manage to have a look."

"This," croaked a voice from behind, "and warm salt water." It was Mrs. Little. She was standing with a tray of cool drinks. She placed a bottle of witch hazel by his feet.

"We exchanged battle scars," she explained. "I noticed his before we went indoors. I've given him a couple of garters for his socks. You'd think I'd given him the moon."

"The children in Little Weirwold have been quite spoiled, it seems," commented the doctor. "I was up at the Grange last night treating ingrowing toenails. There are two large families up there, nineteen children in all. Nancy and the maid had to delouse half of them. Bags of bones, aren't they, dear?" Nancy nodded.

"Thank you for yer advice," said Tom, standing up. "I won't keep you from yer work any longer."

Mrs. Little gave a loud laugh, which deteriorated into

a spasm of coughing. She took another drag of her cigarette.

"I'm the one that's doing the work!" she exclaimed.

"Well, I am supposed to be semiretired," protested the doctor lightly. "Anyway, it's too damned hot to be digging."

Nancy shrugged helplessly at Tom.

"Is it fer an air-raid shelter?" he inquired.

"Yes. And when those bombs start falling he'll be the first to dive into it."

"If there are any, I shall remain in bed," retorted the doctor. "I might as well die in comfort. Don't you agree, Tom?"

Tom had until now pooh-poohed the whole idea of building a shelter. After all, they were in the country. But with the extra responsibilities of Willie living with him . . .

"There's the boy to think of," he said. He picked up the witch hazel. "How much do I owe you?"

"On the house," said Nancy.

Tom called Willie and Sam. After another battle with the gate they walked to the end of the lane and on to the road into the sunlight.

Willie was perspiring heavily. Tom touched his cheek and found it was cold. They passed a small, red-brick house with a tiled roof. It had a playground and was backed by a field.

"That's your school, William."

Willie glanced at the row of potted plants on the windowsills. The school was quite unlike the dark-gray building he had attended in London.

The road brought them to the center of the two rows of thatched cottages. Mrs. Fletcher and a neighbor were standing outside one with a huge sunflower growing in front of it. It was one of the few cottages that housed a wireless. A small crowd was gathered in and around the garden listening to it.

"You go and post yer card," said Tom. "The post office is near the shop. I'll meet you there." And he left Willie and headed towards the group of listeners, with Sammy at his heels.

Willie walked slowly past the cottages. All the windows had been flung open.

"Mornin', William," chorused two voices behind him. An elderly couple were leaning over their garden gate. Their cottage stood immediately opposite where Willie was standing.

"We knows yer name from Mrs. Fletcher," said the old man. He wore a crisp white collarless shirt with the sleeves well rolled up, and his baggy gray trousers were held up with a piece of string. His wife was in a flowery cotton dress with a lilac-colored apron over it. Their skin was as wrinkled and brown as an old football, and on their heads were perched steel helmets. Both carried gas-mask boxes over their shoulders.

"Lookin' fer the post office, dear?" said the old lady. "You be standin' right at it."

"You go in, boy. Be all right," added the old man.

"We hope you'll be very happy here," chimed in the old lady, "don't we, Walter?"

"Yes," he agreed. "We do."

"We're the Birds," she said.

"You go on in," he said. "Go on."

Willie knocked on the door.

"Go on in, dear," they chorused.

Willie opened the door and stepped in. He found himself in a room at the end of which was a small counter with a piece of netting above it. To his right were stacked stationery and pens, jigsaws and wool, needles, scissors and assorted oddments, and to his left candy and bottles of pop.

Standing next to the netting was a young boy. He was leaning on a wooden sill, writing intently. A young man in his twenties, with short-cropped hair and glasses, was sitting behind the netting talking to him.

"They'll never read that," he said.

"Yes, they will," the boy replied.

Willie edged forward to see what was happening. The boy was holding a magnifying glass over a postcard and writing on it.

"Mother's got one of these, too," he said, waving the glass vaguely in the direction of the postmaster. It was the boy's appearance that attracted Willie's attention. He was taller than Willie but at a guess about nine years old. His body was wiry and tanned and he had a thick crop of black curly hair, which looked badly in need of cutting. All he wore was a baggy pair of red corduroy shorts held up by braces, and a pair of battered leather sandals. Several colored patches were sewn neatly round the seat of his pants. Willie could not take his eyes off him.

"Can I help you, son?" said the postmaster.

Willie blushed and slid his card across the counter. The man glanced down at it.

"Stayin' with Mr. Oakley, eh? You'll have to watch yer p's and q's there."

Did everyone know that he couldn't read? He glanced across at the strange boy again. His nose was practically touching the card, he was so close to it. He smacked his lips. With a flourish he drew a line at the bottom, screwed on the top of his fountain pen and hooked it into a buckle on his braces.

"Have you a blotter, sir?"

The postmaster slid a piece over to him. "Anything else?" he remarked wryly.

The boy gave a small frown.

"No, I don't think so, thank you." He blotted the card and slid them both under the counter. "When will it arrive, do you think?"

"Tuesdee, mebbe."

"That's ages," the boy moaned.

"Shoulda sent it sooner, then," said the postmaster.

The boy looked aside at Willie. His white teeth and brown oval eyes stood out in stark contrast against his dark tanned skin. He smiled, taking in Willie's crumpled gray shorts and jersey. Willie turned quickly away and walked out the door, his ears smarting. Tom was standing on the stone steps of the shop at the corner, waiting for him.

"There you are," he said. "Comin' in or not?"

He nodded and walked towards the shop, past three women who were talking outside.

He looked inside the door and stepped in. Boxes, sacks and colored packets were piled along the right side of the store. On the left was a long wooden counter with scales at one end and a large wicker basket filled with loaves of bread. Crates of fruit and vegetables were stacked at the other end. Above the boxes and sacks on the right were shelves with cups, plates, saucepans, bowls, nails and an assortment of colored tins on them. Willie peered outside to see if he could catch a glimpse of the strange boy from the post office.

"Thanks, Mrs. M," said Tom, talking to a middle-aged couple behind the counter. "I'll drop in that tobacco for you tonight, Mr. Miller. Tea, sugar, flashlight batteries and elastic, you reckon?"

"Sure as eggs is eggs," said the man. He caught sight of Willie standing by a sack of flour. " 'Ere, wot you want?" he cried angrily. "Eh?"

"Don't be too 'arsh," said his wife.

"Be soft with this London lot and they take you for a ride. I had cigarettes, chocolate, fruit, all sorts stolen when that last batch of kids come in."

Willie blushed and backed into the sack.

"Boy's with me," said Tom.

"Oh," said Mr. Miller, taken aback. "Oh, sorry, Mr. Oakley. That's different then."

"William, come over here and meet Mr. and Mrs. Miller."

"Pleased to meet you, dear," said Mrs. Miller, who was endowed with so many rolls of fat that her stomach almost prevented her from reaching the counter. She leaned over. Taking hold of Willie's hand in her soft pudgy one, she shook it.

Mr. Miller, a short, stocky man with thinning mouse-colored hair, leaned over and did the same. As Tom and Willie were leaving, Mrs. Miller lumbered towards them, polishing a large apple in her apron.

" 'Ere you are, me dear," she said to Willie. "This is fer you." Willie gazed at it, dumbfounded.

"Go on, take it, boy, and say thank you to Mrs. M," said Tom.

"Thank you," he whispered.

They left the shop and headed back along the road, Sammy behind them. They were outside Mrs. Fletcher's cottage when someone began shouting at them.

"Mr. Oakley! Mr. Oakley!"

A short ancient gentleman with a droopy mustache was running towards them. He was wearing an Air-Raid Precautions uniform.

"That's Charlie Ruddles," muttered Tom. "He's in the A.R.P. Thinks he's goin' to win the war." The old man came puffing up to them.

"Where's yer gas masks then? Yous'll be in trouble if you don't carry one. Don't you know war's goin' to be declared any second?" And he waved at Willie. "He should have one, too."

"All right, all right," said Tom, and continued to walk up the road, with Charlie still shouting after them.

"Yous'll wake up one of these mornin's and find yerself gassed to death," he yelled.

"All right," shouted back Tom over his shoulder. "I said I'll get one."

They walked past the cottage with the sunflower. People were still standing outside talking intently. Willie stared at them, puzzled. Why did they appear so anxious?

"Come on, William," called Tom sharply. "Don't dither! We's got to go into town."

Equipped

— 🌿 🌿 —

Dobbs clopped slowly past cornfields and cottages, bees and cream-colored butterflies. Tom and Willie sat in the front of the cart. They had left Sammy behind to collapse in the cool darkness of the tiled hallway. Willie clutched the long wooden seat, and as they jolted over the rough cobbled road, his eyelids drooped. Suddenly he gave a frightened start, for he had nearly fallen asleep and the ground below seemed a long distance away. Tom pulled on the reins and they came to a halt.

"Here," he said, "you hop in the cart and take a nap." He helped Willie into the back and threw him an old rug to cover himself with, for he still looked terribly pale. As soon as the rhythmic motion of the cart began, Willie fell into a disjointed sleep. His thin elbows and shoulder blades hit the sides of the cart at frequent intervals, so that he would wake suddenly, only to fall back exhausted into a chaotically dream-filled sleep. He was just about to be attacked by a horde of anxious faces when he felt himself being gently shaken.

"We's comin' into it, boy. Raise yerself."

Willie staggered to his feet and hung on to the side of the cart. They jogged past a river that was sheltered by overhanging trees. It curved and disappeared from view behind some old buildings.

"Remember any of this?"

Willie shook his head. "No."

They halted at a blacksmith's. Tom stepped down and lifted Willie after him. He untied Dobbs and led her

into a large dark shed. Willie heard him talking to someone inside. It wasn't long before he reappeared and
swiftly removed his haversack, bags and boxes from the
back of the cart. He placed a hand on Willie's shoulder.

"We got a lot to do, boy. You reckon you can keep
up?"

Willie nodded.

Tom handed him one of the two small buff-coloured
boxes and they both slung them over their shoulders
and set off. They passed a bicycle shop and a cobbler's
and turned a corner into the main street. It curved round
a large square.

"On market days that be filled with all kinds of stalls,"
said Tom.

In the center of the square was a stone archway with
a clock in its wall, and on the ground below, surrounding
it on four sides, were wooden benches.

They stopped outside a newspaper shop. Two plac-
ards were leaning up against the walls. Poland Invaded!
read one, and Turn your wireless low. Remember, someone
might be on duty, read the other. The door of the shop
was already propped wide open.

"Hot, ent it?" said a tiny old lady from behind the
counter. "Your usual is it, Mr. Oakley?" she added.

Tom nodded.

She reached up to a yellow tin of tobacco on one of
the shelves. A pile of comics caught Willie's eye. Tom
glanced at him.

"One candy and one comic," he said sharply.
"Choose."

Willie was stunned.

"Don't you hurry, sonny," said the old lady kindly.
"You jes' takes yer time." She pointed up at some of
the many jars. "We got boiled ones, fruit drops, farthin'

chews, mints, there's lollies, of course. They's popular.
There's strawberry, lemon, lime and orange."

Tom was annoyed at the long silence that followed
and was just about to say something when he caught
sight of Willie's face.

Willie swallowed hard. He'd never been asked to
choose anything ever.

"A lolly, please, Miss," he said at last.

"What flavor?"

He frowned and panicked for a moment. "Strawberry," he answered huskily.

The old lady opened the jar and handed one to him.
It was wrapped up in black-and-white-striped paper and
twisted like a unicorn's horn.

"Now what comic would you like, dear?"

Willie felt hopeless. What use would a comic be to
him—he wouldn't be able to understand the words. He
loved the colors, though, and the pictures looked so
funny and exciting. He glanced up at Tom.

"I can't read, Mister Tom."

"I know that," he replied shortly, "but I can, after
yer Bible."

Willie turned back to look at the comics, so that he
missed the surprised expression on Tom's face. The
words had leapt out of his mouth before he had had a
chance to stop them. He felt a mixture of astonishment
at himself and irritation that his rigid daily routine was
going to be broken after forty undisturbed years. Willie
at last chose a comic with his lolly, and Tom paid for
them. It was his first comic. His hands shook as he held
it.

"Get movin', boy," barked Tom's voice behind him.
"Are you deaf?" Willie jumped. "Come on," he repeated.

Willie followed him next door into a chemist's shop

and then into a grocery shop. They stopped outside
Lyons' tea house, where there was a selection of cakes
in the window. A man in uniform sat at a table nearby,
with a young, weeping girl. Willie looked up at the
shadow that the man's body was casting across her face.

"Later, perhaps," said Tom, thinking that Willie was
eyeing the buns.

As they were crossing the square, Willie tugged at
Tom's sleeve.

"Mister Tom," he said urgently. "Mister Tom, I knows
this place. I remember. That's where I were yesterday."

They looked across at the railway station. A group
of young soldiers were standing outside talking excitedly, their bulging kit bags leaning up against their legs.
A batch of children accompanied by a young woman
and the Billeting Officer who had brought Willie had
walked past them and were heading towards the Town
Hall. They shuffled forward in a dazed manner holding
hands, their labels hanging round their necks. They were
a motley bunch. Some with rosy cheeks in brand-new
coats and sandals, some thin and jaundiced, wearing
clothes that were either too small or too large.

"Come on, William," said Tom. "I got a list of things
a mile long fer the draper's."

The draper's shop stood on the sidewalk opposite.
Next to it was a toy shop.

"You want to look at the toys while I go in here?"

Willie shook his head. He didn't want to be left on
his own.

"As you please," said Tom, and they stepped into
the darkness of the draper's.

The shop was piled high with rolls of materials. Tom
and Willie inched their way between them. At the end
of a roofless tunnel they found themselves standing in

front of a long, high wooden counter. A smartly dressed, middle-aged man was cutting a piece of cloth.

"Good morning, Mr. Hoakley," he said cheerfully. "Blacks hall right, hare they?"

Tom grunted in the affirmative.

A sound of light organ music came from a large wireless at the end of the counter.

"For the latest news," the draper explained. "I must say, this waiting is getting hon my nerves. That Chamberlain's so slow. We're ready for 'Itler. I ses let's get on with it and stop this shilly-shallying."

"I been hearing that blessed organ music on and off all blimmin' day," said Tom grumpily. "Can't he play no other instrument?"

"That's Sandy Macpherson," said the draper. "Wonderful man. Holding the B.B.C. together hin this national time hof stress, Mr. Hoakley."

"Sure he ent causin' it?" retorted Tom.

"Oh, Mr. Hoakley," said the draper. "I'm sure you don't mean . . ." His words were cut short at the sight of Willie's dull, sandy hair on the other side of the counter.

"He's with me," said Tom quickly. "I brung a list from Mrs. Fletcher for materials." He pushed a list across the counter. "Boy's only got what he's standing up in."

The draper beamed. "A pleasure, Mr. Hoakley. I'll 'ave to measure 'im myself. I'm a bit short staffed hat present." He flicked the long tape measure from around his neck and eyed Willie.

"There's not a lot of 'im, his there?" he remarked disappointedly.

Willie craned his head over the counter and watched him measuring and cutting two rolls of gray and navy flannel. A roll of corduroy lay at the end of the counter. He reached out and touched it. It felt soft and firm. He let his fingers drift gently over the ridges. Tom caught sight of him.

"Might as well bring out several colors of that cordeeroy," he said.

The draper looked surprised. "Really. Oh well, if you say so, Mr. Hoakley."

"Two colors you can have, William. Takes yer choice."

The draper laid out rolls of green, brown, rust, navy, gray and red. Willie eyed Tom's green trousers. He pointed to the green roll and after a pause to the navy.

"Good," muttered Tom. The boy's beginning to think for himself, he thought.

Willie smiled nervously and leaned with his back against the counter to look at the other materials. There were crimsons and ambers, turquoises and sea greens, materials of every shade and texture.

Tom leaned down and Willie found himself being fitted for suspenders.

"We'll have these braces," Tom said, placing them on the counter.

Willie continued to gaze at the materials. He loved the reds, but Mum said red was a sinful color.

"I've to go to the bank," he heard Mister Tom say, "so I'll give you a deposit, like."

"No 'urry, Mr. Hoakley. I'll be 'ere hall day."

The draper chatted about rising prices, 'Itler and the price of butter while Tom grunted in acknowledgment.

"Called hup this morning," Willie heard him say, "so if you know anyone who'd be looking for a job, let me know. I'll heven take a young girl," he said, "if she's bright. . . ."

He wrapped the material in sheets of brown paper.

Willie longed to touch it, but it was put under the counter and he quickly followed Tom back through the dark tunnel of materials and out into the daylight.

Next door was a shoe shop. It was packed with people buying up stout shoes. After a wait in the queue Tom at last managed to get served.

"Boots," he said, indicating Willie's feet.

Willie sat on a chair as his feet were placed in a measuring gauge.

"Leather's a bit stiff at first," said Tom as Willie stood up in a solid pair of brown ankle boots. "But we'll get some linseed oil to soften them up."

A huge lump seemed to burn Willie's chest. It slowly rose into his throat.

"Are they fer me?" he asked.

"Well, they ent fer me," answered Tom shortly.

The assistant put them in a paper bag and Tom handed them to Willie.

They stepped off the sidewalk outside and crossed over to another group of shops that curved around the square. Two men were building a warden's post with sandbags. A large poster hung above them advertising A.R.P. outfits. Tom stopped at the corner where the shop stood and looked across at the Fire Station. It stood next to the Town Hall. A queue of men was standing outside, soberly reporting for duty.

A trickle of sweat rolled down the side of Tom's face. He mopped it with his handkerchief. The heat was stifling. There was no hint of a breeze anywhere. He felt a tug at his trouser leg.

"What is it?" he grunted.

Willie was pointing to a tiny shop down the small road they had just crossed. It was on the corner of a cobbled alleyway off the road. The front of the shop was unpainted varnished wood with faded gold lettering above it. In the front window was a display of paint-brushes arranged in a fan. Tubes and colored pots and boxes were scattered below.

Tom's heart sank. He hadn't been in the shop since Rachel had died. It was her favorite place. For forty years he hadn't been able to bring himself to venture into it again. There had been no reason anyway. He didn't paint. He remembered how pleased she would be at the mere thought of a visit.

"Paint has a lovely smell, ent it?" she'd say. "And a lovely feel." And he would laugh at her soft, nonsensical way of talking.

"What about it, William?" asked Tom quietly. "You wants to take a look?"

Willie nodded feverishly.

"Only in the window, mind. I ent got time to dally inside."

Willie gazed at the shop dreamily as he crossed the road. A car hooted at him.

"Mind where you's goin'!" yelled the angry driver.

"Boy's in a daze," murmured Tom.

Willie peered in the window and wiped away the mist his breath was making on the glass.

There were boxes of colored crayons and wax, lead pencils and paints in colors he never knew existed. Large empty pads of white paper lay waiting to be filled in. He looked lovingly at the paintbrushes. There were thin elegant ones for the most delicate of lines ranging out to thick ones you could grip hard and slosh around in bold, creamy-colored strokes.

Tom stood behind him and stared over his head into the shop. He remembered how Rachel used to spin with delight in there. Her long black hair, which was always tied back in a knot at the nape of her neck, would spring constantly outwards in a curly disarray whenever she was suddenly excited. She could look at a row of colors for hours and never be bored.

"If I painted the sky," she had said one day, "I could go through life paintin' nothin' else, for it's always changin'. It never stays still."

He looked down at Willie, who was making shapes with his finger on the misted window.

"What you doin'?"

"Drawrin'," said Willie. "It's one of them brushes."

Tom peered at it. "Humph!" he retorted. "Is it?"

He turned abruptly away and Willie followed him up the lane and back onto the main street. They stopped outside a library.

"Best join," said Tom, "if you's goin' to stay, that is."

They opened the door and entered a large expanse of silence. Someone coughed. Willie tugged at Tom's trouser leg.

"What is it?" he whispered in irritation.

"Mister Tom," he whispered, "why is it so quiet?"

Tom sighed in exasperation. "So's people can hear theirselves read."

They walked up to a large wooden table covered at each end with a pile of books. A tall, thin, angular woman in her thirties sat behind it, her long legs stretching out from under it. She wore spectacles and had fine auburn hair that was swept back untidily into a bun. She looked up at them and allowed her glasses to fall from her nose. They dangled on a piece of string around her neck.

"I've come to join him up," said Tom indicating Willie. "He's with me."

Miss Emilia Thorne gazed at Willie, stared at Tom and then took another look at Willie.

"With you?" she asked in astonishment. "With you!" she repeated. "But you're . . ." She was about to say, "a bad-tempered, frosty old . . ." but she stopped herself.

"I'm what?" asked Tom.

"You're . . . so busy."

Too busy, she thought. He never helped or joined in any of the village activities and had ignored all the signs that a war was approaching. She leaned over the table and gasped. They were both carrying their gas masks. She blinked and looked again. There was no mistaking it. The buff-colored boxes were hanging over their shoulders. Mr. Oakley, of all people, was wearing a gas mask!

"We ent got all day," said Tom sharply. "I'll leave the boy here. I got shoppin' to do."

Willie paled. Tom took a look at his face and groaned inwardly. How had he allowed himself to be landed with such a sickly, dependent boy? But Willie was sick with excitement, not fear. Even though he couldn't read, the sight of books thrilled him.

" 'Ow many's he allowed to have?"

"Three," answered Miss Thorne.

"Let him choose two with pictures and . . ." He paused for an instant. He never liked asking anyone favors.

"Yes?" said Miss Thorne.

"Choose one that you think would be suitable for me to read to him, like. He ent learned yet. And I've forgotten what young uns like, see." He cleared his throat awkwardly. "One has to do one's dooty, don't one?"

"Yes, of course, Mr. Oakley," she replied hastily. She watched Tom leave the library.

"Now," she said, producing a pale-blue card. "What's your name? Your address I know."

Meanwhile, Tom stepped out of the coolness of the bank. It was ominously close. People were still huddled in groups in the square, talking anxiously. Out of the corner of his eye he saw some wirelesses in a shop window. He paused in front of them.

"Echo," he read, "Bakelite." There, on display, was a small ten-by-four-inch wireless. It was run on batteries that had to be recharged. Ideal for someone like him who had no electricity. It was made of light wood with two large circular openings, one with a fretted front, the other fitted with a dial. Something to think about if he had to leave the boy on his own, like. Lot of money, though.

He stopped at the corner and glanced down at the tiny alleyway where the artist's shop stood. He hadn't time, he thought, and he set off briskly towards the blacksmith's, his rucksack and his bags already bulging. He had also a box of groceries to pick up, and some wooden and cardboard boxes that he thought would be useful for Willie's room.

Within half an hour he was back at the library. He peered through the glass at the top of the door. Willie was kneeling on a chair absorbed in books, his elbows resting on a long wooden table. Miss Thorne towered beside him, pointing at something on one of the pages. Tom hesitated for a moment and then walked hurriedly along the small road back towards the artist's shop.

"Forty-odd years," he muttered, staring into its window. "Is that how long it is?"

He pushed the door ajar. It gave a loud tinkle. Even

the same bell, he thought. He paused for an instant and then stepped inside.

Willie felt a hand touch his shoulder. It was Tom. He was carrying a parcel.

"Ready to go now," he said quietly.

Willie had his finger on a large letter. "That's an O, ain't it, mister?" Tom bent down to look. The book was filled with pictures of a marmalade-colored cat. "That's right," said Tom. "You knows yer alphabet then?"

"I nearly knows it." He looked up quickly. "Mister Tom," he asked timidly, "will you help me?" He looked down at the book, clenched his hands and held his breath. Now he'd be in for it. Don't ask help from anyone, his mum had said. He waited for the cuff around the ear.

"Yes," said Tom. "I expect I can talk to Mrs. Hartridge or whoever's your teacher and ask what you need to practice."

Miss Thorne interrupted him. "Don't go working him too hard. Looks like he could do with some of our country air."

"He'll git plenty of that," snapped Tom. "There's veg to plant and Dobbs to look after, and weeding."

Miss Thorne said no more. Poor boy, she thought, away from his loving home and now dumped with an irritable old man.

Tom picked up Willie's three books and gave them to him to carry. The one Miss Thorne had chosen was Rudyard Kipling's *Just So Stories.*

"It's not very educational, I'm afraid, Mr. Oakley."

"Did I say I wanted somethin' educational?"

"No, Mr. Oakley."

"Then don't put words in my mouth."

"No, Mr. Oakley," and she suppressed a smile.

After they had left, she stood in the doorway and watched them walking down the main street past the square.

"What an odd couple," she whispered to herself. "Wait till I tell May!"

"Run," roared Tom, and he and Willie tore down the pathway to the cottage. They were only just in time. The sky gave one almighty shake and split open. Rain and hail bounced on the tiled roof with such venom that Tom and Willie were quite deafened. They had to shout to make themselves heard. Sam growled and barked out of the front window.

Tom put the blacks up, lit the lamps and began unpacking the parcels.

"These are pyjamas, William," he said, lifting up two blue-and-white-striped garments. "You wear them in bed."

"Pie-jarmers," repeated Willie, copying Tom's way of speaking.

"That's right. Now," he said, "you going to sleep in the bed tonight?"

Willie looked startled.

"Bed's for dead people, ain't it?"

Tom stood up. "Come with me."

Willie followed him across the passage to Tom's bedroom. He hovered in the doorway.

"Come in," he said. "Don't dally." Willie took a step in. "See this here bed? I've slept *in* it for forty yer or more and I ent dead yet, and that basket at the end is Sammy's bed, when he's a mind."

They returned to the front room and, after a light

tea of eggs and toast, Willie changed for bed and positioned himself by the armchair, next to Tom. The rain continued to fall heavily outside, rattling the windows unceasingly.

"I'll have to fairly shout this story," yelled Tom above the noise.

Willie sat in his crisp new pyjamas. It had felt strange the previous night going to bed without wearing his underpants; but this odd suit felt even stranger.

"Mister Tom," he said, "ain't you goin' to read from the Bible?"

"Didn't you like it from me head then, like last night?"

"Yeh," said Willie, "yeh, I did."

"I shouldn't think you'd understand all them long words anyways."

"No, Mister Tom," said Willie, feeling deeply relieved at not having to pretend anymore. "Can I have 'Noah's Ark' again?"

Tom related the tale for the second time and followed it with the daring exploits of Pecos Bill from the comic Willie had chosen.

After a cup of cocoa, Willie brushed his teeth over an aluminum bowl and then dashed out into the garden to the little wooden outhouse, wearing his mackintosh and a new pair of gum boots while Tom sheltered him with an umbrella.

They carried the mattress upstairs between them. Tom placed a rubber sheet on it and made the bed over it, Willie helping him when he was able.

"There," Tom said when they had finished. "You can wet the bed till kingdom come."

"Mister Tom," whispered Willie, "ain't you angry wiv me?"

"No," Tom grunted. "When I first had Sammy he

peed all over the blimmin' place. Takes time to settle into a new place and its ways."

He turned down the blankets and Willie climbed in between the sheets. Sammy sat on the bump where his feet were.

"I put yer comic and library books on yer table."

"Thanks, Mister Tom," and he bent down to pick up the book with the marmalade cat in it. Tom watched him tracing words with his fingers.

"Ten minutes."

But Willie didn't hear. He was lost in the colored pictures. A loud knocking came from downstairs. Sammy leaped off the bed and started barking. Tom quickly checked that the blacks were firmly on Willie's window and disappeared down the ladder, holding a squirming Sammy in his arms. Willie raised his head for a moment to listen.

"Good evenin', Mrs. Fletcher," he heard Tom say in a surprised tone. "Come in."

He turned back to his book, and soon Tom reappeared to blow the lamp out. The room was blanketed in darkness until the blacks were removed.

"Good night, William," he said, tousling Willie's hair. "Pot's by the bed if you wants it."

Willie was exhausted. His head whirled with the names and faces of all the people he had met that day. He was just thinking about the boy in the post office when he fell instantly into a deep sleep.

Chamberlain Announces

꙰ ꙰

"Mornin'," said Tom, appearing at the trapdoor.

Willie opened his eyes and looked around. The sun was gliding in long flickering beams across the wooden floor.

"Mornin'," he answered.

"So you slept *in* the bed last night. Good."

Willie gave a tight smile, which faded rapidly when he realized that the trousers of his new striped suit were soaking.

Tom strode across the room. "Come and take a good sniff of this day," he said, pushing open the window. Willie blushed and clung to the top of the blankets. "Never mind about them sheets and jarmers. I got a tub of hot water waitin' for them downstairs." Willie climbed out of bed and joined him at the window.

"Reckon that storm's washed a few cobwebs away."

They rested their elbows on the sill and leaned out. It was a tight squeeze.

Beyond the little road at the end of the graveyard stretched green and yellow fields, and on the horizon stood a clump of woods. Tom pointed to some trees to the right of it.

"The big Grange is over there. Nope, can't see it. When the leaves fall from the trees you'll jes' be able to make it out. And over there," he said, pointing to the left of the fields to where a small road wound its way up a hill, "is where one of yer teachers lives. Mrs. Hartridge's her name."

"Mister Tom, how many teachers is there?" asked Willie.

"Two. Mrs. Hartridge teaches the young uns and Mr. Bush the old uns."

"How old's old?"

"Eleven, twelve up to fourteen. Sometimes a clever one goes to the academic high school in the town. See them woods?" he said. "There's a small river flows through there to where the Grange is. 'Tis popular with the children round here."

They stared silently out at the gentle panorama until Sammy began running up and down the pathway and yelping up at them.

"Wants attention, he does," murmured Tom, drawing himself away from the window. "We's got another busy day, William. Got to start diggin' a trench fer the Anderson shelter this afternoon. That'll put muscles on you."

They stripped the bed between them and carried the sheets downstairs. Tom gently washed Willie's body again and smoothed witch hazel onto the sore spots.

An assortment of clothes was lying on the table. Mrs. Fletcher had brought them round the previous night. David, her youngest, had grown out of them, and although he was younger than Willie he was a head taller. Tom handed him a white shirt from the pile and tied one of his own ties, a brown tweedy affair, around his neck. Willie's gray trousers seemed more crumpled than ever, but with the braces attached to them they at least felt comfortable. He tucked the long tie into them. Tom handed him a new pair of gray woolen socks, and Willie pulled the garters over them.

"I put some oil on them boots last night," he said as Willie stood, his feet encased in them. "Yous'll have to do them yerself tonight."

Tom had to be in the church early, to see Mr. Peters, the vicar. He went on ahead while Willie staggered on after him. It was difficult for him to move in his new boots. They cut into his ankles and he couldn't bend his feet to walk in them, but apart from the slight discomfort, he felt very protected and supported in them. They clattered on the flagstoned pathway, and it pleased him to hear himself so clearly. His bony legs, which usually felt as if they would collapse beneath him, felt firmer, stronger.

He found the back door of the church already open and Mister Tom talking to a tall, lanky man with piebald black and gray hair.

"Ah, William," he exclaimed, turning towards him. "Mr. Oakley tells me that you're going to give us a hand. Those are the hymn books," he continued, indicating a pile of red books on a table by the main door. "Put four on each bench, and if there are any over, spread them across the rows of chairs at the front and at the back. Do you think you can do that?" Willie nodded. "Good." He turned back to Tom. "Now, where's the best place acoustically for this wireless of mine?"

Willie walked over to the table and picked up some books, feeling totally bewildered. Mum had said red was an evil color, but the vicar had told him to put them out so it couldn't be a sin. He had also said that he was good. Mum had told him that whenever he was good she liked him but that when he was bad, she didn't. Neither did God or anyone else for that matter. It was very lonely being bad. He touched the worn, shiny wood at the back of one of the pews. It smelled comfortable. He glanced at the main door. Like the back door it was flung open, revealing a tiny arched porch outside. Sunlight streamed into the church and through the stained-glass windows, and a smell of grass and flowers permeated the air. A bird chirruped intermittently outside. P'raps heaven is like this, thought Willie.

He laid the books out neatly on the benches, his new boots echoing and reverberating noisily around him, but the vicar made no comment and went on talking quite loudly, for someone who was in a church.

He was arranging the books in the back row so that they were exactly parallel to each other, when two boys entered. They were both three or four years older than him. They sat on the second row of choir benches to the left of the altar.

Suddenly it occurred to Willie that the church would soon be filled with people. He hated crowds and dreaded the Sunday service and its aftermath, which was usually a good whipping. He felt a hand on his shoulder. It was Mister Tom.

"Stay with me, boy," he said in a low voice, and Willie gratefully followed him into one of the pews.

Within minutes, the tiny church was flooded with men, women and children. Four more boys sat by the altar. On the right of the altar were three men. Willie recognized Mr. Miller from the corner shop and the young man behind the mesh in the post office.

In the pew opposite Willie were two ginger-haired girls—obviously twins—trying to smother their giggles. Their long carrot-colored hair had been fought into plaits while the remainder stuck out in frizzy, uncontrollable waves. They wore pale lemon-and-green summer dresses with short puffed sleeves and a cross-stitching of embroidery round their chests. Their faces and arms were covered with the biggest freckles Willie had ever seen. Like him, they carried their gas masks over their shoulders. A lady at their side glared down at them.

She must be their mother, Willie thought. Sitting next to her was a tall man with bright red hair, and beyond him a young dark-haired girl.

Mr. Peters and his wife stood by the main entrance greeting the congregation as they entered. Their three teenage daughters, their cook and the assortment of evacuees they were housing filled two of the pews in front.

A hacking cough from the porch heralded the arrival of Nancy Little and the Doctor. Willie gave a short gasp. She was wearing trousers to church! He watched the vicar's face, waiting for the thunderous "thou shalt be cast into the eternal fires" glare, but he only smiled and shook her hand. He was surprised to see Miss Thorne behind them.

"Mister Tom," he whispered urgently, tugging at his sleeve. "Does that book lady live here?"

Tom nodded.

A short, dumpy woman in her forties accompanied her. "That's her sister, Miss May," Tom said in a low voice. "They lives in one of them cottages with the straw rooves. Thatched, that is. They got a wireless."

Willie turned to find the Fletchers with two of their sons moving into their pew. Mrs. Fletcher leaned towards them.

"Mr. Oakley," she whispered, "I begun the balaclava."

Tom frowned her into silence. It was Willie's birthday on Thursday, and he wanted it to be a surprise.

The wireless stood on a small table below the pulpit. The vicar fiddled with one of the knobs and the church was deafened with "How to Make the Most of Tinned Foods," before it was hurriedly turned off. The twins had caught the eye of one of the boys sitting in the front row of the choir. He was a stocky boy of about eleven with thick, straight, brown hair. With heads bent and shaking shoulders, the three of them buried their laughter in their hands.

Mrs. Hartridge and her uniformed husband entered. Willie gazed at her, quite spellbound. She was beautiful, he thought, so plump and fair, standing in the sunlight, her eyes creased with laughter.

"Them be the Barnes family," whispered Tom as a group of men and women came on in behind them. "They own Hillbrook Farm. Biggest round here fer miles."

Mr. Fred Barnes was a brick-faced, middle-aged man whose starched white collar seemed to be causing him an obstruction in breathing. Three healthy-looking youths and two red-cheeked young women were with him. His wife, a short, stocky woman, was accompanying two evacuees, a boy and a girl.

"Trust ole Barnes to pick a strong-lookin' pair," muttered Tom to himself.

Lucy and her parents sat in front of Tom and Willie. She turned and smiled at them, but Willie was staring at the colors in the stained-glass windows and didn't notice her.

When everyone was reasonably settled, Mr. Peters stood in front of the congregation and clasped his hands.

"Good morning," he began. "Now I know we have several denominations gathered here today, especially amongst our new visitors, who I hope will be happy and safe inside our homes. If any one of you is troubled or needs help, please don't hesitate to contact me or my wife. And now if you would all open your hymn books at number eighty-five, we shall sing 'Lead thou me on.'"

Mr. Bush, the young headmaster of the village school,

was seated behind the pulpit at the organ. He gave an introductory chord. Willie didn't know the tune, and as he couldn't read he couldn't even follow the words. He glanced aside at the ginger-haired twins. They were sharing a hymn book and singing. He envied them.

"La it," he heard Tom whisper. "Go on, la it."

Willie did so and soon picked up the melody until he almost began to enjoy it. The hymn was followed by a passage from the New Testament, another hymn from the choir and some simple prayers. The vicar looked at his watch and walked towards the wireless. All eyes were riveted on him, and anyone who had seating space sat down quietly.

The wireless crackled for a few moments until, after much jiggling with the knobs, the voice of Mr. Chamberlain, the Prime Minister, became clear.

"I am speaking to you," he said, "from the Cabinet room at Ten Downing Street. This morning the British Ambassador in Berlin handed the German Government a final note stating that unless we heard from them by eleven o'clock that they were prepared at once to withdraw their troops from Poland, a state of war would exist between us.

"I have to tell you now that no such undertaking has been received and that consequently this country is at war with Germany."

A few people gave a cry. The rest remained frozen into silence, while others took out their handkerchiefs. A loud whisper was heard from the brown-haired choirboy: "Does that mean no school?"

He was silenced very quickly by a frown from Mr. Bush, and Mr. Chamberlain's message was allowed to continue undisturbed.

"I know that you will all play your part with calmness

and courage," he said. "Report for duty in accordance with the instructions you have received. . . . It is of vital importance that you should carry on with your jobs. Now may God bless you all. May he defend the right. It is the evil things that we shall be fighting against— brute force, bad faith, injustice, oppression and persecution—and against them I am certain that the right will prevail."

Mr. Peters turned the wireless off. After what seemed an interminable silence he spoke. "Let us pray."

Everyone sank to their knees. Willie peered over his clasped hands in the direction of the choir. The brown-haired boy had caught the eyes of the twins again and was desperately attempting to relay some kind of message to them.

After prayers, various announcements were made from the pulpit. Volunteers and those already involved with the A.R.P. or Civil Defense work were asked to meet at the village hall. Women and children were to report at the school in the morning to make arrangements for the care and education of the evacuees.

After the service, when everyone had filed outside, Willie looked around for the strange curly-haired boy he had seen at the post office. The brown-haired choir-boy was already in deep discussion with the twins. He was joined by several other children, but there was no sign of the post office boy anywhere. He felt a hand tugging at his shirt sleeve. It was Lucy. She gazed shyly at him, her large red cheeks and wide bulging lips spreading out beneath two round blue eyes. "'Ulloo," she said.

Willie shuffled in his boots and dug a toe into the grass. "Hello," he said in return.

An awkward silence came between them, and he was

more than grateful when Mister Tom called out to him.

"Go and put the kettle on," he yelled. "I got to see the vicar."

Willie turned quickly and stumbled hurriedly down the path, leaving Lucy to stare silently after him until he had disappeared into the cottage.

The lid of the kettle rattled continuously, causing the living room to be enveloped in clouds of dense steam. Willie had tried vainly to lift the kettle from off the stove and, having succeeded only in burning his hand, he waited anxiously for Mister Tom's return. Tom didn't bat an eyelid at the warm fog. He strode into the room and, picking up the kettle with an old cloth, proceeded to make a pot of tea. It wasn't till he had put three mugs on the table that Willie realized that there was a third person in the room. A short, stocky, middle-aged man with thinning brown hair, a ruddy face and a twinkle in his eyes was standing at the doorway eyeing him. He blushed.

"Come on in, Mr. Fletcher," said Tom brusquely. He and Mr. Fletcher sat at the table and Willie took one of the mugs and perched himself on the stool in front of the stove. He felt very self-conscious and stayed gazing at the fire while the two men talked about widths of trenches. He pricked up his ears at one point, for he knew that they were talking about him.

"Oh yes, he'll manage all right," he heard Tom say. "Have to muck in like the rest of us." He glanced in his direction. "William," he said, "yous'll have to get yer hands dirty today. You don't mind a bit of muck and earth, I don't s'pose?"

"No, Mister Tom," said Willie.

This was a different world altogether. For a start, his mother had always taught him that it was a sin to work or play on the Sabbath. Sundays were for sitting silently with a Bible in front of you. And for another thing, if he got any dirt on his clothes he'd get a beating. His classmates had called him a sissie because he had never dared to dirty himself by climbing a wall or joining in any of their rough-and-tumble games. And, in addition to having to keep his clothes clean, his body was often too bruised and painful for him to play, apart from the fact that he didn't know how to.

"Mister Tom?" he asked after Mr. Fletcher had left. "Wot about me clothes gettin' dirty?"

"You can take yer shirt off. 'Tis a good hot day."

Willie shuffled nervously on the stool. "What's up now?" Tom said curtly. "Them bruises is it?" Willie nodded. "Wear yer gray jersey then. Mind," he added, "you'll be drippin'. And put yer old socks on."

After a meal of meat-and-potato stew, of which Willie only managed a few mouthfuls, Mr. Fletcher returned accompanied by his two teenage sons. They were carrying spades and measuring sticks.

Tom pointed sadly to a patch of grass in the back garden. "Best start there," he said, " 'Tis a reasonable distance from the latrine."

They cut and stripped the turf away in small neat squares, and then after measuring the ground they slowly and laboriously began to dig. Willie was given a small spade, and after an hour of removing a tiny section of earth he began to forget that he was surrounded by strangers and gradually became absorbed in his digging. Mister Tom had told him not to be afraid of the earth, but it was still wet from the previous night's rain and occasionally he let out an involuntary squeal when his spade contacted a worm. This made the others laugh and yell "Townee," but they went on digging and

Willie realized that there was no malice in their laughter.

In the middle of digging they all sat down for a mug of tea. Willie helped hand the mugs around. The two youths, he had learned, were called Michael and Edward. Michael was the elder. He was dark haired, with a few strands of hair on his upper lip. Edward, the younger, was stockier. He had brown wavy hair and a hoarse voice that was in the process of breaking.

Willie sat at the edge of the shallow trench and clung tightly to his mug. The insides of his hands smarted under the heat of it. Suddenly he gave a start. Footsteps and the sound of a boy's voice were approaching the hedge. Maybe it was the post office boy. He turned sharply to look. Two boys leaned over the small gate. They were Michael and Edward's younger brothers. One of them was the brown-haired choirboy, and his younger brother was a smaller, dark-haired version of him. Tom gave his usual frown at the appearance of uninvited intrusion.

"May I has yer worms, Mr. Oakley?" inquired the choirboy.

Tom grunted and the smallest fled immediately. "Daresay you can, George. Come on in."

"Thanks, Mr. Oakley," he said enthusiastically, and he swung the gate open.

In his hands was a large tin. He walked over to the trench and began scrutinizing the piles of earth. Willie watched him in horror as he picked up the wriggling worms and put them inside the tin. Within minutes he was helping with the digging. He turned shortly to discover Willie staring at him. "You's one of them townees, ent you?" he said. Willie nodded. "Ent you hot in that jersey?"

George had stripped off his shirt as soon as he had

joined in. Willie shook his head, but the telltale beads of sweat that ran down his flushed face belied the gesture. His jersey clung to his chest in large damp patches.

"You looks hot, why don't you peel off?"

Willie grew more reticent and mumbled out something that George couldn't hear.

"What?" he said. "What did you say?"

"Boy's got a temperature," interrupted Tom curtly. "Best to sweat it off."

Willie didn't look at George anymore after that, but continued digging with extra fervor. Later in the afternoon, Mrs. Fletcher appeared with lemonade and cakes for everyone, and George left, soon after, with a full tin of worms.

Sammy watched them digging from a corner of the garden. He was miserable at being left out. He had tried to help earlier but was only yelled at angrily for filling the hole with earth.

When the trench was completed, Willie sat on the grass to watch the others fix the Anderson shelter inside it. Sammy lay by his feet. The six steel sheets were inserted into the two widest sides of the trench and bolted together at the top, forming a curved tunnel. Michael and Edward placed one of the flat pieces of steel at one end and Tom and Mr. Fletcher fixed it into place. This was the back of the shelter. It had an emergency exit, which they all had a try at unbolting.

Willie was so absorbed that he didn't notice his knees were being licked, and unconsciously he rested his hand on the back of Sammy's neck.

Tom and Mr. Fletcher fixed the next flat piece onto the front of the shelter. Cut inside it was a hole, which was at ground level. This acted as a doorway.

"William," said Tom turning, and being surprised to

see him sitting with Sammy in a fairly relaxed manner, "like to have a try out of this doorway?"

Willie rose and wandered over towards the entrance. He put his head cautiously through the hole and stepped gingerly inside. It was dark and smelled of damp earth. Tom joined him. The shelter curved well above his head so that they could both stand quite comfortably inside. Tom crawled back out into the sun and pulled Willie out after him. He thanked Mr. Fletcher and his sons for their help and shook their hands.

"Pleasure," said Mr. Fletcher. "We must all help one another now."

"William," said Tom after the Fletchers had left, "I'm afraid we ent quite finished yet. We jes' got to cover this with earth. Got any strength left?"

Willie felt exhausted, but he was determined to keep going. He nodded.

Between them they started to cover the shelter until it was time for Tom to leave for a meeting in the village hall.

"Don't keep on fer long," he said as he swung the back gate behind him, but Willie continued to pile the earth on, leveling it down with his hands. It was exciting to see the glinting steel slowly disappear under its damp camouflage. He was so absorbed in his task that he didn't notice dusk approaching. His hands and fingernails were filthy, his face and legs were covered with muck, his clothes were sodden and he was glorying in the wetness of it all. He was in the middle of smoothing one piece of earth when a shadow fell across his hands. He looked up quickly and there, half silhouetted in the twilight, stood the wiry, curly-haired boy he had seen at the post office.

Zach

_¥ ¥_

"Hello!" he said brightly, grasping Willie's hand. There was a loud squelching of mud as he shook it.

"Sorry!" gasped Willie in embarrassment.

The strange boy grinned and wiped his hand on the seat of his shorts. "You're William Beech, aren't you?" Willie nodded. "Pleased to meet you. I'm Zacharias Wrench."

"Oh," said Willie.

"Yes, I know. It's a mouthful, isn't it? My parents have a cruel sense of humor. I'm called Zach for short."

The strange boy's eyes seemed to penetrate so deeply into Willie's that he felt sure he could read his thoughts. He averted his gaze and began hurriedly to cover the Anderson again.

"I say, can I help? I'd like to."

Willie was quite taken aback at being asked.

"I'm rather good at it, actually," Zach continued proudly. "I've given a hand at the creation of several. I wouldn't mess it up."

"Yeh," replied Willie quietly, "if you want."

"Thanks. I say," Zach said as he dumped a handful of earth on the side of the shelter, "I'll show you around. Do you like exploring?"

Willie shrugged his shoulders. "I dunno."

"Is it your first visit to the country?" But before Willie could reply the boy was already chattering on. "It's not mine exactly. I've had odd holidays with friends and my parents, but this is the first time I've actually sort of *lived* in the country. I've read books that are set in the country and, of course, poems, and I've lived in towns *near* the country and gone into the country on Sundays or when there was no school." He stopped and there was a moment of silence as they continued working. "You've not been here long, have you?" he asked after a while. Willie shook his head. "Else I'm sure I would have seen you around. You're different."

Willie raised his head nervously. "Am I?"

"Yes, I sensed that as soon as I saw you. There's someone who's a bit of a loner, I thought, an independent sort of a soul like myself, perhaps." Willie glanced quickly at him. He felt quite tongue-tied. "You're living with Mr. Oakley, aren't you?" He nodded. "He's a bit of a recluse, I believe."

"Wot?" said Willie.

"A recluse. You know, keeps himself to himself."

"Oh."

"I say," said Zach suddenly, "we'll be at school together, won't we?"

Willie shrugged his shoulders again, "I dunno." He felt somewhat bewildered. He couldn't understand this exuberant friendliness in a boy he'd only had a glimpse of once. It was all too fast for him to take in.

"I expect you think I'm a bit forward," remarked Zach.

"Wot?"

"Forward. You know. But you see my parents work in the theater, and I'm so used to moving from town to town that I can't afford to waste time. As soon as I see someone I like, I talk to them."

Willie almost dropped the clod of earth he was holding. No one had ever said that they liked him. He'd always accepted that no one did. Even his mum said she only liked him when he was quiet and still. For her to like him he had to make himself invisible. He hurriedly put the earth onto the shelter.

"I say," said Zach after a while, "I can't reach the top. Is there a ladder indoors?" Willie nodded. "Where is it?"

"In the hall. It's Mister Tom's."

"He won't mind, will he?"

"I dunno," whispered Willie, a little panic-stricken.

"I'll take the blame if there's any trouble," said Zach. "I say, maybe we can finish it and put the ladder back before he returns. It'll be a surprise then, won't it?" Willie nodded dumbly. "Lead the way, then," cried Zach. "On, on, on," and with that they made their way towards the back door.

Meanwhile, after walking in almost total darkness with no lights to guide him save the fast-darkening sky, Tom reached the village hall. It came as quite a shock to enter the brightly lit building. He shaded his eyes and blinked for a few seconds until he had adjusted to the change. There were far more people than he had anticipated, and the buzz of excited chatter was quite deafening. He tried to slip in unnoticed but it was too late. He had already been spotted by Mrs. Miller.

"Well, Mr. Oakley," she burbled. "This is a surprise!"

He turned to frown her into silence.

She was decked out in her Sunday best. A pink pillbox hat was perched precariously on her head, and pinned to its side was a large artificial purple flower. It hung half suspended over her mottled pudgy cheeks. The hat could have been a continuation of her face, Tom thought, the colors were so similar.

He cleared his throat. "Vicar called the meeting, so here I am."

"Yes, of course," said Mrs. Miller.

He glanced quickly round the hall. Some of the older boys were already in uniform, their buff-colored boxes slung over their shoulders. Mr. Peters, Charlie Ruddles and Mr. Bush were seated in front with Mr. Thatcher and Mr. Butcher. He slipped quietly to the back of the hall, catching sight of Nancy and Dr. Little, and acknowledged their presence with a slight gesture of his hand.

He attempted to stand inconspicuously in a corner but it was useless, for most of the villagers nudged one another and turned to stare in his direction. Tom, as Zach said, kept himself to himself. He didn't hold with meetings or village functions. Since Rachel's death he hadn't joined in any of the social activities in Little Weirwold. In his grief he had cut himself off from people, and when he had recovered he had lost the habit of socializing.

"Evenin', Mr. Oakley," said Mrs. Fletcher, who was busy knitting in the back row. "Left the boy, has you?"

"With Sam," he added, by way of defense.

He had been surprised at Sam's willingness to stay, and had even felt a flicker of jealousy when the dog had flopped contentedly down in the grass beside the boy's feet.

Although most wireless owners had opened their doors so that people could listen to the King's message, Mr. Peters talked about it for those who had missed it. He mentioned the regulations regarding the blackout and the carrying of gas masks, and Mr. Thatcher, the tall, ginger-haired father of the twin girls and their dark-haired sister, spoke about the procedure of action during an air raid.

Gum boots and oilskins were given out and ordered for volunteers.

It was decided that the first aid post would be at Dr.

and Nancy Little's cottage and that the village hall was to be the rest center.

Mrs. Miller threw her puffy arm into the air and volunteered to run a canteen for any troops that might pass through. This suggestion was greeted with howls of laughter at the idea of anyone bothering to take a route that included Little Weirwold. However, Lillian Peters, seeing how hurt Mrs. Miller was, said that she thought that it was a good idea and suggested that a weekly gathering of the evacuated mothers and their infants would also be an excellent idea. Mrs. Miller sat down beaming, because she believed she had thought of it herself.

Mr. Bush announced that Mrs. Black had agreed to help at the school, as there would be an extra seventy children attending. Mrs. Black was a quiet-spoken old lady who had been retired for seven years.

"Goin' to have her hands full with some of that town lot," Tom remarked to himself.

Several people volunteered for being special constables, but Tom remained silent. His life had been well ordered and reasonably happy, he thought, because he had minded his own business. The last thing he wanted was to turn himself into a do-gooder, but he realized very quickly that most of the volunteers were genuinely and sincerely opening their hearts and homes.

Mr. Thatcher stood up to talk about fire-watching duties.

"No one is allowed to do more than forty-eight hours a month," he said. "Just a couple hours a day."

Tom raised his arm.

Mr. Peters looked towards the back of the hall in surprise. "Yes, Tom?" he asked. "Did you wish to say something?"

"I'm volunteering, like," he said.

"I beg your pardon," said Mr. Thatcher in amazement.

"I'll do the two hours a day. Early in the mornin' like, or teatime. Can't leave the boy alone at night."

"No, no, of course not." Tom's name was hurriedly put down.

There was a murmur of surprise and enthusiasm in the hall. A tall, angular figure stood up. It was Emilia Thorne.

"Put mine there too," she said. "And while I'm about it, anyone who would like to join our Amateur Dramatics Group is very welcome. Meetings now on Thursdays, which means you can still attend practices at the first aid post on Wednesdays."

Soon a dozen or so hands were raised, and after their names had been written down and details of what their duties would involve, the meeting was brought to a close.

It was dark when Tom stepped out of the hall. He strode away towards the arched lane while the sound of chatter and laughter behind him gradually faded. He recollected, in his mild stupor, that Mrs. Fletcher and Emilia Thorne had spoken to him and that the doctor had asked after William and had said something about their boy being over at his place.

It was pitch black under the overhanging branches, and it wasn't until he reached the gate of Dobbs's field that he was able, at last, to distinguish the shapes of the trees, and Dobbs and the wall by the churchyard. He swung open the gate and shut it firmly behind him. "Bet Rachel's 'avin' a good laugh," he muttered wryly to himself, for not only had he volunteered for fire-watching duties, but he had also volunteered the services of Dobbs and the cart, since there was news of petrol rationing. He strolled over to the nag and slapped her gently.

"I'll has to get you a gas mask and all, eh, ole girl. Seems we're both up to our necks in it now."

The stars were scattered in fragments across the sky. Tom stared up at them. It didn't seem possible that there was a war. The night was so still and peaceful. He suddenly remembered Willie.

"Hope he's had the sense to go inside," he mumbled, and he headed in the direction of home. He opened the little back gate and peered around in the dark for the shelter. He would have bumped into it if he hadn't heard voices.

"William! William! Where is you?"

" 'Ere, Mister Tom," said a voice by his side.

Tom squinted down at him. "Ent you got sense enough to go indoors? Yous'll catch cold in that wet jersey."

A loud scrabbling came from inside the Anderson and Sam leaped out of the entrance and tugged excitedly at his trousers. Tom picked him up, secretly delighted that he hadn't been deserted in affection. Sam licked his face, panting and barking.

"It was my idea," said a cultured voice. "To keep at it."

"Who's that?" asked Tom sharply.

"Me, Mr. Oakley," and he felt a hand touch his shirt-sleeve.

Tom screwed up his eyes to look at Zach. He could make out what looked like a girl in the darkness.

"I just thought it was a shame to go inside on such a night as this," he continued, "so I persuaded Will to partake of my company for a while."

"Who's Will?" asked Tom bluntly.

"My name for William. He told me he was called Willie, but I thought that was a jolly awful thing to do to anyone. Willie just cries out for ridicule, don't you think? I mean," he went on, "it's almost as bad as Zacharias Wrench."

"What?" said Tom.

"Zacharias Wrench. That's me. Zach for short."

"Oh."

Willie stared at their silent silhouettes in the darkness for what seemed an eternity. He could hear only the sound of Sam's tongue lathering Tom's face and a gentle breeze gliding through the trees.

"Best come in," said Tom at last.

They clattered into the hallway. Tom put the blacks up in the front room, crashed around in the darkness and lit the gas and oil lamps. After he had made a pot of tea, they sat near the stove and surveyed each other.

Willie's face, hair and clothes were covered with earth. His filthy hands showed up starkly against the white mug he was holding. Zach, Tom discovered, was a voluble, curly-haired boy a few months older than Willie, only taller and in bad need, so he thought, of a haircut. A red jersey was draped around his bare shoulders, and a pair of frayed, rather colorful men's braces held up some well-darned green shorts. Apart from his sandals, his legs were bare.

"You finished the shelter then?" said Tom.

Willie nodded and glanced in Zach's direction. "He helped."

"By the feel of it, you done a good job. How'd you reach the top?"

There was a pause.

"Wiv the ladder," said Willie huskily.

"Yes," interspersed Zach, "that was my idea."

"Oh, was it now?"

"Yes."

"You put it back then?"

"Oh yes. It might be a bit earth stained, though."

Tom poked some tobacco into his pipe and relit it. "Where you stayin' then? You ent from round here."

"With Dr. and Mrs. Little. I've been here for about a week now."

"Oh," said Tom. "I haven't seen you around."

"I haven't seen you around either," said Zach.

Willie choked on a mouthful of tea and Zach slapped his back. He flinched. His skin was still bruised and sore.

"I say," blurted out Zach with concern, "you're not one of those delicate mortals, are you?"

"No, he ent," said Tom sharply. "Leastways, not for long."

Zach glanced at the clock on the bookcase and stood up. "I say," he exclaimed, "it's nine o'clock. Thanks awfully for the tea, Mr. Oakley. May I come round tomorrow and see Will?"

"Up to William, ask him."

Willie was so exhausted from the day's labors that he didn't know whether he had dreamed the last remark or not.

"Can I?" said Zach earnestly. "I've a marvelous idea for a game."

"Yeh."

"Wizard! Callooh! Callay!"

With a great effort he attempted to pull his jersey on over his head. He tugged and pulled at it until it eventually moved over his nose and ears, causing his hair to spring up in all directions like soft wire.

"Phew!" he gasped. "I did it. Mother says I mustn't grow any more till she's collected enough wool to knit me a bigger one." He tugged the sleeves of the jersey down but they slid stubbornly back to between his wrists and elbows.

"Good night, Sam," he said, giving him a pat.

"William," said Tom, "see yer friend out."

Willie got sleepily to his feet and followed Zach into the hall, closing the door behind him.

"Ow!" cried Zach as his knee hit the stepladder. Willie opened the front door. The sky was still starry and a cool breeze shook the grass between the gravestones. He shivered.

"Your jersey's awfully damp," said Zach, feeling it. "Don't go catching pneumonia." He glanced cautiously round the graveyard. "Just looking for spies," he explained. "Look, about my idea. You know Captain McBlaid?"

"D'you mean Charlie Ruddles?"

"No," said Zach excitedly, "Captain McBlaid of the Air Police."

"Is he the prime minister or somethin'?"

"No!" He took another look around. "I'll tell you more about it tomorrow. Roger, wilco and out."

Willie watched him walk down the path and towards the church, then pull himself up over the wall and disappear. Who was Roger Wilco and what did he mean by out? he thought. He stepped back into the hall and felt his way back to the living room.

In front of the stove stood the large copper tub. Tom was pouring hot water into it while Sam was hiding under the table and eyeing it suspiciously.

"Don't worry, Sam. It ent fer you."

He looked down at Willie. "You'll be stiff tomorrer. Best have a good soak."

Willie stared in horror at the bubbling water and

backed towards the table. He watched Tom lift two more saucepans from the stove and empty them together with a handful of salt into the tub.

"Come on then," he said.

"Is it fer me clothes, Mister Tom?"

"It's fer you,"

Willie swallowed. "Please, mister. I can't swim. I'll drown."

"Ent you never . . ." But he stopped himself. It was a stupid question. "You don't put yer head under. You sit in it, washes yerself and has a little lean back."

It took some time before Willie allowed himself to relax in the water. Tom handed him a large square bar of soap and showed him how to use it. He then proceeded to wash Willie's hair several times with such vigor that Willie thought his head would fall off. A drop of soap trickled into his eyes and he rubbed it, only to find that he had created more pain.

After this ordeal Tom left him to have a soak, and slowly Willie began to unwind. He held on to the sides of the tub and let his legs float gently to the surface. The gas lamp flickered and spluttered above him, sending moving shadows across the walls.

He gave a start, for he had been so relaxed that he had nearly fallen asleep. Tom handed him a towel, and after he had dried himself and had his hair rubbed and combed and had put his pyjamas on, he sat down on the pouffe by the armchair while Tom sat ready to tell him a story. Sam spread himself out on the rug between them.

"I'm goin' to look at the story first and then tells it in me own way, like I done with Noah. That suit you?"

Willie nodded and hugged his knees.

"This is the story of how God created the world."

And he began to talk about the light and the darkness, the coming of the sky and the sea, the fish and the animals and of Adam and Eve.

After this he made them both some cocoa and began the first of the *Just So* stories.

"I haven't read these for years," he said, leaning over to Willie. "Come and look at these pictures."

Willie rested against the arm of the armchair and listened to "How the Whale got his Throat." This was a slow process, for Tom had to keep stopping to explain what the words meant, and several times had to look them up in a dictionary.

Willie lay in bed that night, tired and aching, but the aches were very pleasant ones and as he slept he dreamed that Adam and Eve were being chased by a large whale and that he stood in the garden of Eden wondering if God was nubbly and ate infinite sauce and sagacity.

An Encounter over Blackberries

They slung the rubber sheet and pyjamas over the washing line and peered into the shelter.

"Water," murmured Tom. "I might have known. We'll have to keep a stirrup pump close by." He patted the side of the strange earthy mound. "I'll put some more earth on today and then we can plant a few turnips and such in it. Ever growed anything afore?" he said, turning to Willie.

Willie shook his head.

"Always a first time. Come with me. I'll show you somethin'."

Willie followed him out of the back gate and across the tiny road, Sam scampering after them. Instead of turning left towards the village they went on to the right. They hadn't walked very far when they came to a tiny dirt track off the road.

The aching that Willie had first felt on waking was beginning to ease up—apart from his ankles, which were still a little sore from his boots. A sudden burst of energy rose up inside him. It excited and frightened him. He had always been good at keeping still. It was wicked not to, he knew that, but now he felt a desperate desire to leap and jump. He pressed his lips together and, clenching his fists and frowning, he tried to numb the strange new feelings away.

Tom caught sight of the flush of excitement burning in his cheeks.

"Race Sammy to the gate," he said, pointing to one a hundred yards ahead of them. "I'll hold him to give you a head start."

"Run, d'you mean?"

"Well, I don't mean fly. Now when I ses go, you jes' go."

He whistled for Sam and held him squirming and wriggling in his arms.

"You got rabbit and bone fever, ent you, my boy?" he said, as he struggled to hold him.

Willie fixed his eyes on the gate and held his breath.

"Right," said Tom. "On yer marks, get set, go!!"

Willie shot forth, half running, half stumbling. He clenched his fists even tighter. Bang! He fell with a hard thud onto his knees. Pushing himself up, he staggered on, feeling angry and desperate inside. In his heart he wanted to run properly, but his stupid legs were letting him down. He heard Sam barking behind him.

"Go it," shouted Tom. "Go on, William!" and, before he realized what he was doing, he was running too.

Willie propped himself up against the gate gasping for breath while Sam sat nonchalantly by his feet, an easy winner.

"Cheer up, boy," said Tom. "It ent the end of the world."

But to Willie it was. He was a sissie after all. It was true what his classmates called him. He was a Willie Weakling. A huge lump of misery welled up into his throat and he stiffened his jaw so that he wouldn't disgrace himself by crying.

"What's up then?" asked Tom. "Miserable because Sam beat you, eh?"

Willie nodded and stared at the ground.

"Can't expect to be good first time. Takes practice. Sam's had more'n you. Anyways, you beat me, didn't you?"

Willie looked up and gave a brief smile.

"Yeh, yeh, I did!"

"You needn't look so pleased about it," said Tom in a disgruntled manner. He swung the gate open. "Well, what do you think?"

Willie found himself standing in a large field. On one side were rows and rows of furrowed earth with tufts of green leaves sticking out of them, and on the other, far side stood a large cluster of trees dripping with apples and pears.

"There's taters, cabbage, beans, peas, sprouts, turnips, all sorts! We'll have to pick them all pretty sharpish. You can help me when it's time."

He closed the gate and they set off back down the dirt track towards the cottage.

They were leaning over the shelter putting more earth round the walls when Zach arrived.

"You walk through Dobbs's field?" asked Tom sharply.

"Yes, and I shut both gates."

Tom gave a grunt.

"Can Will come out and play?"

"He's out already, ent he?"

"Yes, I s'pose he is," said Zach thoughtfully. "It's a figurative expression that I haven't really given a lot of thought to."

"Where'd you git all yer queer words from?"

"Are they queer?"

"Well, they ent normal."

"So I've been told often and oft." He gave a sigh. "I say, Will, what on earth have you done to your hair?"

Willie looked blankly back at him, and pushed his fingers through it. His scalp didn't itch anymore. It tingled.

"Wot's wrong wiv it?"

"Nothing. It's just a different color, that's all. I didn't realize you were so fair."

It was true. The lank look had disappeared and it did look lighter.

"Go and play, William," said Tom.

"Play?"

"Yes, play."

"Excuse me, Mr. Oakley," interposed Zach. "Before we go, may I have a look-see inside the shelter? I'd like to see what it looks like in daylight."

"Please yerself," answered Tom, but before he could warn Zach about the waterlogged floor the boy had already leaped down inside. There followed a loud squelching sound and his feet sank as if in quicksand.

"Don't you never look before you leap?"

"Occasionally. Didn't this time though, did I?"

Tom turned at the sound of the back gate opening. A rather disgruntled-looking George walked towards them, his hands stuffed into his pockets.

"Mr. Oakley," he said, "me and the twins is goin' blackberryin', like, and takin' a picnic." He glanced quickly at Willie. "Would William like to come with us? Mum ses, she's makin' enough fer us all."

"I say," said Zach, poking his head out into the sunlight. "Can I come? I'd bring some food too."

George stared at him in horror. He sighed inwardly. These townees were queer folk, he thought. They talked different. Their ways were odd. It was bad enough having to ask the one called William to come. He was intrusion enough. Drat his mum.

"Please," pleaded Zach earnestly.

"All right."

What else could he say? He felt irritated. He knew the twins would be furious with him.

"There's just one small problem," said Zach. "I'm afraid I'm a bit like Buster Keaton at the moment."

George looked at him blankly. He's a queer one, he thought, no doubt about that.

"Yes. Look at me."

He pressed his arms to his side and leaned forward on a diagonal without falling over. "I say," he said, after having created no response. "You do know who Buster Keaton is, don't you?"

"Are you goin' to stay down there all day?" grunted Tom.

"That's what I'm trying to tell you. I'm stuck. I need a pull." They all grabbed hold of him, and after a lot of yelling from Zach and one almighty heave, they yanked him out and fell backwards in the grass on top of a yelping Sammy.

"Thank you," said Zach, struggling back to his feet. He looked down at them. His sandals were encased in a large quantity of glutinous mud. He lifted one foot up and placed it heavily in front of the other, making a slow progression to the gate.

"I say," he said, twisting his body round. "Where shall I meet you?"

"Outside the shop," grunted George. "In an hour's time."

"Right-ho!" And he slowly squelched his way through the gate and out of sight.

An hour later the twins and George were waiting on the corner with their baskets, bags and gas masks. Willie caught sight of them as he turned the corner. He stopped for a moment and looked around for Zach. He caught sight of a dark-haired boy in a bright red shirt and green shorts coming out of the shop. He gave a sigh of relief and started walking again. Zach had seen him and was waving frantically. George and the twins turned to look at them. Willie felt painfully self-conscious. Zach ran down the road to meet him. His sandals had been scraped clean, but they still looked pretty dingy.

From the moment they joined the others outside the shop, it was obvious that the twins were sulking. George mumbled incoherently to them.

"This is Will," said Zach, introducing him to the two girls. "I've forgotten which one of you is Carrie and which one is Ginnie."

"I'm Carrie," said the one in the sky-blue dress.

"And I'm Ginnie," said the one in the lemon color.

"Hello," said Willie huskily.

This was followed by a long and tense silence. George stood in the middle of the two pairs, feeling very awkward and uncomfortable. He had guessed right. The twins had been furious with him for inviting the two evacuees. In their opinion, from the little they had seen and heard, one of them spoke too little and the other too much. It was rotten of George to ask them.

George cleared his throat. "Well," he said, "s'pose we'd best get started."

They turned and headed down the lane towards Ivor's farm.

Willie held an empty bucket and a small bag, while Zach carried a basket and satchel. They walked on behind the others.

"I say," he said excitedly to Willie. "You should have seen Mrs. Little's face when I walked in. She threatened to plant potatoes in my feet." He nudged Willie and glanced at George and the twins walking ahead. "They're a bit stuffy, aren't they?" he whispered.

"Stuffy?" said Willie. "Wot d'you mean?"

"Unfriendly."

"But they asked us to go on a picnic wiv 'em."

"M'm. I suppose so."

He nudged a sore spot on Willie's arm.

"Anyway," he confided, "we'll have a bit of fun, eh?"

Willie was unsure about that. He wished his tongue wasn't quite so dry and that the skin round his neck didn't feel so very tight.

They came to Ivor's farm. Lucy and her friend Grace Bush were playing in front of the house. They ran up to the gate and climbed up onto it. Mrs. Padfield was hanging out washing.

"Hello!" she said. "Where are you all off to?"

"Blackberryin'," said George.

Lucy caught sight of Willie. Her eyes slowly expanded.

" 'Ullo," she said shyly to him.

Willie shuffled with embarrassment and avoided her large gaze.

Stupid girls, he thought angrily to himself. Stupid, stupid girls.

"Fred and Harry are doin' a bit this afternoon. They's helpin' their Dad at the moment, seein' as there's no school fer a bit. Best not to go to your patch. Be nothin' left." Mrs. Padfield smiled and carried on with her work.

"We'll drop some in for you," said Carrie, "won't we, Ginnie?"

Ginnie nodded.

"Have a good day then."

Lucy watched them going down the lane. She would dearly have loved to have joined them but they were all older. They wouldn't want someone as little as she. She felt a tug at her dress.

"Come on," said Grace impatiently. "I want to play."

The others veered round a corner and came to a large field. The girls walked off in one direction to some hedges on the far side, leaving George with Willie and Zach.

"Who's in the doghouse, then?" asked Zach. "You or us?"

George gave a smile. "Come with me," he said. "I'll find you a good spot." He pointed to some bushes. "See them red berries?"

"Rather," said Zach. "They look delumptious."

"De-what?"

"Delumptious. That's a mixture of delicious and scrumptious."

"Well, anyways," continued George, undaunted by Zach's interruption, "if you eats any of them you'll die. Them's poisonous. Don't eat nothin' till you've shown me. Look, there's a good un," he said, pointing to a hedgerow dripping with blackberries. "You pick there. I'm off to find a patch of me own."

An hour later, after scratching their arms and legs and staining their hands and mouths with juice, they sat down in the grass and passed a bottle of lemonade around. The girls looked a little less sulky and stared at the two townees. Willie was embarrassed. Zach, however, enjoyed the attention.

"How'd you do that?" asked Carrie, pointing to Willie's leg. He paled for an instant, thinking perhaps that his socks had slid down, but they hadn't. She was referring to the graze on his knee.

"I fell," he whispered.

"Looks nasty," said Ginnie.

Willie glanced at her and looked hurriedly away. When they had quenched their thirst a little, they returned to the bushes to pick more berries, staying a little closer to each other. Slowly, they started to talk—except for Willie, who only listened. Mum had said that if he made himself invisible people would like him and he wanted that very much.

He learned that Carrie liked reading books, climbing trees and exploring, that Ginnie liked naming and pressing wild flowers, knitting and sewing, and that they both liked swimming. George was keen on fishing and his mother had, on three occasions, cooked fish that he had caught. If they were tiddlers he always threw them back. He liked swimming too and in the summer had built a raft, but it had disintegrated in the middle of the river while he and the twins had been sitting on it. He also played cricket, and had already earned himself a bad reputation by smashing two windows in the village.

Zach said he liked acting, and reading adventure books and poetry. He also liked swimming and cycling. He said that he wrote stories, though he had to admit that he had never got further than the first two pages.

Willie, meanwhile, not only remained silent during these conversations, but picked his berries slowly so that they might forget that he was there, but he reckoned without Zach.

"Will!" he said, suddenly entering into his silence. "What do you like?"

He was just about to shrug off the question with "I dunno" when he noticed that George and the twins were looking at him for an answer. He sucked a bit of juice from one of his fingers and tried to think of something to say. He couldn't read or write. He couldn't swim or ride a bicycle. He had never made anything and he couldn't tell the difference between one flower and another. He couldn't play cricket or any other game for that matter and he had never been fishing. He began to panic. The others would get bored with waiting and go off on their own without him. He swallowed hard and looked up at their faces. They didn't look bored. He relaxed a little and then he remembered something.

"I likes drawin'."

"I'm hopeless at it," said George. "All my people have tiny heads and huge arms and legs."

"Like you," said Carrie.

Ginnie laughed.

"Get on with you," retorted George. "That's not true!"

"Could you draw me?" asked Zach.

"I dunno. I could have a go."

"I'm starvin'," said George, interrupting the conversation. "Let's eat."

They gathered together under a tree and spread the food out. There were scones that had been spread with butter and jam, meat sandwiches, marmalade sandwiches and egg sandwiches. After they had consumed these, they each had a slab of apple-and-black-currant pie and some chocolate cake. This was followed by more lemonade.

For Willie it was his first taste of chocolate cake, scones and fruit pie. He couldn't manage half his share, but he was helped by the others, especially George, whose appetite was bottomless.

After they had eaten and sunbathed a little, they cleared everything away and moved to another hedge to pick more berries. Their baskets were soon full, and, feeling tired, they made their way home.

Willie felt as if his arms would surely come out of

his sockets with the weight. His bucket and bag were overflowing. He puffed and panted behind the others, gritting his teeth with the effort of trying to keep up with them.

After George had left his basket at home he gave Willie a hand. He felt so ashamed of his weakness, but George didn't ridicule him at all. He seemed pleased to help. They walked down under the archway of trees to the Littles' cottage, stood outside the gate chatting to Zach and went on down the lane. As they came to the rectory George stopped.

"Look!" he said, gazing up through the trees. "Look! There's a swallow."

Willie screwed up his eyes and peered upwards. All he could see was a bird. A swallow to him was something you did when you ate food or you did to stop yourself from crying. He couldn't see how that could be in the sky.

They opened the gate into Dobbs's field. George put down the bucket and strode over to her to give her a pat. Willie hovered behind him. He took a few steps towards her and raised his hand to touch her neck, but she gave a little shake of her head and that set him stumbling backwards. He'd wait till he was with Mister Tom again.

George climbed over the gate while Willie opened and shut it neatly behind him. They walked through the garden to the back door when a voice called to them from behind. It was Tom. He was leaning out of the shelter.

"Afternoon, Mr. Oakley," said George.

"Afternoon, George."

They came over to where he stood and peered inside. The earthen floor was covered with planks and on either side were two rough bunk beds. A tin with one side cut out of it hung from a hook at the back. Fixed inside was a candle. Underneath it stood an orange crate on top of which were two flower pots. One was placed like a lid on the other and had a hole in the base. Inside this was another candle. Above their heads over the entrance was a rolled piece of dark canvas. A potted plant hung in a nearby corner.

"Cor!" gasped Willie. "Ain't it fine?"

"Best to be comfortable," said Tom, and he gave a short cough to hide his pleasure.

"Proper job," agreed George.

They took turns to walk around inside and sit on the bunks, and then George left to go home for tea.

Willie spent the evening with Tom, washing and bottling the blackberries and eating some of them for supper. He sank into an even deeper sleep that night with the knowledge that he, Willie Beech, had survived a whole day with four other people of his own age and he had made jam.

School
— ❧ ❧ —

Willie sat down to breakfast in a clean gray shirt and jersey, pressed gray shorts and polished boots. He stared out at the graveyard. It was a dull day.

"Eat up, boy. Soon be time to go to school," said Tom, placing a paper bag on the table. Inside were two apples and a thick egg sandwich.

"You can come back here for dinner if you wants, or have it with the others. Best take yer cap and mackintosh. Looks like rain." He picked up Willie's label from the top of the bookcase and handed it to him.

They walked together through Dobbs's field and Tom stood by the gate and let Willie walk on his own up the lane. Zach was sitting on the Littles' dilapidated gate waiting for him. Willie met him and turned to look at Tom. They waved to each other and Sammy immediately shot forwards.

"Samuel," said Tom firmly. "Here!" The dog stopped, glanced at his master and then bounded back to him. Tom picked him up and watched the two boys disappear round the corner.

George and the twins were standing in a crowd outside the village hall. Two old cars drew up with eight children and two anxious-looking mothers inside.

"I say," said Zach. "It's awfully crowded, isn't it?"

"It ent usually like this," said Carrie.

"They've had to get an extra teacher," added her sister.

"And," said George, "we have to share the school

with some Catholics. We're havin' it in turns. Look!"
He pointed in the direction of two nuns surrounded
by a horde of children. "If it stays like this we ent goin'
to have much school at all," and he grinned with pleasure.

The five of them went into the hall together. The
blackout curtains, which were rolled neatly above the
windows, stood out starkly against the light-green walls
and wooden skirting boards. Mr. Bush was seating the
small children cross-legged on the polished wooden
floor. The older children were to sit in the back half
of the hall, which was filled with rows of chairs. At the
front end was a small raised platform with curtains on
either side.

"I say," said Zach excitedly. "There's a stage!!"

"Quickly," said George, tugging at one of Zach's well-
darned sleeves, "let's grab them chairs afore the big
uns get them."

They ran towards them, Willie following as fast as
he could, climbing over several small children on the
way.

Everyone else had grabbed seats at the back, and when
it was too late, George suddenly realized why the particular seats they had chosen had been left empty. They
were sitting in the front line of chairs. The rest of the
children were seated on the ground, so that all five of
them were now very exposed.

"Drat it," cursed George. "I got some toffees I was
goin' to slip in me mouth."

Mr. Bush and Mrs. Hartridge were talking to an elderly
lady.

"That's Mrs. Black," whispered Ginnie. "She must
be the extra teacher."

Mr. Bush dealt with the older children first and placed

a few evacuees with them at the back. It was very noisy. There was a lot of shouting and shuffling amongst the newcomers, most of whom were feeling bored and restless and had spent too long in the country already.

Mr. Bush announced the times when the older ones were next needed and dismissed them.

George, Carrie and Ginnie were to be in Mrs. Hartridge's class again. She was taking the eight- to eleven-year-olds. The twins had had their tenth birthday in the holidays and George was eleven.

Mrs. Black was to have all the local children and non-Catholic evacuees from five years old to eight.

Willie watched Mrs. Hartridge approach him and Zach. Zach told her his age, which was nine, and spelt out his name, apologizing for it at the same time. She smiled. Willie handed her his label and said nothing. Her long flaxen hair was coiled up in a thick plait at the top of her head. Willie gazed with pleasure at her soft, pink-cheeked face and then suddenly his heart fell.

She leaned over to Zach and said, "Now, Zacharias."

"You can call me Zach if it's too much of a mouthful."

"I think I can manage, thank you. Now tell me, what were you doing at your last school? You can read and write, can't you?"

At this juncture, Willie's ears filled up. Zach's chattering was only a faint rumbling echo in the distance. He felt her hand on his shoulder.

"Now, William," she said. "How about you? Can you read and write?"

He remained silent. He didn't dare look at the others. What would they think of him?

"What did you say, William?"

"No," he answered, and he picked at one of the nails

on his fingers and stared at the floorboards wishing he could disappear into them.

"Oh, I'm sorry about that, William. I would have liked you in my class. You'll have to go and sit with Mrs. Black's class," and she pointed to the little ones seated on the floor. Willie looked up in anguish and quickly down again.

The burning inside his ears seemed to spread into his jaw. He rose as if in a daze, found a space on the floor and sat down. He clasped his hands tightly together and bowed his head. He felt utterly humiliated.

Mrs. Hartridge's class was dismissed. They were to have school in the afternoons and wouldn't be starting until Friday.

Willie was left with Mrs. Black, and she and the remaining children filed over to the school. There were two girls even older than him who also couldn't read, but it didn't make him feel any better. One of them ignored everyone including Mrs. Black, and just filed her nails and stared out of the window.

Tom was weeding the graveyard when Willie returned. He watched the dejected figure walk past him into the cottage and, after allowing a few minutes to elapse, followed him in and discovered him sitting at the table in the living room, his bag of apples and sandwich lying untouched.

"I could just do with a cuppa," he said brightly. "You too, William?"

Willie gave a nod.

Tom pushed a mug of tea towards him. "How was it then?"

Willie scraped the toes of his boots together.

"Bad, was it?"

Willie nodded.

"Best tell me then."

Willie raised his head. It was difficult to look at Tom without his lips trembling.

"I'm with the babies."

"Oh, and whose class is Zacharias in then?"

"Mrs. Hartridge's."

"Why ent you? You're near enough the same age, ent you?"

"Yeh, but he can read." He paused. "And write."

"And the ones that can't are with Mrs. Black, that it?"

"Yeh."

"I see."

Tom stood up and looked out at the freshly weeded graveyard.

"Mrs. Black'll teach you to read. Did you learn anythin' today?"

"Gas drill," he mumbled.

"What's that?"

"Gas drill," he repeated, only louder. "We did gas-mask drill." He blew the top of his tea and sipped it. "There ain't even enough pencils."

Tom had seen some of the roughnecks that gentle old Mrs. Black would have to deal with. Most of her time, he reckoned, would be taken up trying to keep discipline.

"We'll begin this evenin'," he said sharply. "That do?"

"Wot?"

"Learnin' to read and write. I'll teach you to write yer own name fer a beginnin'."

Willie's eyes stung as the ground moved in a gentle haze beneath him. He beamed. "Aw, mister" was all he could manage to say.

Tom was surprised to find a lump in his own throat.

"Go and have a run with Sammy," he growled huskily. "I'll get supper."

Sammy, who had sensed Willie's misery and had until now remained motionless, began to bark and run after his tail.

"Go on with you, boy," said Tom.

Willie rose and clattered down the hallway. He ran through the gate, down the lane and across to the dirt track faster and faster, leaping and jumping. He wanted to yell for joy, but when he tried he couldn't get any sound out. He felt annoyed at first, but then he realized that he was running far better than he had been the previous day and that he wasn't even trying. It takes time and practice, that's what Mister Tom had said.

After supper had been cleared, Tom put a piece of paper and a pencil in front of Willie. On the paper were several straight lines and in between each pair was a series of dots.

"Now, William," said Tom. "You jes' join up the dots from the top downwards, and when you done that yous'll have written yer name. Now jes' takes yer own time."

Willie held the pencil nervously and then pressed it hard onto the paper. The lead snapped. Tom sharpened it again.

"Easy now," he said, handing him back the pencil. "You got plenty of time."

Willie stared frantically at the paper.

"I can't," he said. "I can't."

Tom looked sharply at him. Willie was frightened. His face had turned quite pale and beads of perspiration had broken out across his forehead.

"I won't beat you, if that's what's bothering you. Come

on, let's have a go," he added reassuringly. "I'll sit beside you and tell you how yer doin'."

Willie placed the lead on the paper and slowly followed the dots down and up, down and up, making the letter W.

He sat back and looked at it.

"It's bad, ain't it? Ain't it, Mister Tom?"

Tom peered at it. He was surprised.

"No," he said with honesty. "No, it ent," and Willie knew by the certainty in his voice that he was telling the truth.

"Ain't it?" he queried.

"No," Tom repeated. "It certainly ent. You go on. You's doin' fine."

Willie returned to the dots, and apart from the occasional wobble he wrote "William" in a remarkably smooth hand.

"That's good," said Tom.

"Is it?"

"Do it again."

Willie continued following the dots between the lines and then stopped.

"Mister Tom," he said. "I can look at my name and draw it. Is writin' like drawrin'?"

"I don't think so. Show me what you mean."

Willie found a clean unlined space, looked at what he'd done, drew two straight lines and wrote "William" in between them.

"Those lines are almost straight," gasped Tom. "Where'd you learn to do that?"

"Nowhere," said Willie. "I jes' looked at 'em and done it."

Tom was speechless for a moment. When he had recovered, he picked up a pencil and ruler, drew two straight lines, wrote "Beech" in between them and handed the pencil to Willie.

Willie drew the two lines again and, while carefully scrutinizing the new word, copied it.

"That's very good," remarked Tom.

"Is it?"

"Don't you know?"

He shook his head.

"You've jes' written yer name, boy."

"Have I?" And he stared down at the letters. He couldn't understand why those shapes were his name. Tom took his hand and made him point to the letters, going from left to right, sounding out each one. Willie joined in the second time round.

"Good," said Tom. He was about to suggest that he have a break when Willie pointed to the letters and sounded them out on his own. He became stuck at the double-e sound.

"Wot was that one agin, Mister Tom?"

"ee."

"B . . . ee . . . Wot's that?"

"ch."

He started again and succeeded in sounding all the letters through.

"You picked that up very quick," said Tom. "Very quick."

"It's copyin', though, ain't it?"

"Yes, I suppose so."

"Mister Tom," said Willie after some thought, "ain't that bad?"

"Copyin'?"

"Yeh."

"Not when yer learnin'," said Tom. "Only if yer bein' tested, like."

"Oh," he said, "I thought it were bad."

There was a knock on the front door. Sam started barking.

"Now who can that be?" said Tom.

"Mister Tom?" said Willie. "Does that mean that I won't go to hell if I copy?"

"Hell!!" said Tom in amazement as he strode out of the room. "Don't be daft, boy. Whatever put such a thought in yer head?"

Willie felt enormously relieved and returned to his writing. He was interrupted by voices in the hallway. He turned, and George and the twins walked in.

"Before you ses anythin'," said Carrie as Willie stood up, crimson, "we've jes' come to tell you that we're miserable about you not being in our class and that we still wants you to come round with us like."

"Yes," interjected Ginnie.

"And," said George, "yer not to feel bad about not bein' able to read and that. Anyway, it ent all that good when you can. You jes' gits given more lessons."

Carrie, at this juncture, gave him a poke.

"What we wanted to tell you," she continued, "was that we's goin' up the woods on Saturdee and we was wonderin' if you'd come with us like."

Willie opened his mouth to speak but was interrupted by another loud knock. Tom was hardly out into the hallway when in burst Zach.

"Will," he said breathlessly and stopped in midstream. "I say, what's going on here? Is this a party?"

Tom closed the door and was about speak when a further volley of knocks were hammered on it and Charlie Ruddles, the warden, strode angrily in.

"The front door wuz open, Mr. Oakley, and I saw a definite chink of light from where I wuz situated."

"Oh, and where would that be, Mr. Ruddles?" asked Tom, a little perturbed at so many dramatic entrances in one evening. "Would that be from lying on the hall floor with yer nose under the door?"

The twins at this point turned hurriedly away and bit their lips. Charlie stood back aghast. "I won't go into the legalities, Mr. Oakley. There were a definite chink. Don't you know there's a war on!" And with that he slammed the door and everyone except for Willie, who was feeling somewhat stunned, erupted into gales of laughter.

Birthday Boy
❦ ❦

Willie leaped out of bed. It was the beginning of his sixth day in Little Weirwold. He pulled back the blankets, peeled back the cotton and rubber sheets and struggled down the ladder with them in his arms. Sammy was yapping and jumping up and down, waiting for him at the bottom.

"Mornin'," said Tom, appearing at the back door. "Happy birthday!" He expected Willie to ask if there had been any post, but there was no response.

Willie dressed and helped Tom wash his sheets and pyjama trousers. They had decided, the previous evening after "Cain and Abel" and "How the Camel Got His Hump," that every day Willie would get up a little earlier than usual to practice writing and reading before leaving for school.

When he had finished his chores, he sat down at the table and copied out "I am William Beech" over and over again until Tom, after much effort, finally persuaded him to go for a run and exercise Sammy. He had only just disappeared down the graveyard path and out of sight when the postman arrived at the back gate.

"A birthdee boy, is it?" said young Matthew Parfitt.

"Anything from London?" asked Tom.

Matthew shook his head. " 'Fraid not. I got parcels though, and cards and this." It was a basket with fresh eggs, a newly baked loaf of bread, a pat of butter and some rashers of bacon inside. "Tis a birthdee breakfast from the Padfields."

Tom took the cards and parcels, together with the basket, indoors. It was a shame that there was nothing from the boy's mother, but then it was only Thursday and perhaps since war had been declared the post was being delayed. He hurried into the front room.

Willie returned flushed and breathless, followed by Sammy. He flung open the door and was about to say something when he caught sight of the table.

On top of a red-and-white-checkered tablecloth were two of the best plates, cups and saucers. In the center stood a jam jar with flowers in it, and surrounding Willie's place were parcels and envelopes.

"Happy birthdee," said Tom.

"Are they fer me?" he asked in astonishment.

" 'Tis where you usually sit, ent it? Go on, open them. I'll read out who they're from."

Willie picked up a soft brown-paper package and with trembling fingers slowly untied the string. Inside lay a green woolen balaclava helmet, a green sleeveless pullover and a pair of navy-blue corduroy shorts.

"Like to try them on?" said Tom.

Willie climbed out of his thin gray ones and stepped into the navy pair. Tom fixed the braces onto them. The shorts were a little loose round the waist.

"Soon fill out, though," said Tom. He put the pullover on over Willie's shirt. "Stand back and let's have a look at you."

The top was also a little long, but not so that it looked foolish. The shorts hung comfortably down to the base of his knees. He beamed.

"Feel good, do they?"

"Yeh. They got pockets too," he said, plunging his hands deep into them. He glanced at the balaclava. "Wot's that?"

" 'Tis a balaclava. Keeps yer head and ears warm when the wind's nippy."

"Can I put it on now?"

"If you want."

"Who give it me?" he asked as he pulled it over his head.

"I did, but Mrs. Fletcher made it."

"Ta," said Willie in thanks, and he gratefully touched the soft wool of the pullover.

"Ent you goin' to open the rest?"

The next parcel contained some Chiliprufe underwear from May Thorne, whom Willie had never even met. Emilia, her sister, had given him an illustrated copy of *The Wind in the Willows*. Inside she had written, "To William on his ninth birthday. For Mr. Oakley to read to you until you can read it yourself."

Willie held it tightly to his chest. "Is it fer me to keep?"

Tom nodded.

His own book. His very own book. The only other book he owned was the Bible, and that was old and dusty and had previously belonged to someone else. This book was new. The pages were crisp and white and were filled with the most marvelous pictures of animals wearing clothes.

He placed the book carefully to one side and continued to open the other parcels. There was a white china eggcup with a gold rim from Connie and Walter Bird, a boy's comic annual with lots of pictures and games in it from Dr. and Nancy Little, and a card game from the vicar and his wife. In addition to the parcels there were seven birthday cards.

Willie was completely overcome. He sat down and stared at the gifts quite speechless. Tom, meanwhile, took a large parcel out of the cupboard and placed it in front of him.

"That's me present from me to you."

"But you give me this," he said, indicating his pullover, "and these shorts."

"This is something different like."

Willie unwrapped the parcel and gave a start. There, before his eyes, lay one large and one small sketch pad. Pages and pages of untouched paper. There were two paintbrushes and three pots of paint. One brush was a medium-sized one, the other was thin and delicate. The paints were red, yellow and blue.

"If you mix them," said Tom, "you can also git orange, purple, green and brown."

Wrapped up in tissue paper were a pencil, an eraser and a sharpener. Something was carved at the end of the pencil. It looked familiar. He traced it slowly with his finger. "William Beech."

He looked lovingly at the paints and brushes and swallowed a pain that had risen at the back of his throat.

"I take it you like them," murmured Tom. "I chose them meself, like."

He glanced out at the window at the oak tree, where Rachel and his son were buried. She used to hug and kiss him when he gave her presents. She loved painting, wild flowers and pretty lace, sweet jams, freshly brewed beer. Since her death he had never wanted to touch anything that might remind him of her. Trust a strange boy to soften him up. The odd thing was that, after he had entered the paint shop, he had felt as if a heavy wave of sadness had suddenly been lifted from out of him. Memories of her didn't seem as painful as he had imagined.

"Thanks, Mister Tom," said Willie huskily. "I'll look after them real proper."

After a birthday egg-and-bacon fry up, Willie ran off to school. Tom met him outside at lunchtime, as there were no classes for him in the afternoon. They visited the people who had given him presents so that he could thank them personally. It would save the agony of trying to write letters, and Tom thought it would be a good opportunity for Willie to meet them. As for Tom, everyone was very surprised to see him, for he rarely visited anyone.

They strolled back home down the tunneled lane and called in at the Littles' cottage and the vicarage on the way. Willie had looked around for the twins and George, but they were nowhere to be seen. Even at the Littles' there was no sight of Zach.

P'raps they've gone blackberryin', he thought and for a fleeting moment he wished that he was with them.

"How about stayin' outside this afternoon?" suggested Tom suddenly. "It's a fine day." His words were immediately contradicted by the appearance of a dark shadow across the sky. "Drat them blimmin' clouds," he muttered. Sam raced on ahead of them and waited at Dobbs's field. Willie couldn't wait to begin drawing. He'd start with the gnarled old oak tree in the graveyard. That would be fine. But before they had reached the back gate a few drops of rain had already plopped warningly on their heads.

"I'll have to draw inside," said Willie to himself.

Tom grunted and then suddenly hit on an idea. "How about the church?" he exclaimed. "Of course, you could draw in there."

"Yeh," agreed Willie. "Yeh, I could."

He wrapped his mackintosh carefully round the small

sketch pad and fled down the pathway to the church, arriving in the nick of time, for as he closed the heavy arched door behind him, a slow drizzle of rain swept across the village and surrounding fields.

He stood quite still for a moment. It felt odd to be alone in a church. He would have felt nervous if it hadn't been raining. The sound it made rustling outside in the trees made him feel comfortable and protected. He stared up at the windows and then caught sight of the pulpit. Slinging his mac over the back of a pew, he sat down and rested his feet on the one in front. He placed the sketch pad on his knees, flicked open the first page and began to draw.

He didn't hear the rain suddenly stop. He was conscious only of the pulpit and his sketch pad. The rest of the church had ceased to exist for him. Neither did he hear Zach repeatedly calling him from outside, or the sound of his footsteps running up the tiny pathway to the back door.

The door opened slowly and Zach peeped in. He had never seen the interior of a church before. He slipped quietly in and glanced up at the windows and walls until his attention was drawn to a mop of fair hair sticking out from behind one of the back pews. He was just about to speak when he became aware that Willie was absorbed in some task. He took a few paces forward and leaned over Willie's small thin shoulders. His shadow fell across the pad. Willie jumped and turned round, hurriedly placing his arm over the picture, but it was too late. Zach had already seen it.

"I say," he gasped, full of admiration, "that's magnificent."

Willie shyly flapped the cover of the pad over the drawing.

"You must show the . . ." but he checked himself. "Didn't you hear me call you? I practically tore my throat out yelling for you."

Willie shook his head.

"Er . . ." said Zach thoughtfully, feeling a little stumped for words. "Er, Mr. Oakley says that he'd like to er . . . converse with you. Er . . . talk about the time of day. That sort of thing. He's waiting for you now."

"Is he?" said Willie in surprise, and he picked up his mackintosh. "Is it still rainin'?"

"It finished an age ago," groaned Zach. "Hurry up or the . . ." He stopped. "Er . . . or . . . it might start again."

They stepped outside. Pink clouds with white-tipped edges were gliding across the sky. Willie stopped and gazed up at them.

"Come on!" said Zach impatiently.

They walked down the path towards the front door. Blacks are up early, thought Willie, as he approached the cottage. He heard Sammy give an excited bark from the front room and then it immediately sounded muffled. Odd, thought Willie, but he shrugged it off and hung his mackintosh on his peg.

"Oh, do hurry," said Zach, who was standing waiting at the door. Willie looked at him.

"Wot you waitin' for?" he asked.

"You go in first," and with that Zach pushed open the door and immediately the whole room erupted into:

> *"Happy birthday to you,*
> *Happy birthday to you,*
> *Happy birthday, dear William,*
> *Happy birthday to you."*

The twins, George, their mothers, Lucy and her mother and Tom were all standing in the front room singing, while Sammy sat in the middle and howled.

A large banner with "Happy Birthday William" on it hung above and across the stove.

On the table stood two jellies, one red and one green. There was a plate of chocolate wafers, a plate of potted meat and fishpaste sandwiches and a plate of fairy cakes. In the center of the table was an iced cake with nine lighted candles on it. So that was why the blacks were up, thought Willie.

Zach was the first to break the ensuing silence.

"Was it a surprise?" he burst out. "Was it a real surprise? Did you guess?"

It was obvious from Willie's astounded expression that he had had no idea at all.

So this was what a birthday party was like. He had heard people at school talking about them. He looked towards Tom for help.

"You gotta blow the candles out, boy."

"And if you manages to blow them all out at once you can make a wish," said Carrie.

Willie leaned over, took a deep breath and blew. Six candles went out the first time, the remaining three the second time. Everyone applauded.

"You can still have a wish," said Zach, "when you cut the cake, only you mustn't talk till after you've made it and it must remain a secret else it won't come true and . . ."

"We'll be 'ere till doomsday if you go bletherin' on," said Tom.

Willie held the knife above the cake, screwed up his face till he had thought of a wish and then plunged the knife into the icing.

Mrs. Fletcher, Roe Padfield and Mrs. Thatcher sat on the low cupboard by the door, and Tom pulled the table out so that everyone could squeeze round on three chairs, a stool and the arm of the armchair. They had just sat down when Zach suddenly let out a cry.

"I nearly forgot. You haven't seen Will's picture."

Willie was still holding his sketch pad tightly under his arm. His face turned pink.

"You drawn a picture?" asked Tom.

"I'll say."

"You never stop saying," said Tom abruptly.

"Can we see it?" said Carrie.

"Please," added Ginnie.

Willie lifted the cover up shyly. George came and stood by his side and gave a low whistle.

"I told you, didn't I?" said Zach.

Tom leaned over their heads and peered down. It was a copy of the carved eagle on the pulpit. Its strong stubborn wings were swept back in a magnificent curve. Around it Willie had added rain so that it appeared to be flying against a great wind.

"That's a fine hand you have there, William," said Tom quietly. "A fine hand."

Willie blushed crimson.

"When I'm a famous author will you do my illustrations?" said Zach.

"I thought you was goin' to be a famous pilot this mornin'," retorted George.

"Well," said Zach, a bit put out, "I can write about my daredevil air exploits, can't I?"

They all settled down to eating while Willie, amidst all the chatter and laughter, found himself an object of praise. After tea there were more presents. A jigsaw puzzle from the twins, colored pencils from Zach, candy from George and some small cakes from Lucy.

"She baked them herself," said her mother.

Lucy gazed up at him. She was bursting with adoration. Willie didn't know how to treat her. The cakes were lovely, though.

"Ta," he said awkwardly, and she gave him one of her voluminous smiles.

After playing several party games, everyone finally returned home. Tom and Willie stood outside and watched them leaving. They turned back into the sitting room and closed the door.

"Mister Tom," said Willie, touching his sleeve. "It's the best . . . it's the best . ." but he never finished. The excitement and food simply welled up inside him and he gave a short gasp and vomited all over the carpet.

The Case
— ❦ ❦ —

During the next seven weeks the leaves floated and
twirled from the trees, and a light hoarfrost covered
the fields in the early mornings.

Matthew Parfitt, who was in the reserves, had been
called up, and May Thorne, to the surprise of everyone,
volunteered to deliver the post. She unearthed an ancient bicycle from some forgotten shed corner and proceeded to ride it from cottage to cottage, her sackful
of letters stuffed compactly into a basket in the front.

"I thought that they were extinct," Zach had said on
first seeing her riding it. "Looks like a fossil on wheels.
I am, of course, referring to the bicycle frame and not
Miss May," he added.

Michael Fletcher, who had signed up in September,
had at last, after much impatient waiting, also been called
up. He and John Barnes traveled into Weirwold together
to catch the train.

Mrs. Miller had been rushed into the hospital with a
concussion after having walked into a tree in the pitch
dark. When news of the event reached the graveyard
cottage, Willie overheard Tom muttering something to
the effect that it was a wonder the tree didn't have to
be taken too.

Meanwhile, the government had asked for a money
contribution from the parents of evacuees. Since many
parents were miserable at being separated from their
offspring and it would be a struggle for some to pay
money for their misery, they finally decided to have them

home again. Half of the evacuees in Little Weirwold and the surrounding area had already left. This meant that the classrooms were not so crowded, but there was still a shortage of paper and pencils. Willie longed desperately to be in Mrs. Hartridge's class, even though he had since grown quite fond of Mrs. Black.

Every day before and after school he faithfully practiced reading and writing, and occasionally when Emilia Thorne returned from the library she would pop round, when Tom was out on fire duty, and sit with him. She soon discovered that he had a remarkable aptitude for learning words, especially if he liked them. She started to teach him rhymes and poems, and then she would write them down on scraps of paper so that he could follow the letters through when he was on his own.

By now Tom had related the whole of Genesis to him and had read the *Just So Stories* twice. He and Willie were now in the middle of Exodus and had just begun *Grimm's Fairy Tales*.

Willie and Zach managed to see each other every day as well as weekends and odd evenings, and they, the twins and George would walk and play in the fields together.

One dull afternoon, on the last day of October, Zach and Willie were kneeling on the window ledge in the sitting room of the Littles' cottage. A slow icy drizzle of rain splattered and ran in tiny rivulets down the window.

Zach squinted through the glass and wiped his breath away from the pane.

"Where is he?" he moaned. "He's taking an age." He turned despondently from the window. "It'll soon be dark and then we won't be able to see him coming at all."

He was cut short by a loud knocking at the front door.

"Yippee! Wizzo!" yelled Zach, leaping up and running out of the kitchen. "Callooh! Callooh! Callooh! Callay!"

He switched the hall light off, stumbled to the front door and flung it open. His face fell. It was George and the twins.

"There's a welcome," said Carrie.

"It ent arrived, has it?" said George as they stepped into the dark hall.

Zach slammed the door behind them in a disgruntled manner and turned the light on.

"We can only stay for an hour," said Ginnie.

Mrs. Little leaned against the kitchen doorway, a freshly lit cigarette in her hand.

"You'll have to take them upstairs, Zach. First aid begins in fifteen minutes."

Zach groaned.

"Unless, of course, you want to volunteer to be a body."

"No, thanks," said Zach hurriedly. "Quick, let's go."

The five of them scrambled up the narrow carpeted stairway.

"And don't forget to put up the blacks," yelled Mrs. Little after them. "I don't want Charlie Ruddles wagging his finger at me again."

"I won't," answered Zach.

Zach's room seemed more like a study than a bedroom. One wall was filled to overflowing with medical books, and against the back window overlooking the Littles' straggly but unsuspectedly organized garden stood a large rolltop desk and chair. Along the wall opposite the bookcase was a bed, and under the front window, which looked out over the tiny arched lane and fields, was a small table with a photograph of a young dark-haired woman and a slightly older man with large penetrating eyes and a broad grin. They each had an arm around the other. On the floor beside Zach's bed was a small pile of books.

The twins perched themselves on the bed, Zach sat on the chair by the desk and George and Willie sat cross-legged with their backs leaning against the bookcase. Carrie picked up some of the books.

"To Save His Chum," she read aloud. *"Stalky and Company. The Golden Treasury of Verse, Great Actors I Have Known*—what an odd mixture!"

"Not at all," exclaimed Zach.

"Well, I think it's odd."

There was another loud knocking from downstairs. Zach leaped from his chair.

"It's Mister Tom!" said Willie suddenly, and he flushed at having betrayed his excitement so openly.

Zach gave out a yell, threw the bedroom door open and almost flung himself down the stairs. The others clattered on behind him.

Tom was standing in the hallway, his cap and overcoat covered with a thin layer of drizzle.

"I've tried to keep it dry," he said, indicating a large battered suitcase by his feet. "Best to wipe it, though."

He looked at Willie. "S'pose you'll be wantin' to stay fer a bit, eh?"

"Yeh, can I?"

"I'll collect you in thirty minutes. Mind you come immediate, like."

Zach and George dragged the case up to the bedroom and laid it on one side. It was a brown leather case with two straps that buckled on either side of the handle.

The leather was soft and faded with age. Both sides of it were covered by labels of all colors and shapes with the names of towns and countries on them. Two thick pieces of cord were tied horizontally and vertically around it.

"Has you been to all them countries?" asked George.

"My parents mostly. They used this when they were one-night-standing and eventually they gave it to me."

"One-night-standin'?" repeated Willie.

"Yes. There are some companies that perform in a different venue every night."

"Venyew? What's that?"

"A place. A place where a show is going to be performed. Usually the show is already booked in advance. Anyway," continued Zach, "my parents kept their ordinary clothes in one suitcase and their costumes and makeup in another."

"Does your father wear makeup?" asked George.

"Sometimes," answered Zach, still struggling with the cords. "Gosh, they certainly did a good job on this."

"Do you mean like a lady?" said Willie.

Carrie burst out laughing.

"Here," said Ginnie, "I'll help you," and she knelt by Zach, who was by now hot with frustration. He leaned back on his heels and looked at Willie.

"Haven't you ever seen a show?"

Willie shook his head.

"Me mum ses that theaters and pitcher houses are dens of sin."

"Rot," exclaimed Zach. "I was practically born in the theater. I was breast-fed in theater dressing-rooms."

Willie blushed. "That's swearing," he said.

"I learned to walk and talk in theaters," said Zach. "And I'm not sinful, am I?"

"You're just an angel, ent you," said Carrie, her hands clasped.

"And you're cracked," said Zach. "Come on, let's open this beastly case."

At last the stiff damp straps were unbuckled and the two large clips unfastened. Zach threw back the lid in triumph and the twins and George gathered round to look at the contents. Willie hesitated.

"Come on, Will," said Zach, seeing him hang back. "I want to show off to everyone."

"When do you stop?" remarked Carrie.

Zach gave her a withering glance, but it was so over-dramatic she and the others burst out laughing. He gave up and looked inside the case. An envelope with "Zach" written on it in bold lettering was stuck to the inside of the lid. He tore it off and ripped open the envelope.

"It's from Mummy and Daddy," he yelled.

"Surprise, surprise," said George. "Come on. We've got to go home soon. You can read that later."

"Oh, all right," said Zach, stuffing it into his pocket.

The case was packed very tightly. He peeled off a large piece of newspaper from the top and unwrapped five small parcels, inside which lay several home-baked cakes.

"I ent never seen cakes like that afore," said George.

"My grandmother taught my mother to make these when she was a girl."

Underneath were two jars of pickled herrings and three bars of chocolate.

"Wizzo!" he yelled, pulling out an assortment of much-loved and battered objects. "Books!"

"What you want with those?" said George. "Thought you'd have enough of that at school."

Carrie began to flick through them. Willie tapped

Zach's shoulder, but he had already read his mind and he handed him a couple.

The words were laid out in a strange manner.

"It's all talkin'," said Carrie. "There ent no description."

"There's some in the dialogue," explained Zach. "The words have to set the atmosphere, you see. They're plays."

"How d'you play wiv 'em?" asked Willie, his curiosity aroused.

"You are an ass, Will. They're theater plays. Scripts." He pointed to the lines. "See here, that's that character's lines and that's the other person answering. Actors learn them off by heart and then they rehearse them masses and masses of times until it sounds as if they've just thought of them."

George held up one thick battered tome.

"*The Complete Works of William Shakespeare.* Ugh!" and he dropped it in disgust.

"How dare you!" cried Zach, picking it up hastily. He looked at Willie, sensing that he wouldn't have heard of him. "William Shakespeare was one of our greatest playwrights. A playwright is a man who writes plays like the one in your hand, only he wrote plays nearly four hundred years ago and people still go and see them being performed."

"William Shakey," said Willie quietly to himself.

"Shakespeare!" hooted Carrie.

"William Shakespeare," he repeated. "William." So he had the first name of somebody famous.

The next article that Zach dragged out was a stiff black circular object. He shook it and in one second it became a shiny top hat.

He placed it on his thick wiry hair and cocked it slightly to one side. Everyone was terribly impressed. He then pulled out a small black suit. The jacket of the suit curved in at the waist, and at the back were two buttons above a pair of tails. There was a stiff white object called a dicky. It was a collar and bow tie and the front of a shirt. Dangling from it were two thin cords to be tied at the back. Zach put it on, and when the jacket was done up it looked as if he was wearing a proper dress shirt. Imitation white cuffs were attached to the ends of the jacket sleeves.

"Proper job," remarked George.

Ginnie examined the whole suit very closely. She turned back the sleeves to see exactly how the cuffs had been sewn in.

Zach unwrapped a pair of objects wrapped in newspaper.

"My taps!"

He held up a pair of shiny black patent shoes. On each sole were two pieces of metal, one at the tip and one at the heel.

"What kind of shoes is they?" asked George, puzzled.

"Tap shoes. You've seen Fred Astaire dance, haven't you? Well it's . . ." He stopped. The others were all shaking their heads from side to side.

"I've heard of Fred Barnes," said George. "He owns the Big Farm up at . . ."

"Will. You're a Londoner. You must have seen him at the pictures."

"I ain't allowed," emphasized Willie. "I don't do that sort of thing."

Zach was astounded. He thought the whole world had heard of Fred Astaire.

"Well, there's only one way to explain tap." He moved the case to one side, rolled back the carpet and told the others to sit by the bookcase. He then put the shoes on and laced them up. He did look strange in the elegant black shoes, darned woolen socks, threadbare shorts, top hat and tails.

"Now this is what's called a tap spring," and he lightly tapped his right foot along the floorboards and hopped neatly onto it, leaving his left leg raised slightly behind him. Carrie smothered a giggle. He glared at her.

"If you don't want to see what it's like I shan't bother wasting my time." Ginnie gave her sister a dig in the ribs.

"Come on," said George. "Take no notice of her."

If it hadn't been for Willie's attentive expression Zach would have stopped.

"All right," he said. "Here goes. And a one, two, three, four, five, six, seven, eight." And with that he danced around the room, his shoes tapping rhythmically on the floor, springing and twirling around, and as he tapped and stamped, he yelled out, "Shuffle hop, cramp roll, Buffalo."

He concluded the dance with a double spin, springing sideways in the air and kicking his feet sharply together, and as he did so he landed in a heap on the bed.

George, the twins and Willie broke out into applause. Zach grinned sheepishly at them.

They were interrupted by the entrance of Mrs. Little. She stood and, brandishing a hefty piece of ceiling plaster in her hand, glared at them.

"Zach," she said, looking directly at him, "I presume you are responsible for this."

He looked up at her from the bed, his cheeks flushed with the exertions of his performance, the taps on his shoes exposed to her scrutiny.

"Sorry, Aunt Nance," he began earnestly.

"I know it's difficult," interrupted Mrs. Little, "but we don't want to treat real casualties just yet, so keep the noise down, will you?"

Zach nodded, and she opened the door out onto the landing and closed it behind her. They sat silently and listened to her footsteps fading away down the staircase. Zach undid his shoes.

"Never mind," said Ginnie quietly. "You can show us again, another time."

"Not if this wretched drizzle continues and we have to stay indoors," he said. "It's awful having to creep around all the time."

"You was fine," broke in Willie. "You was really fine."

Zach beamed.

"Come on, slowcoach," urged George.

Zach hurriedly unpacked a soft, flat parcel.

With a flourish he pulled out a jersey of many colors. The body and sleeves were knitted in colored squares, red, yellow, green, black and orange. He struggled out of his old jersey and put it on. He even had to turn up the sleeves.

"Wonderful, isn't it?" he remarked. But the others could only stare at him in speechless amazement.

"You ent goin' to wear that, is you?" said George.

"Whyever not?"

"Well, 'tis a bit bright, ent it?"

"You'll have Charlie Ruddles after you with blackout curtains," said Carrie. Ginnie giggled.

Zach turned to Willie.

The jersey had a polo-neck collar in red. The cuffs and the waistband were ribbed in the same color. Willie thought that next to Zach's deep complexion and black hair the red looked pleasing.

"I think it's fine," he said quietly, and Zach knew he was speaking truthfully.

There were socks in the case, a scarf, a cape and colored tights, scraps of material and a pair of old black ankle boots with a label hanging on them. It read, "Found these in the theater wardrobe. No use for them. Too small. Have had them resoled. Hope they fit you. If too big you can always stuff the toes. Love, Mum."

Zach closed the case and passed the cakes around.

"Where shall we meet next time?" he asked.

"What's wrong with here?" said Carrie.

Zach pointed his thumb downwards.

"There's always something going on here in the evenings. If it's not first aid it's the Knitting Socks for Icelandic Seamen Club."

"Well, there ent much room in our place," said George. "I share with David an' he's bound to keep comin' in to see what we's doin' and Edward hasn't had a room of his own ever. Now that Mike's gone he guards it like it were a blimmin' gold mine."

Zach turned to the twins.

"How about your place?"

The twins looked at each other.

"We've a room between us," said Ginnie, "but there's Sophie."

Sophie was their eight-year-old sister.

"She'd be nosin' in on us," said Carrie.

Willie remained silent. He had a room. It was terribly private and precious, though. Dare he risk inviting them and asking Mister Tom's permission? After all, he was still wetting his bed. He would hate the others to find out.

"Zach," he began huskily. He cleared his throat. "There's my room."

"Of course," he cried. "I'd forgotten. Could we meet at your place?"

"I'll ask Mister Tom," Willie said, flushing slightly.

"Well, that's that settled," said Zach with finality. Willie was not so sure. "What's the next game to be?"

"Not Tarzan again," said George. "I've had enough of bein' an ape."

"Actually," said Zach, "I've got another idea brewing. How about Sherlock Holmes? You could be Moriarty, George."

"The archenemy?"

"Yes," said Zach, surprised. "How did you know?"

George raised his eyes. He was always the archenemy and Carrie was invariably his evil assistant.

"Does that mean I has to die or be rescued again?" said Ginnie.

"Well, not exactly," said Zach, a little perturbed. "Anyway, as I was saying, Will, you could be . . ."

"Dr. Watson," chorused George and the twins.

Willie was always Zach's faithful assistant, and it was quite obvious, as soon as Sherlock Holmes was mentioned, that Zach would be the famous deerstalkered detective.

"How about sittin' in a tree waitin' for badgers," suggested George. "Or seein' if Spooky Cott is really haunted?"

Spooky Cott was the name given to a deserted cottage. It was surrounded by an undergrowth of tangled bushes and trees. Over the years, several people had reported hearing strange sounds emanating from it. George and the twins dared not venture near it except in the broadest of daylight, and even then they usually fled at first sight of it.

"At night?" asked Ginnie, and she shivered.

"Yes, with a torch."

"Blackout regulations."

"Drat," said George.

"Goodness," Ginnie gasped, catching sight of the clock. "We'll have to go. We'll be in trouble if we don't run for it."

She, Carrie and George grabbed their coats and fled out of the room and down the stairs.

"When shall we meet?" whispered Zach urgently after them.

"Friday?"

Friday was agreed.

They hurriedly whispered their good-byes to each other, and after the front door had been closed Willie followed Zach back into his bedroom.

"Now," said Zach, jumping onto the bed, "I can read my letter," and he pulled out the crumpled envelope from his shorts. "You don't mind, do you?" he said, glancing at Willie, who had sat down beside him.

"No," answered Willie, "course not."

He wriggled back farther on the bed till he was leaning up against the wall. He could hardly believe that Zach was his special friend. Zach said he was a good listener and that he was a sensitive being. Willie had thought being sensitive was being a sissie. Zach didn't think so. He admired him for it. Admired him!

He glanced over at Zach. He was lying sprawled across the pillow leaning on his elbow, his head propped to one side, reading the letter. There seemed to be pages.

His own mother had written to Little Weirwold only once since his arrival eight weeks ago, and the letter had been addressed to Mister Tom. He had read it out to him but he knew that he'd left out bits.

He had actually written a letter of his own to her. His first ever. He'd even addressed the envelope, bought the stamp by himself and posted it. I expect she's been too busy to answer, he thought, what with the war and everything. For a brief moment he thought of his home in London and brushed the memory aside.

There was a knock on the front door downstairs and the sound of Mrs. Little opening it.

"That's Mister Tom," said Willie, moving off the bed. Mrs. Little called up to him.

"I got to go."

"Bother," said Zach.

They were at the top of the stairs when Zach touched his shoulder.

"Don't forget about the room, will you," he whispered.

Willie shook his head and ran down the stairs.

Tom was waiting for him at the bottom. Willie put his gabardine and cap on and slung his gas-mask box over his shoulder.

The sky was almost black when he and Tom stepped outside. A strong wind tore through the trees, whipping the branches fiercely to one side while the rain swept across their faces. Tom put up the umbrella.

"Best hang tight to my arm, boy," he yelled and together they leaned forward and tramped through the long wet grass to wrestle with the Littles' gate.

Willie clung firmly to him. He pulled his cap down over his eyes, but the wind whistled bitterly through his ears.

They passed the Bush family's cottage and struggled by the vicarage. The leaves flew and scattered around in fragments, brushing their bodies and sticking to their wet cheeks.

They fought with the long gate into Dobbs's field and Tom checked that she was sheltered. The wind tried to wrench the umbrella from his hands. He hung grimly on and wrestled with it until he could lower it in front of them. Half running, half walking, they fled through the back garden, narrowly missing the Anderson, and threw themselves into the passageway, the leaves swirling in after them.

They slammed the door behind them and panted and smiled in the darkness. It was as if someone had suddenly turned off the sound.

Tom opened the sitting-room door and the silence was broken by Sammy as he came bounding out, leaping up at the pair of them barking excitedly. Willie hung his gabardine and cap on his peg while Sammy stood on his hind legs and placed his paws on his stomach. Willie ruffled his fur.

"Has he been fed?" he asked.

"No, lad, I left it fer you."

Willie grinned happily. It was one of his jobs to feed Sammy in the evenings.

After he had fed him, he wiped his boots dry with an old rag, put the kettle on and sat down at the table with pencil and paper.

" 'Tis late fer that," said Tom.

"Just ten minutes," pleaded Willie. "Mrs. Black ses if I can do me letters and me capitals better, I can start joined-up writin' soon."

"No longer, though."

"Ta," and with that he began writing.

Tom made the tea and took down two large white mugs from hooks hanging by the window. One had a letter T on it, the other a letter W.

Since Willie was so desperate to be accepted in Mrs. Hartridge's class, Tom had been helping in every possible way. He had stuck labels in various places so that Willie would associate an object with a word, until after a time Willie labeled them himself. He glanced at all the bits of paper hanging higgledy-piggledy on the furniture and walls. He hoped that Willie would manage to get into Mrs. Hartridge's class before she left. It had been announced only a month ago that she was expecting her first child and would probably be leaving after the spring term.

He glanced at Willie, who had now finished writing. He was sitting quietly, drinking his tea.

It wasn't until after he had gone to bed that Willie asked about the room. He had remained subdued for the rest of the evening, glancing at Tom and looking away. It was Tom who finally coaxed it out of him.

He had gone up as usual to turn Willie's lamp down and had found him sitting up in bed with one of his library books lying open on his knees. Instead of tracing the pages with his finger as he usually did, he was staring vacantly into space. Tom came over to him, closed the book and put it on his table.

"Now then," he said, crouching under the rafters and seating himself comfortably at the foot of the bed, "what's it all about, eh?"

Willie looked at him, startled.

"What's eatin' you? You been in a brown cloud ever since supper."

Willie took a deep breath.

"You see," he began, "Zach made the ceiling fall on

Mrs. Little's head and Edward won't let George in his room 'cos of the war and Zach ses they're knittin' boots in the sittin' room and the twins ses they might, only . . ."

"Slow down," said Tom, "and gets to the point."

"Mister Tom," he said breathlessly, "could I have George and Zach and Carrie and Ginnie up here in this room?"

"Don't see why not. They been thrown out of their homes?"

"No. It's jes' there ain't much room at George's and Zach ses . . ."

"No need to explain. This is your room. You does what you like, only," he warned, pointing his pipe in Willie's direction, "if there's any mess you has to clear it up. Understand?"

"Yeh. Course," said Willie.

"When is they wantin' to come?"

"Fridee."

"Fridee 'tis then."

Tom stood up and kissed Willie's forehead. "Night, lad," he said quietly.

"Mister Tom," said Willie, as he turned to turn the lamp down.

"Yis?"

"They don't know about—you know," and he patted the blankets with his hands.

"The bed-wettin'? You ent ashamed of that, is you?" Willie nodded.

"Ent no need to mention it. I'll makes yer bed up before the evenin' so's they won't see the rubber. That do?"

"Yeh. Ta."

The room was blanketed in darkness until Tom removed the blackout curtain.

"Night," he said again, and he disappeared down the steps, closing the trapdoor after him. Willie leaned his head back on his upraised hands. He glanced at the slanting windowpane. The rain was running down the glass in tiny sparkling rivulets. He snuggled down into the warm blankets. He had never thought that he would ever come to love the rain, but he did now. The last thing he remembered before falling asleep was the *patter, patter, patter* of it gently and rhythmically hitting the tiled roof above his head.

Friday

— ⚘ ⚘ —

Mrs. Fletcher was bending over the last of a bed of weeds, hoping finally to rid herself of them before her husband returned from the potato harvesting. Her thoughts were interrupted by the sound of heavy footsteps and loud barking. She looked up vacantly. It was Tom Oakley. Easing herself gently to her feet, she leaned slowly backwards. Her spine gave a soft cracking sound.

"Back early, ent you?" she remarked. "Yous ent finished, has you? I ent started tea fer Ben yet."

"He's stayin' on," said Tom. "I decided I'd come home early tonight. Boy's got friends comin' round. Your George fer one."

"So he said."

Tom grunted.

"I jes' thought I'd be around like, in case the boy needs anythin'. Tends to git overexcited."

A strand of auburn hair fell across Mrs. Fletcher's eyes. She brushed it aside.

"Don't seem so long since his birthdee, do it?"

"Two months," commented Tom absently, and he gazed down the road remembering how he had watched Willie's thin little hunched body stumbling after Sammy on that first day.

"You heard from his mother yet?"

"I had a letter last week. Mostly about him bein' bad and me watchin' him, like. I wish he would be bad. He says 'yes' or 'dunno' to every blessed thing I ses."

Mrs. Fletcher laughed.

"I wish George would."

She picked up a bucket filled with weeds.

"What about this six shilluns contribution then?"

"That's what she wrote about. Ses she can't pay yet but it'll be on its way. Ses it means she won't be comin' to see the boy fer Christmas."

"Shame on 'er," tutted Mrs. Fletcher.

"Oh, I dunno," said Tom. "He's changed quite a bit in these last few weeks."

So has you and all, thought Mrs. Fletcher.

"Yes," he went on, "I almost fancy he's grown a bit. It won't do him no harm to be out of his mother's apronstrings fer a bit longer. She puts the fear of the divil into him anyways."

He leaned across the gate in a confidential manner.

"Do you know, Mrs. Fletcher, last week he laughed. It were a bit of a nervous one like, but he actually laughed. It were the first time I ever heard him do it. Didn't think he had a sense of humor in him."

Mrs. Fletcher looked steadily into his eyes. His forehead had lost its furrowed look. The deep pitted wrinkles above his eyes had softened outwards. Behind his scowling manner was a kindly old man, and if it hadn't been for the arrival of a rather insipid little boy, she might never have known, nor might anyone else for that matter.

A breeze shook a half-naked tree, causing a handful of leaves to cascade into the garden.

"Well," said Mrs. Fletcher, "now that you're here you might as well take the jersey and socks. I finished them last night."

After Tom had collected the woolens, he walked home

feeling remarkably relaxed. Sammy ambled leisurely in front of him while he stopped intermittently to pick up sweet chestnuts on the way.

Willie had scraped the potatoes, chopped up carrots and turnips, buttered a few slices of oddly cut bread and filled Sammy's bowls with fresh water and scraps. His boots were laid out on a newspaper, and had been scraped and polished. He was sitting cross-legged on the floor giving a finishing touch to them when Tom walked in. He looked up and rubbed his forehead excitedly, leaving another smudge of brown shoe polish above his nose.

"I finished me readin' book today and I starts the last one on Mondee. And Mrs. Black ses I can do joined-up writin'," he added, scrambling to his feet. "By mid-term I might have finished the last one. Then I can read good enough fer Mrs. Hartridge."

"Good. You've worked hard fer it and you're bright."

"Bright?"

"Got it up here," said Tom, tapping his head with his hand.

It was after they had cleared supper and were sitting by the range with a cup of tea that the first person to arrive knocked at the front door. Willie, whose stomach had been steadily growing tighter, almost spilled his tea over his shorts. He was wearing the new jersey that Tom had collected from Mrs. Fletcher. It was navy blue with a rolled-top neck. The cuffs were well turned back and the jersey came halfway down his shorts.

"Ent you goin' to answer it then?" said Tom.

Willie placed the mug carefully on the table and made his way nervously out of the door and down the small dark passageway.

It was Zach. Willie was glad that he had come first.

He showed him into the living room, where Sammy greeted him, wagging his tail.

"Unusual jersey, that," commented Tom. It was the first time he had seen Zach's "Joseph" jersey.

"Unique, I'd say," replied Zach.

"I'll go put the blacks up and light the lamp," said Tom.

Willie and Zach waited at the foot of the ladder while Sammy scrabbled around the first rung.

A square of amber light shone down on them from the open hatch.

"I say, it's magnificent!" gasped Zach. "Like rays from Heaven."

Tom climbed down the ladder.

"All yours," he said.

Sammy by now had wormed his way up to the third rung, where he was floundering and panting breathlessly.

"You want Sam with you?"

"Won't you be lonely without him, Mr. Oakley?" asked Zach.

Tom was a little taken aback at this candid question.

"No. I can do some jobs that he gits in the way of. But if he becomes a nuisance, William," he added, "you bang on the floor and I'll pick him up."

"Ta," said Willie gratefully, and between him and Zach they carried Sammy up the ladder.

Willie had grown used to the changes in his room, so that he was pleasantly surprised at Zach's excitement over it. Two of the walls were covered with his drawings and paintings, and on one wall were shelves that Tom had fixed up for his clothes and treasures.

Zach gazed round at the tiny wooden bed under the rafters. The flickering lamp above their heads and the patches of color round the walls gave the room a cozy lived-in air.

After a brief glance at the two boxes of apples stacked in the corner, he sat on the end of the bed with Willie and talked about the poem he was writing.

It was in "the epic vein," which for him meant a long rhyming poem about knights in armor. Sammy, who had been sitting quietly by their feet, jumped up and began barking. There was a loud knock on the open trapdoor and Carrie and Ginnie's heads came into view.

"Ent it beautiful," commented Ginnie.

"Like a workroom of one's own," sighed Carrie enviously.

They were interrupted by an impatient voice from below.

"Stop spoonin'. I want to see. Hurry up."

They clambered up onto the floor followed eagerly by George, who practically fell over them in his clumsy desire to get in. All three of them stared silently at the walls.

"You never done these, did you?" said George.

There was a drawing of the oak tree, two brave attempts at Sammy, a painting of five children blackberrying, one of a library with people sitting and walking round and several sketches of boots and flowers and half-eaten sandwiches.

"Sheer genius, aren't they?" said Zach thrusting his nose upwards. "Wizard choice of friends I have, don't you think?"

"Why has you got all them words written under them?" asked George.

Willie flushed.

"Is it fer learnin' to read?" said Carrie.

He nodded. "I starts the last readin' book on Mondee, and joined-up writing."

"I say, well done," exclaimed Zach.

"Don't know why yer botherin'," grunted George. "You gits to mess around more in your class. Anyways, if I could draw like you, I wouldn't bother about nothin' else."

"Anythin' else," corrected Carrie. "And you don't bother about anythin', anyways."

"I does. They jes' don't teach interestin' things at school. Who wants to read books? Books ent no good. They don't feed animals and plow fields, does 'ey?"

Carrie groaned. "You'm jes' pig ignorant."

"Good," said George. "I likes pigs and pigs is useful."

"Are you two going to spend this evening ranting again?" interrupted Zach.

It was obvious to everyone from the moment they sat down that Zach was bursting to tell them something.

"Come on, reveal all," said Carrie, imitating his theatrical way of speaking.

"Guess what!" he half squeaked. "Miss Thorne is producing a children's Christmas show for the war effort and she needs all the help she can get."

Ginnie gasped. "I couldn't go onstage. I'd hate it."

"You needn't act in it. You could help backstage."

"You could do your sewin'," suggested George.

Ginnie's face lit up. "I could make costumes."

"Well spoken, that man," said Zach. "That's a wizard idea."

George cleared his throat and beamed. "I does have the odd unbeatable one," he said smarmily.

"I'm glad to hear that," said Zach, "because I'm going to ask you for another good suggestion."

George visibly swelled with pride. "Go ahead," he said.

"What are *you* going to do in the show?"

George's face fell. "Me!" he spluttered. "Me! I ent doin' no fancy theatricals with ole corny Thorny. She's nutty as a fruitcake."

"Coward," said Carrie.

"I ent goin' to do it," he protested. "And that's a fact."

"I vote we bring this meeting to order," said Ginnie sharply.

Zach looked at George.

"Well," he said. "Are you going to be courageous or not?"

"Coward," repeated Carrie.

"Oh, all right," said George crossly. "I'll do it."

"Wizzo. That's two."

"What about you, Zach?" asked Carrie.

"Oh, I expect I'll volunteer for one of the leads," he said, leaning back and crossing his long brown legs nonchalantly. He turned to Willie.

"I ain't been near a theater. Me mum ses . . ."

"It isn't exactly a theater," interrupted Zach earnestly. "It's the hall. It's just that we're going to make it into a theater."

"Yeh, but . . ."

"You needn't perform. You could help with the scenery."

"Paintin', like," said Carrie.

Willie smiled nervously. "Yeh, all right."

"I'll volunteer too," said Carrie, "I don't care what I do so long as I don't have too many lines to learn."

"Wizzo," yelled Zach. "That's the five of us."

He studied Sammy, who was chewing the toe of one of his large stuffed boots.

"No," said George and the twins in unison. Zach looked at Willie.

"You'll have to ask Mister Tom," Willie said.

"Three against two," said Carrie.

"Oh, all right," he sighed wearily, "I give in."

"My turn now for news," said George. "We's goin' to have a big Carol Service in the church on Christmas Eve. Mr. Bush started rehearsin' us last night and he could do with some extra voices, like."

Carrie opened her mouth.

"Boys only," he added.

"Ent it a blimmin' cheek," she exclaimed angrily. "Boys gits all the chances. The academic high school in Weirwold only takes boys," she said in protest to Zach, "and they never bother to put girls in fer it. And here's me dyin' to go and him," she said waving a finger at George, "havin' all the chances, and him hating books."

"Mebbe now there's a war on it'll be different for girls," said Ginnie, gently touching her sister's arm. She knew how much learning meant to her.

"I hope so. But it don't seem no different being at war really, do it? 'Cept there's more goin' on in the evenin's with first aid and the like."

There was a short silence.

"Well," said George, glancing at Willie and Zach, "you two interested?"

"I'd like to," said Zach, "but I never go to church so it'd be a bit strange if I sing in it, won't it, me not even being a Christian."

"Ain't you a Christian?" asked Willie in alarm.

Zach shook his head. "No. I thought you knew that."

Willie expected at any moment to see the tips of two red horns slowly emerging from under his hair, but they didn't.

"You could always ask the vicar," suggested George.

"But what if I had to say your prayers. I might have to say things I didn't believe in. It leaves me in a bit of a dilemma, don't you see."

"Di-what?" said George.

"Quagmire," said Zach, and he gave a sigh and threw his hands up in the air. "I mean I'd really like to, but I've already been shouldered out of the Nativity play. It's rotten, rotten luck. I know the story quite well too. I mean your Jesus that you believe was God was Jewish, wasn't he? Joseph, his father, was Jewish and so was his mother. And here's me dying to act and I can't be in it because I'm Jewish."

"Now you know how I feel about the high school," said Carrie.

"Oh, git the handkerchiefs out fer a weep," groaned George, pretending to play the violin.

"I'll do it," said Willie suddenly. "I'll s-s-sing."

George beamed.

"Rehearsals every Thursdee. I'll give you a hand in the readin' if you gits stuck."

"We need to do somethin' a bit more excitin', like," said George impatiently. "Let's go lookin' fer badgers or even their holes. How about it? Who's for goin'?"

"I'd like to," blurted out Willie.

They all stared at him in surprise. It was unusual for him to volunteer without persuasion.

"I'll come too," said Zach. "I don't know anything about badgers, but it might be useful. Who knows, perhaps one day I may have to play one."

Carrie and Ginnie looked at each other.

"We'll come too," they sighed in a tone of resignation.

"I ent forcin' you," said George.

"I say," said Zach. "What was that mysterious place you were talking about at Aunt Nance's?"

Ginnie paled. "Spooky Cott," she whispered.

"Couldn't we go and look at that as well?"

George and the twins gave no answer, and Willie felt a cold prickle crawl up his back and into his hair.

"Oh come on," cried Zach. "It can't be that frightening, can it?"

All three of them nodded silently.

"We ent bin there for two years now," said George.

"I say, what happened?"

"Nothin' you could exactly put yer finger on, like," said Carrie ominously. "But there was a strange eerie feeling in the air. The trees"—she swallowed—"the trees, they seemed to groan and wave their arms about."

"Let's go. I mean, if we all go together we can protect each other."

"When was you thinkin'?" asked George in an unusually timid voice.

"How about tonight!" whispered Zach, and he gave a shrieking imitation of a cackling witch.

George and the twins yelled and Willie clutched Sammy, who had started barking.

Zach gave a long ghostly moan and raised his hands. With wide, blank eyes he shuffled towards them. They stumbled backwards. Willie tried to calm Sammy, who was jumping about excitedly.

"That's enough," said Ginnie crossly.

"Oh, all right, spoilsports," Zach said, feeling disgruntled, and he sat down, missed his cushion and landed with a painful thump on the floor. This time it was the others who laughed. He rubbed his bottom vigorously, looking very hurt.

They were interrupted by a knocking on the hatch.

Willie lifted it up to find Tom standing on the steps, with a large tray in his hands. On it was a jug of lemonade, five cups, a plate of ginger snaps and a bowl of nuts. Beside it was a small saucer of salt.

"Hot chestnuts," yelled Willie. "They has them in London when it's Christmas. I seed them sell them in the streets lots of time, but I ain't never tasted them like."

"Thought mebbe you could use them."

"Rather," cried Zach. "Mister Tom, you're a real brick."

"Am I?" Tom mumbled. "Humph!"

He looked around at their delighted faces and began to feel embarrassed.

"You'd best eat them afore they gits cold."

Sammy wriggled into his arms and pushed his head underneath Tom's chin.

" 'Ad enough have you, boy?" he said, picking him up, and with that he gave them all a brisk wave and disappeared down the steps, closing the hatch quickly behind him.

"He's a real decent sort, Will," said Zach. "You're awfully lucky being landed on someone like him."

Willie smiled. He'd known that since that first bewildering day.

"I'm lucky too," he went on, "with the doctor and Aunt Nance."

"That's 'cos they're daft like you," said George through a mouthful of ginger snap.

"I don't think Christine and Robert King are very

happy," said Ginnie. "They's stayin' at one of the tenant cottages at Hillbrook Farm and they has to earn their keep. 'Specially now that John's gone."

"Robert fell asleep in history on Monday," said Carrie.

"Don't blame him," said George.

"And Christine told me," continued Ginnie, "that Mr. Barnes threatened to have their dog put down if they didn't work hard enough."

"Here, have a chestnut," said Carrie, flinging one into her sister's hands.

"Yes, let's eat," added George.

The meeting ended with everyone feeling very satisfied. They scrambled down the ladder, yelling their good-byes. Will watched them as they ran through the graveyard and climbed over the wall to the lane. He closed the door, walked into the living room and sank happily into the armchair.

Tom glanced at him. The last time Willie had had so many children at the cottage he had been sick. Tonight he looked healthily tired.

"Let's have a look at that ole arm of yours," he said.

Willie sleepily pulled his jersey and shirt off and slid to the edge of the armchair. Tom squatted down in front of him. Very gently he cleaned a sore and put some ointment on it. It was the last one.

"This time next week, should be gone," he muttered, but Willie didn't hear him. His eyelids were already fluttering into sleep.

Tom helped him into his pyjamas, carried him up the ladder on his back and put him to bed.

When Willie woke the next day, there was something altogether unusual about the morning. He lay in bed for some time and stared up at the ceiling trying to puzzle it out. Finally he gave up and clambered out of bed. It was only when he started automatically to strip it that he realized what it was that was so different. There was no need for the sheets to be washed that day. They were dry.

The Show Must Go On
❧ ❧

November had been a damp and drizzly month, bringing shorter days and causing aggravation to those people who found it increasingly difficult to travel in the blackout.

Tom had meanwhile dug up his turnips and set to work hedging, digging ditches and helping out with the other farms, when the extra labor was needed. Willie would return from school to find the living room filled with the musky perfume of freshly cut branches burning in the stove.

All evacuees had left the village and outlying countryside, except Willie and Zach, Robert and Christine King up at Hillbrook Farm, and the four Browne children at the vicarage.

David Hartridge had become a fullfledged pilot and was looked upon as a hero. His few short visits to the village caused great excitement.

While Little Weirwold was returning to normalcy, events in the larger world continued to escalate. Hitler had escaped a bomb blast in a Munich beer cellar. German aircraft had parachuted mines into the Thames estuary. A British merchant cruiser had been sunk by German battle cruisers. Finland had been invaded and Helsinki had been bombed.

But these events of war didn't really disturb Little Weirwold except for Miss Emilia Thorne, who had to recast the Christmas show as each evacuee left for home.

It was now the first week in December. The last of

the swallows had gone long ago, and now the black outlines of rooks could be seen flying around the plowed fields looking for grubs. Cold icy winds swept under the gaps of cottage doors, rattling them fiercely. It looked as though it would be a hard winter.

Willie had completed the last of the "Learning to Read" books. His reading was up to standard for Mrs. Hartridge's class and his writing was progressing well. He now needed to learn his tables up to six times and also be able to do multiplication, addition, subtraction and division, tens and units, shillings and pence and have a basic knowledge of simple weights and lengths. It all seemed quite endless.

Tom had thought that once Willie finished his final reading book, he wouldn't want him to read to him anymore, but Willie loved to sit back and listen to his voice, and so the stories continued. They had now almost finished Exodus and were in the middle of *The Wind in the Willows*.

With Christmas only three weeks away the days were hectically filled making presents, hanging up decorations and rehearsing.

The show that Miss Thorne was producing was an adaptation of *A Christmas Carol* by Charles Dickens.

Zach was playing Bob Cratchit, Mr. Fezziwig, the ghost of Christmas present and the ghost of what might be. Carrie was cast to play Mrs. Fezziwig and the young woman who had fallen in love with the youthful Scrooge, while Ginnie hid in the school happily making costumes with Miss Thorne's older sister.

George had been tried out in a variety of parts, but each time he stepped on the stage he would stand with his legs and arms splayed out and drone monotonously.

Miss Thorne suddenly hit upon the idea of casting

him as the ghost of Marley, Scrooge's ex-partner. It would need no acting ability from George.

One winter afternoon, while they were rehearsing, something happened that stunned everyone involved in the play.

Willie had already helped paint the scenery, but had been asked to take over as prompter when Matthew Browne had been suddenly whisked off to boarding school.

He usually sat with the prompt book, next to Miss Thorne. His head still spun slightly as he followed the words and looked upwards intermittently to see, by the expression of a face, if someone had forgotten the lines. But after a while he soon knew large chunks of the play off by heart and could occasionally prompt without looking at the book. It was difficult at first. Initially he whispered the line, but it was embarrassing to have to continually repeat himself, after a series of "pardons" and "whats?" and he soon discovered that if he spoke a line clearly and loudly he wasn't noticed as much.

On this particular afternoon Willie sat as usual with the prompt book resting on his knees, his forehead frowned into a tense concentration. The blackouts were already pulled down over the hall windows. Willie liked it that way. It gave an air of mystery and excitement to the rehearsals.

Carrie was the only one onstage. She stood with her hands clasped tightly together and stared frantically at the curtain rail, her face racked with pain.

"Carrie, dear," said Miss Thorne, "you look as though you've got wind."

"It ent fair," she retorted, scowling fiercely.

"Isn't," corrected Miss Thorne.

"It isn't fair," said Carrie. "I feels daft pretendin' to

speak to someone who ent, *isn't*, there."

Miss Thorne gave a sigh. Her long willowy legs splayed outwards into a balletic second. Although she was terribly fond of the children, she found that working with them was like banging her head against a brick wall. Zach was the only one who showed any real talent, and he was more of a performer than an actor. He played himself all the time, using his characters to display his many theatrical talents. He was still trying to persuade her to have a tap routine in the play.

She stared up at Carrie, slapping her forehead with the palm of her hand.

"Has anyone seen Christine or Robert King?" she asked, turning to the others, who were sitting at the back of the hall.

"No, Miss," piped Lucy.

Robert was playing Scrooge.

"We'll do the crone scene then."

"Christine's in that," chorused three at the back.

"So she is," said Miss Thorne. "This really is too bad. We've two weeks to go and we are nowhere near being ready."

She glanced at Willie. "William, stand in for Christine."

"But it's a girl's part," said George.

"Well, we'll just have to have a male crone for today," replied Miss Thorne in a dangerously quiet voice.

Willie crept nervously onstage with the prompt book in his hand and was joined by the others.

"Begin!"

He read out Christine's part, giving an imitation of all the inflections in her voice, at the same time prompting those around him when they forgot their lines.

"No, no, no!" cried Miss Thorne. She looked around. "Someone else prompt."

"But then he won't be able to say his lines," said Carrie. "Er, will he?" she added nervously as Miss Thorne glared threateningly at her.

"I'll prompt," said Zach.

Miss Thorne didn't think this was too good an idea, but time was precious, so she agreed.

"Now, William," she said. "Do you think you can remember the moves?"

He shrugged helplessly.

"Well, let's try, shall we? And William?"

"Yes, Miss?"

"Imagine that it's very cold and dark, that you're old and hungry and that you love stealing and making trouble for people."

Willie looked at her dreamily.

"Did you hear that?"

He nodded.

"Good. You have the first line. Start when you're ready."

"Ready?" he asked, feeling a little puzzled.

"When you feel that you're that horrible old man."

Willie withdrew into himself. He remembered an old tramp he used to watch down by the underground station near where he lived. He was hunched and he dragged his feet when he walked. He also remembered times when he himself was so hungry that he couldn't stand straight for the cramps in his stomach.

Miss Thorne watched him grow visibly older. His shoulders were pushed up by his neck and his stomach caved in. He looked cold and miserable and bad tempered.

Zach found himself totally mesmerized and placed his finger on the page so that he wouldn't lose his place.

Then Willie began speaking. His voice was harsh and mean. The others onstage stared at him and someone giggled.

"Go on," interrupted Miss Thorne firmly.

The three onstage with Willie joined in as best they could, but they sounded as if they were reading out lines from a schoolbook. Willie continued imagining that his dirty feet were wrapped in rags and newspapers, and when the scene came to an end he shuffled slowly off the stage.

"I say," whispered Zach.

"You'll say nothing for the moment," said Miss Thorne. "Let's do that scene again. You're beginning to get the idea, William."

They rehearsed the scene over and over again, and as they repeated it Willie believed more than ever that he was the old man. He found himself suddenly reaching out and touching someone or making some wild arm movement without thinking. He didn't understand what Miss Thorne meant when she told him to keep a gesture. How could he keep something that just happened?

When Miss Thorne finished working on the scene, he heard his companions sigh with relief.

"I'm fair done in," one of them said.

How strange, he thought, I'm not tired at all. I could easily have gone on.

He came down the tiny steps at the side of the stage and sat beside Zach.

"You're good," whispered Zach.

"Good? How d'you mean?"

"You're a good actor."

Willie didn't understand. He thought that being an

actor was tap dancing and playing the fool. All he'd done was to make a picture of someone in his head and worm his way inside it.

He took the prompt book back from Zach and began his old job again.

For the next half hour the rehearsals took on a sudden lift, and everyone began to dare to try things out without feeling foolish. The only thing that spoiled it was the absence of Robert. He was in nearly all the scenes. Finally Miss Thorne refused to wait any longer and told them to take a short break while she left the hall to make a phone call to Hillbrook Farm.

Willie found himself immediately surrounded. Lucy slipped her hand into his. He flushed and pulled it away.

"Dunno what you're on about," he said quietly in response to their praise. "I jes' pretended I was someone else, that's all."

"I really believed you was that horrible old man," said Carrie in admiration.

But so did I, thought Willie. He was puzzled. He didn't understand why they were making so much fuss.

"You're a natural," said Zach. "When you talked it was like you'd just thought of it. How did you do it?"

"I jes' listened to what someone said and answered them, like."

All the sudden admiration unnerved him. He felt lonely being so different. To hide his fear he asked Zach to tell a joke and do his funny Buffalo step. Zach hesitated at first, but luckily someone who hadn't seen him do any tap dancing egged him on. Willie was soon forgotten and became mixed into the group again.

Zach stopped. He heard Miss Thorne open the outer door of the hall. She flung the inside door to one side, was about to slam it but changed her mind and closed it behind her in a quiet and controlled manner. Her face was pale and she was wringing her hands in agitation.

"Sit down everyone, please."

They did so immediately.

She walked slowly towards her chair, sat down, folded one leg over the other and placed her clasped hands over her knee.

"I'm afraid I've just had some rather bad news. Robert and Christine's mother came early this morning and took them back to London. It seems she felt they were being used as unpaid labor. This means that we have no Scrooge."

"Oh no!" cried Zach amidst the loud wails of disappointment.

"Does that mean we can't do it?" asked Carrie.

There were only two weeks till the performance. They had all helped with scenery and costumes. Did this mean that all their hard work was wasted?

Miss Thorne turned to Willie.

"William," she said quietly, "I'd like you to play the part of Scrooge."

Willie felt an intense tingle pass from his toes to the roots of his hair. He looked up at her. Everyone's face was turned to him as if he was their last chance.

"Will you?"

He nodded.

"Oh, well done," cried Zach. "Hip, hip, hurray!"

"That's enough," interrupted Miss Thorne firmly. "We have a lot of work to do. We'll start with Act One, Scene One. Those not in the scene will have to take turns prompting. We must all pull together and help."

She turned to face Willie. He was standing quite still,

feeling paralyzed and yet at the same time filled with a flood of energy.

"Don't hurry," she said.

"Everythin' has its own time," he whispered, and he blushed. "That's what Mister Tom ses."

"That's right," and she gave him a warm smile. "We'll go through the blocking first. Take my script and pencil for now."

The blocking was all the various moves which made up the pattern of each scene. This was to give it movement and life and to ensure that the focus of attention was never blurred for the audience.

Willie half mumbled and half read the script as he penciled little letters around the sentences. Miss Thorne had taught them all the names of the different stage areas. There was downstage right and left and upstage right and left, up center, down center and of course center plus many others such as "left of so and so."

To the ones who were watching, Willie seemed very bad. He stumbled and droned and scribbled in his book like someone half asleep. But Miss Thorne knew that as soon as he had got rid of the book and started working on the character of Scrooge, he would be very different. It was strange that she had never thought of him before, for she now remembered how quickly he had learned poetry when she was helping him learn to read. But then hardly anyone noticed him when he was around. They only noticed his absence.

She stopped rehearsing when they reached the end of Act One.

"Well done, William," she said encouragingly. "Well done, everyone. You've all worked very hard."

Willie looked up a little bewildered and then back

down at his script. The words were beginning to cease being just shapes and pictures. There was something else in them. He felt breathlessly excited.

"William," said Miss Thorne, interrupting his thoughts. "Keep my script and look over the scene we've blocked. The next rehearsal will be on Monday night after school. We'll block Act Two then."

Willie walked shakily out of the inner door to the porch. Zach had already put on his coat and cap, and was waiting to tell him something, when Ginnie and Miss Thorne's elder sister burst in.

"Whatever's the matter, May?" asked Miss Thorne.

"Haven't you heard the news yet?"

"About the Kings?"

"No. About Mr. Bush."

"What about him. Has he had an accident?"

"Worse. He's been called up!"

"But he's a teacher. They aren't calling them up, surely?"

"It's his own fault. He's on reserves and they say that we already have more than our quota per pupil than most other places."

"Who's going to teach the seniors?"

"I don't know. The vicar, I suppose."

"What about the Carol Service?" interrupted George. "It's on in three weeks' time."

May Thorne turned to her sister.

"What's this about the Kings, then?"

"It's all sorted out. I'll explain later."

"What's been goin' on?" burst out Ginnie.

Zach and Willie slipped out into the darkness.

"I say, Will," said Zach, taking Willie's arm, "a jolly exciting night, eh?"

"Yeh," replied Willie, still dazed.

"I think you're, how do you say it? Fine. Yes, I think you're fine."

Willie smiled.

"We're both jolly jolly fine," Zach yelled and he dragged Willie on behind him. They stumbled and laughed down the tiny lane to the Littles' cottage, where they parted.

Willie walked quickly towards Tom's cottage. He clutched the script tightly under his arm. It felt so good tucked there, so snug and firm under his armpit like it was a part of him. He ran into the cottage, flinging his cap and coat onto his peg.

Tom was sitting at the table, gluing colored paper chains together. He'd hung the clusters of holly that Willie had painted silver onto the walls.

Willie looked up at them.

"Pretty, ent they?" he remarked.

"You's beginnin' to sound like me," Tom said.

Willie stood by the table, holding the script in his hand. Pushing a chair gently to one side, he placed it on the table and sat down.

Tom was unusually quiet. He put the chains down and stood up. Sammy followed him, tugging at his trouser legs. He lifted him up absently, sat in the armchair and stared into the open stove.

"Shall I make us some tea?" suggested Willie.

"H'm," grunted Tom, a little startled. "What?"

Willie walked over to the kettle and filled it with water from the pitcher.

"I'll make us some."

"Yes, that's right, boy, you do that."

Willie suddenly became aware of how pale Tom looked and he felt alarmed for a moment. Perhaps he was ill. Sammy was sitting on his lap panting in a bewildered fashion. He gave a small whine. Tom looked up and caught Willie's worried gaze.

"Is you all right?" asked Willie, sitting on the stool.

"Just had a bit of a wake-up, so to speak."

"Wake-up?"

"You heard about Mr. Bush?"

He nodded.

"I been asked to take over the choir like, for the concert, play the organ. . . ."

"Can you play?"

"Used to when Rachel was alive."

"Who's Rachel?"

"A gentle-hearted wild young girl I once loved."

"Where's she now?"

Tom pointed to the window behind him with his thumb.

"She's the one under the oak tree. Died after she had a baby. She had scarlatina, see. . . ."

"What happened to the baby?"

"Died soon after. Buried together." He glanced at Willie. "Same name as yours, too."

"William?"

He nodded and gave a deep sigh. "It's a long time since I touched that organ. It'll take a good bit of practice."

"You goin' to do it then?"

Tom leaned back and paused for a moment. "Yes," he said at last, and he glanced across at the table. "What's that then?" he asked. "A new book?"

"It's the script of *Christmas Carol*."

"Oh? What you doin' with it then?"

"I've been asked to be in the play."

" 'As you?" said Tom, leaning forward.

"Yeh."

"I take it you's goin' to do it then?"

Willie smiled, his cheeks burning with excitement.

"Yeh."

"Reckon we'll both be needin' that tea extra sweet tonight, eh, boy?"

Carol Singing

꙾ ꙾

"Bah! 'Umbug!" he cried as he paced the floor. It was at least the fiftieth time in the past hour that Willie had uttered the words. He paused and read the nephew's lines, put down the script and began pacing the floor again.

"If I could work me will, every idiot who goes abaht wiv Merry Christmuss on 'is lips should be boiled wiv his own puddin', and buried wiv a stake of holly through his heart. He should!"

Willie sat down on the end of his bed and gave a sigh.

"I nearly got it," he muttered to himself. "I got to be a bit more grumpy."

He rose.

"Nephew!" he said brusquely. "You keep Christmuss in yer own way and let me keep it in mine." He stopped and hit the open palm of his hand with his fist. "No! It don't feel right. I'm a bad-tempered man and I don't like bein' interrupted, like." He began again. "Nephew, you keep Christmuss in yer own way and let me keep it in mine."

A loud knocking at the front door made him jump.

"Blow it!" he grumbled. "Jes' when I wuz gettin' it."

He frowned and walked towards the trapdoor. Immediately he realized how Scrooge must have felt when he was interrupted.

"Nephew," he repeated angrily, "keep Christmuss in yer own way and let me keep it in mine." He gave a loud grunt and looked into his imaginary accounts book. "That's it!" he yelled. "I got it! I got it!"

A volley of louder knocks came from downstairs. Willie threw himself down the ladder and opened the door. It was George. He looked over Willie's shoulder. "Who else is in there?" he asked.

"No one," answered Willie.

"Who you yellin' at then?"

Willie looked at him blankly for a moment.

"Oh," he said, realizing what George was talking about. "I was jes' goin' over me words, like."

"I could hear you from here."

Willie blushed.

"Only from the front door, mind. Don't s'pose no one else did. You comin' then?"

"What?"

"Haven't you remembered? It's Thursdee, doughbag. We got Carols. Thought you'd be there first seein' it's Mr. Oakley's first practice, like."

"Oh, yeh," said Willie hurriedly, and he flung his scarf on. "Am I late?"

"No. We's all jes' a bit early."

Willie slammed the front door behind him. He ran after George along the pathway towards the back entrance of the church. Already there were people seated in the benches on either side of the altar. Tom was sitting at the organ, a large scowl on his face.

Willie caught his eye and smiled at him. He knew that the scowl meant he was just a bit shy.

Edward Fletcher and Alec Barnes came in at the front door and joined the men right of the altar. Edward's voice had now evened out into a wobbly tenor. Alec, a large, dark-haired sixteen-year-old, was looking very embarrassed. Everyone wanted to know if his father had been using the King children as "slave labor" or not.

Behind Alec sat Mr. Miller and Hubert Pullet, the

son-in-law of Charlie Ruddles. He was a poker-faced, pale man in his fifties. Next to him sat the twins' father, a handsome freckle-faced man with thick wavy red hair. Ted Blakefield, a local thatcher, sat beside him. The oldest member of the choir was Walter Bird, still wearing his tin hat and the only one with a gas mask.

George sat in the second row, to the left of the altar, next to two older boys, while Willie joined the younger ones in the front.

Tom stood up and gave two short taps with his hand on the top of the organ.

"We'll begin with 'Hark the Herald,' " he said, smoothing out the pages of his music. He waited until everyone had found their places before playing the short introduction.

After the first few notes he stopped. No one was singing. He leaned around the organ.

"What's the matter?" he inquired.

"We was jes' listenin' to you playin', like," croaked Walter. "You kept in toon, didn't you?"

Tom grunted.

"I ent 'ere to listen to meself. One more time."

The men suppressed a grin among themselves. Still the same short-tempered Mr. Oakley, they thought.

Tom played the introduction once more and they joined in.

"You call that singin'?" he interrupted gruffly. "Sounds like a dirge."

"A dirge, Mr. Oakley?" interspersed Mr. Miller, his balding head shining with perspiration.

"A dirge," repeated Tom. "This is to be a Carol Service, not a funeral. Lift them *up* with yer voices. Don't bury them."

George gave a short laugh and slapped his hand

sharply over his mouth. Tom glared at him.

"Put a bit of that laughin' in yer singin', boy," he said. That was what Rachel would have suggested, he thought, and he sat down and turned to the beginning of the carol.

"Once again."

They lifted up their books and sang with even more fervor.

"Gettin' better. Good cure for insomnia, though. Send at least the first four pews to sleep. Now," he said, turning over several pages, "let's wake them up with 'Glory to the Newborn King.' 'Tis good news."

Willie took a deep breath and pictured in his mind a rainbow, its rays of colored light pouring down from massive clouds.

"In the triumph of the skies," he sang, "Glory to the newborn King."

"Good," said Tom when they had finished. "William, you's gettin' the idea, but you're singin' up to the ceiling. Sing it out front."

He turned to everyone.

"All of yous, sing it out through them doors and through the village."

Mr. Miller wiped his face with a handkerchief.

"I don't think I can sing any better, Mr. Oakley."

"Don't let Hitler hear you say that," replied Tom. "Now, one more time."

They sang it through twice, and then as a contrast followed it with a gentle rendition of "Silent Night." The rehearsal ended with a rousing version of "O Come All Ye Faithful."

"I think that'll do for tonight," said Tom, closing the *Book of Carols.*

"What time is it?" asked Edward.

"It's nine o'clock," cried Alec in alarm. "I've to do the milkin' tomorrow mornin'. Good night, Mr. Oakley. Thank you," he yelled, running out of the church.

Willie left his bench and stood by the organ. George joined him.

"It were a real good rehearsal, Mr. Oakley," he said. "Real good. Weren't it, Will?"

Willie nodded.

George said his good-nights and left the church with the others.

Willie could hear their voices drifting away into the distance, singing "Hark the Herald" and laughing over something. He leaned on the organ.

"I'll play you somethin' I ent played in years," said Tom. "Don't know if I can remember it all. It were one of Rachel's favorites."

Willie rested his chin in his cupped hands and listened.

Unlike the jaunty tunes of the carols, these notes were long and lingering. They throbbed and shook the frame of the organ, sometimes dying to the gentlest and saddest of sounds, only to crescendo and fall again. Willie had never heard anything so beautiful. As Tom lifted his fingers from the organ, the music seemed to sink and fade into the very walls of the church. Tom sat back and flexed his fingers several times until his knuckles cracked.

"Bit out o' practice, like," he said.

"Mister Tom," said Willie, his eyes welling with emotion, "it were real fine."

"Hmph," Tom grunted. "Thank you, boy. Must admit I enjoyed it meself."

New Beginnings

There were usually fifteen pupils in Mrs. Hartridge's class, ranging from nine to fourteen years of age. On this particular Monday there were only ten present. Three children who had a two-mile walk to the school hadn't arrived because of the snow, and Harry Padfield and Polly Barnes were helping out on their parents' farms.

At a quarter to nine Willie had walked in, accompanied by Zach. The twins had followed soon after. By five minutes to nine George had arrived, looking very pale and swollen eyed and wearing a black armband. He smiled weakly at Willie. His brother Michael had been reported "Missing, believed dead." A memorial service had been held for him the previous day, and the village had given the vicar money towards a plaque to be placed in the church.

Willie had stood awkwardly while the others moved into their seats. Mrs. Hartridge had smiled at him and asked him to sit in the front next to a girl named Patsy. They had stood up for prayers and sat down.

"I'm sure we would all like to welcome William Beech to our class," she had said, turning to him. "We know what excellent progress you've made and how hard you've worked."

Willie had tried to cover his embarrassment by scowling, but Patsy had smiled so sweetly at him that the scowl didn't last long. Mrs. Hartridge gave him a history and geography textbook, a spelling and arithmetic book, a nature and English book, a notebook, a pencil and, what thrilled him most of all, his own pen. It had a long slim wooden handle with a nib fastened at the end.

"Take care of it," she had said. "I'll see how your writing is this week, and if it's good enough you can begin writing in ink next week."

Willie had laid the pen carefully in his desk and now his first lesson had begun. First they all had to chant their twelve times tables. Willie managed to get up to six. He had practiced them long enough. By the time the class had reached twelve only Carrie and Ruth were still chanting.

"Same two again," said Mrs. Hartridge. "Hands up who managed to eleven." Three hands were raised. "Ten?" Two more went up. "Nine? Eight? Seven? Six?" Willie raised his hand. "Well done, William. I know you've only learned up to six. Five?" George raised his hand at three but she didn't scold him.

"Today we're going to do long multiplication. George and Frederick, I'd like you to review your tables. William, I'd like you to begin seven times table, and I'll give you some problems of your own. For the rest, take these down," and she walked over to the board and chalked up four problems.

After arithmetic they had an English language lesson on nouns. Willie's head was spinning. He turned to look at Zach and saw Carrie passing him a note. Zach glanced surreptitiously at it on his knee. Checking to see if Mrs. Hartridge was looking, he turned back and nodded. She looked a little scared. Then he saw Zach mouth "Good luck" to her and return quickly to chewing the end of his pencil and scribbling something in his notebook.

"Don't look so worried, William," said Mrs. Hartridge

as she went over the nouns. "It's only your first day. If you're stuck and you need help, don't be afraid to ask. That's what I'm here for."

Willie nodded.

How beautiful she was with her violet blue eyes and her single long flaxen plait. She was wearing a cream-colored woolen blouse, a russet-colored cardigan and a green woolen skirt flecked with browns. She was plumper than usual, round and comfortable.

"Pencils and books away. Time for break. Patsy!"

Patsy was the milk monitor for the week. Mrs. Hartridge had taken to heating the milk, now the weather was so cold. She poured it into cups and Patsy carried them two at a time to the desks.

"Those of you who don't have gum boots or galoshes are to stay in," she said as she handed out the dried socks, but today everyone had.

Willie saw Zach winking at Carrie. Slowly she left her desk and walked up to Mrs. Hartridge's desk, where she was sorting out some books.

"Excuse me, Mrs. Hartridge."

"Yes, Carrie," she said, surprised. "Is there something wrong?"

"Not really."

Carrie took hold of one of her flame-colored plaits and tapped it nervously on her shoulder.

"It's jes' that . . ."

"Yes?"

"Can I speak to you on yer own, like? It's very important."

"Now?"

Carrie nodded.

"All right. We'll go somewhere private."

"Thank you, Mrs. Hartridge."

"When you've all finished your milk, go outside."

Patsy collected the empty cups and took them on a tray down the hall and into a kitchen, where Mrs. Bird washed them.

Zach, Ginnie, George and Willie fled into the playground.

"I say," said Zach, "it's wizard to have you in our class."

"And don't worry about everythin' bein' new," said Ginnie. "We'll help you."

"Ta," said Willie. He was about to grumble about how he felt bottom of the class when he remembered that George's tables were worse than his and that he had just lost his brother. He bit his lip and kept silent.

"Where's Carrie?" said Ginnie. "I saw her going up to Mrs. Hartridge."

"Perhaps they're having a little conflab," said Zach.

"She would have told me if anything was wrong," said Ginnie.

"Oh, there's nothing wrong. Yet," he added mysteriously.

Ginnie was astounded. "Do you mean you know what it's all about?"

Zach nodded. "I'll say I do."

"But—but I'm her sister!"

"She thought you might try and stop her."

"Stop her? Stop what?"

"Well," said Zach hesitantly, "I suppose you'll find out soon enough."

"Find out what?" exclaimed Ginnie in exasperation.

"Go on," said George. "Stop huggin' it all to yerself."

"Yeh. Tell us," joined in Willie.

Zach took a deep breath.

"She's asking if she can take the exam for the high school."

"She never is," gasped Ginnie. "She wouldn't dare."

"She jolly well is."

"But they ent even puttin' in any of the boys for it, they hasn't fer two years."

"So?"

"She's a girl!" cried George.

"I say, is she really?"

"I think it's jes' fine," said Willie.

"You would," retorted George. "You think anything he ses is fine."

"No, I doesn't. It ain't his idea anyway. It's Carrie's."

"Let's not quarrel," said Ginnie, who was feeling a little hurt that Carrie had confided in Zach and not her.

By the end of break there was still no sign of Carrie. Rose Butcher rang the bell and everyone queued up in the playground and filed in. Carrie was sitting at her desk, looking very flushed. Before they could ask her any questions, Mrs. Hartridge had pinned a map onto the board and told them to take out their geography books.

"Turn your desks round to face each other," she said. "Ginnie, go to the cupboard and hand out two sheets of paper to each desk. When you have the paper, tear each one in half."

Ginnie tried to catch Carrie's eye, but she was staring down at her desk. She caught hold of Ginnie's hand and gave it a gentle squeeze.

"Now, which ports do we get our fish from?"

Willie watched the hands go up. He sighed. Everything takes its own time was what Mister Tom was always saying. Maybe if he just sat back and listened he might catch up. The rest of the period was taken up with drawing maps of England, coloring in the sea, putting red dots to mark the ports and drawing little fishes next to them.

After geography came nature study. Here George and Ginnie shone. They loved animals and plants. Carrie knew the odd name of a flower, but Ginnie and George far excelled her and loved identifying them. Willie was very surprised. He had always thought that boys who liked flowers were sissies, but George was the strongest in their group of five. He had already taught Willie a little about the habits of squirrels, moles, rabbits and, of course, badgers. As the boy next to Ginnie was away, Mrs. Hartridge allowed George to join Ginnie, Patsy and Willie.

Rose rang the dinner bell and the five raced out of the classroom, slung their coats, hats and gum boots on and ran out into the snow.

Zach grabbed Carrie. "What did she say?"

"She ses she'll think about it and make inquiries. It'd mean Mr. Peters giving me extra coaching like and havin' to do special work. No girl here 'as ever done one afore, see. So it ent yes and it ent no."

She turned to Ginnie.

"I'm sorry I didn't let on, but I thought you'd try and stop me. I know we always does everythin' together but I wanted to do it on me own and I woulda told you, anyway."

"How would I have stopped you?"

"Oh, you're so sensible. All yous at home think I've odd ideas and that, I didn't want you down on me. And I know that if I really want to go to the high, I've to stop grousin' and do something. If nothin' happens I shall have to think of somethin' else, but at least I know that I've tried."

"Theys'll think you're odder if you gits in," said George.

"Well, I'd rather be happy and odd than miserable and ordinary," she said, sticking her chin in the air.

"Hark at her. She's gettin' snooty already."

"I am not!"

"Let's go eat in my shelter," suggested Zach. "It's freezing out here." And he blew some warmth into his gloves.

They ran towards the little shelter, where Aunt Nance brought them cups of hot black-currant juice.

When they returned to school, Zach took Willie aside.

"How are you liking it?" he whispered.

"I feel very stupid," said Willie.

"Well, you jolly well are not, so don't try telling yourself that you are."

During the first lesson of the afternoon, Mrs. Hartridge read out a passage from *Treasure Island* and wrote up ten questions on the board for them to answer.

"Remember," she said, "that you start your answer with a statement, so that if I say, 'What is your name?' you write, 'My name is John Smith' or whatever."

She came over to Willie to give him an English exercise book and to show him how to lay out the date and the subject. It was difficult for Willie to write the answers, but he managed to finish somehow. They each swapped books with the person next to them and put crosses or checks as Mrs. Hartridge told them the correct answers. When Patsy handed back his book, she stared at him.

"You got eight out of ten," she said in wonder. "And it's only yer first day."

"Who has full marks?" asked Mrs. Hartridge.

Carrie raised her hand and flushed. Mrs. Hartridge smiled.

"Nine out of ten?"

Ruth raised her hand.

"Eight out of ten?"

Zach and Willie put up their hands.

Zach whooped with delight when he saw how well Willie had done. The rest of the class gasped.

"That will do, Zacharias," said Mrs. Hartridge, trying hard not to smile and not succeeding very well.

"Well done, William," she said, and Willie swelled with pleasure. "And now put away your books. Who are the paint monitors this week?"

Zach and a girl called Alison in the fourth row left their desks. Fred cleaned the board.

"The subjects for this afternoon are 'A Rainy Day' or 'A Rainy Night,' and one at a time at the pencil sharpener." She turned to Willie. "From what I hear, I think you'll be all right on your own," and she gave him another of her heavenly smiles. One day, thought Willie, I'll draw you real good. He looked down at the large white sheet in front of him and lifted his pencil from the groove.

Forty minutes later he raised his paintbrush for a moment and looked up while the blackouts were being put up. Dusk was already settling in and everyone had been squinting in the fading light. But after the lights were turned on, Willie resumed painting and grew deaf to his surroundings. Patsy took a glimpse now and then over his shoulder. His picture frightened her a little.

Mrs. Hartridge walked down the aisle looking at each person's work.

"That's very good, Ruth," she said. "You're improving, Frederick. Another heroic rescue, Zach, only this time in the rain. Well tried." She glanced down at Willie's painting and gave a start. She had heard that he was good, but hadn't expected him to be quite as good as she perceived at that moment.

The painting was set at night in a gloomy back street in a city. An old lamppost stood alight on a corner. Squatting down by a wall was a blind beggar in a shabby raincoat, his white stick lying beside him. His cap lay on the street in front of him and he stared out with dead sad eyes.

The rain swept across the old man's face so that his white hair hung limply and rain trickled down his cheeks. Hiding in an alleyway on his right were two grinning boys. They were eyeing the money in the cap.

"That's excellent, William. Do you think you could finish it in fifteen minutes? Then I could leave it out to dry. I'd like to put it on the wall."

Ginnie and George glanced over his shoulder. He was embarrassed at first, but soon became so absorbed in his painting that he continued, oblivious of the clatter of slamming desks, the washing of pots, the laying out of wet paintings on newspapers near to the stove and the cleaning of brushes.

Mrs. Hartridge picked up Hans Christian Andersen's *Fairy Tales* and was about to begin "The Shepherdess and the Chimney Sweep" when Willie raised his hand.

"Please, Mrs. Hartridge. I've finished."

"Good," she said. "Lay it down by the others. You can clear up afterwards."

Willie did so and sank back to listen to the story. When it was finished, Rose rang the bell for the end of school and everyone clustered round the paintings. Afterwards George, Zach, Willie and the twins played in the field behind the schoolhouse. George left early with a headache, and the twins left soon after. Zach and Willie sauntered slowly homewards and talked endlessly outside the Littles' dilapidated front gate. Willie's first day in Mrs. Hartridge's class was over.

One Friday morning, in the first week of March, Willie looked out of his window to find that the snow had thawed completely, and piebald fields of brown earth and tufts of grass now lay exposed all around the village. The river was almost bursting its bank. Two blackbirds cawed their way past the graveyard and headed in the direction of the woods. Willie unfastened his window a little. It was a beautiful day, clear and sunny. He breathed in the cool crisp air and was filled with so much energy that he too felt like the swollen river.

After putting on his clothes and making his bed, he clambered down the ladder with his chamber pot.

"Sammy," he called. "Sam, 'ere, boy."

A loud barking came from the garden. No sooner had he opened the back door than Sam came flying in. Tom stuck his head out of the air-raid shelter. He was pumping out water.

"You looks full o' beans," he said. "You might as well go for a run now. I'll 'as yer breakfast started when you comes back."

Willie ran back into the house, put some coke in the stove, slung on his gum boots, overcoat and balaclava while Sam twirled round and round his ankles. They spurted through the back garden and headed out towards Tom's field and beyond.

"Yahoo!" he yelled. "Yahoo! Yahoo! Yahoo!" And as he sprinted along the lane, he began to laugh. Sam scampered on ahead, showing off, chasing his tail and enjoying Willie's excitement. Eventually Willie turned back and Sammy followed him home. The balaclava hung back from his face exposing flushed cheeks and two red ears.

That Friday was to be a special day. Zach, George, he and the twins had at last arranged to meet at Zach's, after school, to discuss plans about visiting Spooky Cott. They were to bring tea so that they could leave Zach's immediately to go to a meeting in the village hall to hear which play Miss Thorne had chosen to produce next.

After breakfast Willie helped Tom make up sandwiches, and then spent ten minutes going over yards, feet and inches before leaving for school. He met Zach in the arched lane and they talked about the Spooky Cott enterprise and the possible new play.

"I think it's going to be another Dickens," said Zach, as they walked into the school hallway. "Miss Thorne's awfully keen on him."

Alison Blake rang the bell and they sauntered into class.

George had been moved into the second row next to Ginnie, and Carrie had been moved to the back row with the elder ones. Although she was ten she had already reached the standard of a thirteen-year-old. Since most children left at fourteen, Mrs. Hartridge hoped that Carrie would obtain a scholarship—otherwise she would have to spend the next three or four years working on her own. The teacher had spoken to Carrie's parents the weekend after their talk and had explained that Carrie was bright enough to take the exam. Her mother had objected at first.

"What about uniform?" she had said.

Mrs. Hartridge had assured her that there were always

people who were willing to sell uniforms that their children had grown out of.

"And she ent even taken this here examination yet, Madge," Mr. Thatcher had added. "Let's take one thing at a time." Secretly he was rather proud that one of his daughters wanted to take it. The war was encouraging girls to be more independent now. They both finally agreed. Most of her evenings were now spent doing homework and cramming, and her mother allowed her to skip some of the household chores as long as she made up for them after the exam.

Willie had by now settled happily into his new class. He adored being near Mrs. Hartridge, and he watched her stomach gently expand with each passing week. He loved the way she moved and smiled and the soft cadence of her voice.

However, he, like the others, couldn't wait for the hours to fly that Friday. Eventually school ended and they all fled to the Littles' cottage and up to Zach's bedroom. They discussed plans for the Spooky Cott expedition, which was to take place on Saturday, and later made their way to the play meeting. Miss Thorne announced that they would be presenting *Toad of Toad Hall.*

When they had left the village hall, Willie and Zach chatted briefly at the Littles' gate and arranged to meet the following afternoon.

Willie sang as he walked down the lane. He was still bursting with energy. He swung open the gate into Dobbs's field, which was now empty. Dobbs was still in winter residence at the Padfields'. The ground was muddy and an icy wind blew down his neck. He wound his scarf tightly around him and tucked it deep into his overcoat.

"I don't care if there's even an air-raid drill tonight," he said, grinning and twirling around. He ran into the cottage, flinging the back door open, his cheeks flushed with both pleasure and the cold wind. He tore off his coat, balaclava and scarf and burst into the front room.

Tom was standing by the stove. He glanced at Willie and listened quietly to his chatter. While Willie talked nonstop he untied his boots and placed them on newspaper and proceeded to warm his hands by the stove.

Tom didn't make any comment. He gazed down at Sammy, who was slumped miserably over his feet. Willie looked up and noticed that Tom was holding a letter.

"What's the matter?"

"It's from yer mother," he said, indicating the paper. "She's ill. She wants you to go back for a while."

Home
_ ⚘ ⚘ _

Dobbs clopped on towards Weirwold, Tom and Willie sitting on the cart behind her. They hadn't exchanged many words on the journey. They had both felt too numb. Willie held Sammy tightly next to him and stared through blurred eyes down at the leather and brass harness, the moving flank of Dobbs and the rough road beneath them. Occasionally he lifted his head to gaze at the fields, only to look quickly downwards again.

Tom kept his eyes on the road. The blacksmith's at the edge of the village could be seen faintly in the distance. He had tried persuading Willie's mother to come and stay in Little Weirwold, but to no avail. She had written that she only wanted Willie to stay with her for a while till she felt better. He spoke to the Billeting Officer, but there was nothing she could do. Mothers were always taking their children back and they had the legal right to do so.

They left Dobbs and the cart at the blacksmith's. Tom helped Willie on with his old rucksack. It was filled with books, clothes and presents he had acquired during his stay. In the carrier bag that he had carried on his first day were his few original possessions.

Willie trembled. A blast of wind swept into his face and he shivered. Tom squeezed his shoulder firmly and walked with him towards the railway station, holding Sammy on a makeshift leash.

They sat on a bench on the platform and gazed at the hedgerows on the other side of the railway tracks.

"Don't forgit to write, William," said Tom huskily, and with shaking hands he took his pipe out of his pocket and began to fill it.

"No, Mister Tom."

"If you changes yer mind about them paints, you jes' let on and I'll post them."

Willie shook his head. "They belongs at home, I mean at your place. Then they'll be there when I come back. I will come back," he added earnestly, touching Tom's hand. "I will, won't I?"

"You might feel different when yer home. I s'pect yer mother's missed you. Probably why she didn't write much—and William?"

"Yeh."

"Don't expect too much too soon. You ent seen each other for over six months, so things might be a little awkward like, for a while."

Willie nodded.

A cloud of smoke drifted upwards from a clump of trees in the distance. They watched it getting nearer and heard the sound of the approaching train growing louder. They stood up and Mister Tom picked Sammy up in his arms.

"Now you takes care of yerself, boy. You keeps up that ole drawrin'. You've a fine gift. If you runs out of pencils, you lets me know."

Willie nodded and his eyes became misty. He blinked. Tears fell down his cheeks. He gave a sniff and brushed them quickly away.

"Ta," he said.

Tom swallowed a lump in his throat.

"I'll miss you," said Willie.

Tom nodded. "Me too."

They watched the train drawing into the station. A

crowd of soldiers and sailors were hanging out of the windows. Tom opened a door. One of the soldiers, a young lad of eighteen, caught sight of the anxious look in Tom's eyes, and he helped Willie on board.

"Dinna you fret, sir," he said. "We'll find 'im a seat all right."

Tom nodded his thanks and clasped Willie's shoulder as he hung dejectedly out of the door window.

The whistle blew. They choked out their good-byes, waving to each other till the train and platform were out of each other's sight.

"Here you are," said the young soldier.

He had persuaded another soldier to let Willie squeeze into a place by the window.

"Will that do ye, lad?"

Willie nodded, relieved that he could stare out the window. He didn't want anyone to see his face. He placed his rucksack on his knees and hung on to it grimly.

At first the soldier left him alone, but later decided to try and cheer him up.

"What's yer name then?"

"William Beech."

"Where are ye goin'?"

"London."

"Ah thought you bairns were bein' moved oot," he said. "You miss home then, do ye?"

He shrugged.

"That old man yer granda?"

"No," Willie answered, looking up. "He's Mister Tom."

"Is he now?"

Willie's lips quivered.

The soldier paused, sensing that this was not the best subject to talk to the boy about.

"Who are ye stayin' with in London then?"

"Me mum."

"Och, ye'll be glad ta see her then. Your dad called up then, is he?"

"I ent got no dad."

"Sorry aboot that." He paused again. "Tell me aboot yer ma. What's she like?"

Willie was puzzled. What was she like? At the moment she was just a dim memory. She had dark hair. He remembered that much.

"She's got dark hair and"—he thought again—"she's medium size."

"Eyes?"

"Beg pardon."

"Eyes. What color eyes has she?"

Willie didn't ever remember clearly looking at her eyes, but he couldn't tell him that. He must think of something to say.

"Mixed, are they?"

He nodded.

"Does she sing a lot?"

Willie shook his head. The thought of his mother singing except in church was too shocking to contemplate.

They looked at each other silently for a moment.

"What's in them bags then?"

"Clothes and presents, books."

"You like readin' then?"

Willie nodded.

"Ah've not got the patience meself."

"And drawrin'."

"What?" said the soldier.

"I draw, like."

"Oh," the soldier said, and he saw by the sudden

brightness in Willie's eyes and his smile that this would be a good subject to talk about.

"You have any on you then?"

"Yeh."

"Ah'd like to see them if, that is, you're willin'."

Willie nodded shyly and opened his rucksack. He pulled out one of three sketch pads from the back and handed it to him.

The soldier opened it.

"Och," he cried in surprise, "ye can really draw. Och, these are guid, these are really guid. Yer mother must be terrible proud of ye," he added, handing the pad back to him.

"She ent seen them yet."

"Well, when she does, she will be."

"D'you think so?"

"I know so."

Willie eased the sketch pad back into his rucksack. He caught sight of the acting book that Zach had given him and the jawbreakers that George had produced suddenly when he had said good-bye. He didn't want to look at them now. He flicked over the top of the rucksack and did the straps up.

Would his mother be proud of him? he wondered. He began to fantasize around her, only her face was very vague. She became a mixture of Mrs. Fletcher and Mrs. Hartridge. He imagined her waiting on the platform for him. He would wave out the window and she would wave back smiling and laughing, and when he stepped out of the train he would run up to her and she to him and they would embrace. He stopped. He remembered that she was supposed to be ill. Perhaps she would be too ill to fetch him. She might even be dying and, instead of her, there would be a warden or a vicar to meet him and he would be taken to her bedside and she would touch him gently and say how much she loved him and how proud she was of him. He leaned back and closed his eyes. He felt tired. The strain of all the good-byes had exhausted him. He wondered what Zach was doing. He had written the first two verses of another epic poem specially for him. He had it in his pocket. Zach had said that he'd finish it and send it to him in the post or by pigeon.

The train chugged and crawled towards London and Willie soon fell into a sleep that was filled with a multitude of strange dreams.

He felt someone shaking him to consciousness.

"Hey, sleepyhead. Wake up! Wake up, lad! This is London. We're in London. Wake up!"

He opened his eyes expecting to see the light from his bedroom window and Mister Tom looking through the trapdoor, but he saw only the young Scots boy leaning over him against a vague background of khaki and shouting.

He swung the rucksack over his shoulder and lifted the carrier bag. His legs felt wobbly and his clothes smelled of tobacco. As he stepped outside, the cold night air hit him sharply. He buttoned up his overcoat, pulled his balaclava up over his head and put on his gloves. He looked around the platform, which was swarming with soldiers, but there was no sign of his mother anywhere.

A large sergeant stopped and looked down at him.

"Run away, has you?" he boomed in a bone-rattling voice. "You'd best see the ticket man, my lad."

"I ent run away, sir," he blurted out.

"You tell that to the ticket man."

The ticket man was a middle-aged man with a droopy mustache. He took one look at Willie and gave a weary sigh.

"Another one, eh? Don't you lads know it's safer in the country," and he tweaked Willie's ear through the balaclava. "I s'pose you've no ticket. Now let's take down yer address."

Willie pulled a ticket out of his pocket and showed it to him.

"Oh," he said, "oh."

"I'm visitin' me mum, like. She's ill."

"Ah," he said, "Ah, I see! Well. And where is she then? Is she pickin' you up or a warden pickin' you up or what?"

"I dunno."

The ticket man hummed significantly and looked at the sergeant. "I think I can handle this all right, sir. Thanks for your help."

The sergeant touched his beret and disappeared among the soldiers.

"I think we'd best find a warden, my boy."

Willie looked frantically round the station.

"Wait. There she is," he said, pointing to a thin gaunt woman, standing next to a pile of sandbags. He waved and yelled out to her but she started vacantly around neither seeing or hearing him.

"She don't seem to know you, do she? I think you'd best wait here for a while."

"I'll talk to her," Willie said.

"Oh no, you don't," said the ticket man, grabbing his arm, and then he changed his mind. "Oh, go on with you."

Willie ran over to her. "Mum!" he cried. "Mum!"

"Go away," she said sternly. "You won't get no money from me."

"Mum" he repeated, "it's me."

She glanced down and was about to tell him to clear off when she recognized him. Yes. It was Willie, but he had altered so much. She had been looking for a thin little boy dressed in gray. Here stood an upright, well-fleshed boy in sturdy ankle boots, thick woolen socks, a green rolled-top jersey and a navy-blue coat and balaclava. His hair stuck out in a shiny mass above his forehead and his cheeks were round and pink. It was a great shock to her.

"I'm awfully pleased to see you, Mum. I've such a lot to tell you and there's me pictures, like."

She was startled at his peculiar mixture of accents. She had expected him to be more subservient, but even his voice sounded louder.

"I'm sorry," she said. "I'm not very well, you see, and I'm a bit tired. I wasn't expectin' such a change in you."

Willie was puzzled.

He thought that it was his mother who had changed. He had learned new things, that was true, but he was still him.

He studied her face. She was very pale, almost yellow in color, and her lips were so blue that it seemed as if every ounce of blood had been drained from them. The lines by her thin mouth curved downwards. He glanced at her body. She was wearing a long black coat, fawn stockings and smart lace-up heeled shoes. A small shopping bag was now leaning against her leg.

He touched her arm gently. "I'll carry that for you, Mum," he said, picking it up.

She spun round and gave his hand a sharp slap. "I'll tell you what I wants when I wants, and you know I don't approve of touching."

"Sorry," he muttered.

They stood silently and awkwardly as the large noisy station roared around them. Willie felt his heart sinking, and the spark of hope that he had held was fast dissolving. He remembered how kind and jolly Mrs. Fletcher was. He stopped. Mister Tom had said that they would feel awkward at first and that it would take time to get used to each other.

Mrs. Beech, meanwhile, surveyed her small son, her mind racing. She'd be lenient with him for the moment. After all, it was his first evening back and he had a lot to learn before accepting his manly responsibilities.

"Let's go for a cup of tea," she said at last. "You can take my bag."

"Thanks, Mum." And he smiled.

She stepped sharply backwards, horrified. She couldn't remember ever having seen him smile before. She had hoped that he had remained a serious child. The smile frightened her. It threatened her authority. She swallowed her feelings and stepped forward again, handing him her bag.

Everything was going to be fine, thought Willie. He followed her down a tiny back alley to a small café. They sat near the door.

"You look more filled out," said his mother. "Fed you well, did he, that Mr. Oakley?"

Willie sipped his tea. It wasn't as good as Mister Tom's, but it was hot and that was what mattered.

"Yes, he did."

She pointed to his rucksack on the floor. "Where'd you get that from?"

"Mister Tom."

"Oh, and who's he?"

"Mr. Oakley. He gave it me to carry the presents."

One of her hands was outstretched across the table. He went to touch it but quickly changed his mind.

"There's a present for you too."

"I don't need charity, thank you," she said, pursing her lips. "You know that."

"It ent charity. It's for you gettin' well. Mrs. Thatcher made you some bed socks. Pink they are. Real soft. And Lucy's mum and dad put in eggs and butter."

"Butter?"

"Yeh. And Mrs. Fletcher made a fruit cake. She ses she knows you might not feel like eatin' it now but it'll keep for when you do." He was talking an awful lot, she thought. She'd never seen him like this before. Too cheeky by far. She'd soon discipline it out of him.

"And Aunt Nance, Mrs. Little, has sent a bottle of tonic wine."

Mrs. Beech turned puce. "Wine!" she said angrily. She checked herself and lowered her voice. "Wine!" she repeated. "Haven't I told you about the evils of drink? Have you been drinkin then? Who is this debauched woman?"

"It ent like what you buy in a pub, Mum. I asked. She ses it's got iron in it. It'll help you git your strength back. Mr. Little's a real doctor, Mum, and she's his wife."

"What kind of doctor?" she asked suspiciously.

He shrugged.

"One who helps people git better. I was scared of him at first but I ent now."

"Then he can't be a real doctor."

"He is, Mum."

Mrs. Beech was stunned. Her son had answered her back. He had actually disagreed with her.

"Are you arguing with me?"

"No, Mum, I wuz jes' . . ."

"Stop puttin' on that way of talking."

"What way, Mum?"

"And wipe that innocent look off yer face."

"I don't understand . . ." he started.

"You haven't changed, have you? I thought that man would frighten some goodness into you, but it seems he hasn't."

She suddenly grew anxious and a cold panic flooded her limbs.

"He *was* a church man, wasn't he?"

"Yes, Mum. He took care of it, and the graveyard. I told you in my letters."

"Oh, yes. Your letters. Now Willie, I thought you'd grown out of lying."

"But I ent lyin'!"

"Stop talking like that."

He felt bewildered. Like what? he thought.

"That writing was not yours. I know that. That's why I didn't bother to answer."

"But I learned at the school and Mister Tom and Miss Thorne helped me."

"My, you do seem to have taken up a lot of people's time. They must be glad to see the back of you."

"No, Mum, they ent. They . . ." He hesitated. "They . . ."

"They what?"

"They like me." It felt so good to say that.

"That's show, Willie. You're an evacuee and they were just being polite."

"No, Mum!"

"You are committing the sin of pride, Willie, and you know what happens to people who commit the sin of pride."

Willie was growing more and more confused. It was as if he was drifting into some bad dream.

Mrs. Beech tapped the table gently.

"That's enough for now, Willie. We don't want to quarrel on our first night, do we?"

He shook his head.

Willie? That was the other thing that felt strange to him. Nobody had called him that for six months. "Will" felt comfortable and his full name, William, sounded fine, although he had always felt like a Willie inside. Suddenly, now, when his mother referred to him as Willie it was as though she was talking to someone else. He felt like two people. He knew she wouldn't accept the Will side of him, only the Willie, and he didn't feel real when she called him that.

She leaned towards him.

"There's something I've been meaning to tell you, Willie," and she forced a smile which, for some reason, alarmed him, seeing the shape of it under those dead, colorless eyes.

"It's a little surprise, only," she added, "we have to creep into the house. No one must see you. It's—" She hesitated. "It's like a game," and she immediately felt relieved at having thought of the idea.

"No one must see me?"

"No."

"Why?"

She frowned and then put on the smile again. "You'll see. It's a surprise. It'll be spoiled if I tell you."

He nodded. He didn't really feel sick in his stomach. He was just imagining it, wasn't he? It was her that was ill, not him.

"And then you can show me your cake and presents."

"Yeh," he said, visibly brightening. "I can show you me pictures."

She waved him to stop. She didn't want him talking again.

"Yes, of course, but right now I've got a headache. It can wait, can't it?"

They left the café and caught a bus. The windows of the bus were covered with what looked like chicken netting.

"Why is that there?" he asked.

"It's rude to ask questions and it's rude to point. Behave yourself," his mother whispered.

"Missed London tahn, did you, luv?" said the bus conductress as she took their fares. It was the first woman Willie had ever seen working on a bus.

"Borin' in the country, so I hear. All of them cows. Still you know it is safer there," and she winked at his mother. "You miss them, though, don't you, luv."

She nodded, put her arm stiffly round Willie's shoulder and switched on the smile.

"Yes, and he's all I've got."

"Don't tell me. I've five of me own. I've given up sendin' them off. It don't seem worth it, do it really? Nothin' much happenin'. Hardly seems as if there's a war on at all, do it?"

"No," replied his mother politely.

Willie shivered at the iciness of his mother's rigid body. Having her arm round him made him feel nauseous. His own mother made him feel ill. Perhaps he really was wicked after all.

The bus crawled along slowly in the blackout until at last they reached Deptford. They stepped off and the conductress yelled "Good night" to them.

Mrs. Beech led Willie round the back of their street. She told him to hide in an alleyway and watch their front door. As soon as she had opened it and coughed, he was to run in. It was a strange game, thought Willie. He slid his hand into his shorts pocket and felt Zach's poem. It helped him feel less unreal.

He had not been standing long when he heard the cough. Picking up the rucksack and bags, he dragged them across the pavement. His mother whispered angrily to him to hurry up. She was frightened. She didn't want anyone in the street to know that he was back. He stumbled into the front room, which was still in darkness. There was a strong dank smell coming from somewhere. It was as if an animal had opened its bowels or peed somewhere.

"Is it a dog?" he asked.

"Is what a dog?"

"The surprise."

"What surprise? Oh that. No, it's not a dog."

She turned the light on.

The room was darker than Willie had remembered. He stared up at the gray walls. There were two prayer books on the mantelpiece, and one on the small sideboard, still in the same position. In addition to the newspaper over the windows, it was also crisscrossed with brown tape.

"What's that for?" he asked.

"What have I said about asking questions!" She shouted, slamming her hand angrily on the table.

"Don't," said Willie, startled.

"Are you telling me not to . . ."

"No," interrupted Willie. "I meant, don't ask questions. That's what you say. You say I mustn't ask questions."

"And don't interrupt me when I'm speakin'."

They stood, yet again, another awkward silence between them.

Willie turned away from her and then he saw it. A wooden box on a chair in the corner. He was about to ask what it was but changed his mind, walked over to it and looked inside.

"That's the surprise," she said.

He put his hand inside.

"A baby," he whispered. "But why?" He stopped and turned. "It's got tape on its mouth."

"I know that. I didn't want her to make a noise while I was out. It's a secret, you see."

"Is it?" he hesitated. "Is it yours?"

"Ours."

"A present?"

"Yes."

"Who from?"

"Jesus."

He glanced down at the baby. She was very smelly. She opened her eyes and began to cry.

"I'll pick her up," he said, leaning towards her.

"Don't you dare."

"But she's cryin'."

"She's just trying to get attention. She must learn a little discipline."

"But, but," he stammered, "she's only a baby."

"Sit down!" she yelled. "Immediately."

Willie sat at the table.

"Has she a name?"

She brought her fist down hard on the table.

"No! And that's enough questions from you or you'll feel the belt round you."

Willie flushed. The belt! It was still at Mister Tom's. He'd keep his mouth shut. Maybe she'd forget.

"Now, let's see what you've got in those bags. And take that coat off."

He hung it on the back of the chair, stuffing his balaclava and gloves into the pockets. He emptied the carrier bag first. He took out his old sneakers with the tops cut off.

"They got too small," he explained and placed his thin gray jersey, shorts, cap, mackintosh and Bible on the table beside them.

"I see you've still got your Bible," she said. "You've been keeping up with it, I hope, and learning it."

"Yes, Mum."

She leaned back in her chair.

"Recite Exodus, chapter one, verses one to six."

Willie stared at her blankly.

"I don't learn them by rote, Mum. I learns the stories like. I can tell you lots of stories. Old and New Testament."

"I'm not interested in stories. You learned by rote before you left here."

"That's because I listened to the others say it in Sundee School," he explained. "We didn't . . ."

"Undo that other bag."

He unfastened the straps of the rucksack and slowly began to pull everything out. It felt as though he was stripping naked in front of her. All the things that were precious and important to him were now being placed under her scrutiny.

She sat ashen faced and watched him unpack. When he had finished she spoke in a quiet and controlled manner.

"Now I'll ask the questions and you'll give me the answers and no back chat. Where did you get them clothes and boots you're wearin'?"

"Mr. Oakley and Mrs. Fletcher."

"You steal them?"

"No. They were presents."

"You begged."

"No, I never."

"Don't argue. I said you begged."

He took hold of the eggs, fruitcake, wine and bedsocks and slid them across to her.

"Those are your presents," he said.

"You begged those too, I suppose."

"No. I've got a present of me own for you," he added. It seemed spoiled now. His surprise. It had been Mister Tom's idea. He picked up two pieces of cardboard that were strung neatly together and untied them. Inside was a drawing. It was of the graveyard and the church with fields and trees in the background. He passed it to her.

"It's where I lived."

She looked at it. "You steal this?"

"No."

Now she would be pleased with him, he thought.

"No. I drew it meself."

She looked at him coldly. "Don't lie to me."

"I'm not. I did it meself. Look!" And he grabbed a sketchpad that was full of drawings. "These are mine, too," he said, flicking over the first page.

"I haven't time to look at pictures, Willie."

"But I did them meself!" he cried. "Please look at them."

"Willie. You have got a lot to learn. I shall either burn these or give them to charity. I only hope that no one ever finds out what you've done."

Willie stared at her in dismay.

"I didn't steal them, honest, Mum. I did them. I can show you."

"That's enough!" she said, banging her fist on the table again.

The situation was worse than she had ever imagined. It would take a lot of hard work to silence him into obedience.

"And these?" she asked, indicating the books and candy, colored pencils and clothes.

"Presents," he mumbled.

"More presents, Willie? Do you expect me to believe that? Do you expect me to believe that strangers would give you presents?"

"They ent strangers, Mum. They're friends."

"Friends! I'd like to know who these so-called friends are."

"George and Zach and the twins and   "

"Are they churchgoers?"

"Oh yes. George is in the choir. So am I." His face fell. "Was. But Ginnie and Carrie . . ."

"Girls?"

"Yes. The twins are girls. Carrie's working for . . ."

"You play with girls. After all I've said about that, and you mix with girls."

"But they'se fine and they goes to church. They all does, all except Zach."

"Jack? Who's he?"

"Zach," he said. "Short for . . . He bit his lip. Some instinct told him that he was approaching dangerous ground. His ears buzzed and his mother's voice began to sound distant.

"Why doesn't he go to church?" he heard her say.

He tried to evade the question.

"He believes in God, Mum, and he knows his Bible real good."

"Why doesn't he go to church?"

"They ent got one of his sort in the village, see, and anyway"—he faltered for a second—"he thinks that there's more God in the fields and sky and in loving people than in churches and synagogues."

"In what?" she asked.

"In fields and"—he hesitated—"and . . . and . . . the sky."

"No. You said than in churches or what? What did you say?"

"Synagogues," said Willie. "That's what they call their churches."

"Who?"

"Jews. Zach's Jewish."

His mother let out a frightened scream.

"You've been poisoned by the devil! Don't you know that?" And she rose and hit him savagely across the face. He put up his hands to defend himself, which only increased her anger. He reeled backwards in the chair and crashed onto the floor.

"But," he stammered, "Zach ses Jesus was a Jew."

"You blasphemer!" she screamed. "You blasphemer!"

Something heavy hit him across the head and he sank into a cold darkness. He could still hear her screaming and he knew that she was hitting him, but he felt numb and separated from himself. He had become two people and one of his selves was hovering above him watching what was happening to his body.

He woke up with a jerk, shivering with the cold. He began to stretch his cramped legs but they hurt. Opening his eyes, he looked around in the darkness. He knew immediately where he was. He had been locked under the stairs. He peered through the crack at the side of the small door. It was pitch black. His mother must have gone to bed. He shivered. His boots were gone, so were his jersey and shorts. He tugged at his waist and winced as he contacted a bruise. His undershirt had been sewn to his underpants. He took hold of the thin piece of material that lay under his body and wrapped it round himself. He could smell blood. He touched his head and discovered several painful lumps. His legs were sore and covered with something wet and congealed.

The night before, he had been lying in his first and only bed, in his first and only room. He was glad that he had left his paints and brushes there. Mister Tom would take care of them. Mister Tom! He had given him some stamped, addressed envelopes so that he could send him letters. He had also sewn two half-crowns into his overcoat. Would they still be there? Or would his mother sell the coat together with his clothes? He thought of the baby with the tape over its mouth. Maybe if she did sell them it would help the baby. He remembered the books and Zach's poem. She would certainly burn that, since it had Zach's name on it.

He felt as though he was a different person lying there in the dark. He was no longer Willie. It was as if he had said good-bye to an old part of himself. Neither was he two separate people. He was Will inside and out.

For an instant he wished he had never gone to Little Weirwold. Then he would have thought his mum was kind and loving. He wouldn't have known any different. A wave of despair swept through him and he cursed his new awareness. He hadn't been used to this pain for a long time. He had softened.

"Mister Tom," he whispered in the darkness. "Mister Tom. I want you, Mister Tom," and he gave a quiet sob. His ankle hurt. He must have twisted it when he fell. He placed his hand round it. It was swollen and painful to touch. He let go of it and curled himself tightly into a frozen ball, praying that soon he would fall asleep.

The Search
✠ ✠

The cottage seemed very quiet without William. Tom missed the sound of his boots clattering along the tiled hallway and his chatter at night. In the days that followed his departure Tom found himself glancing at the table to share something he had read, only to realize that the chair where William usually sat was unoccupied. He felt the old familiar emptiness that he had experienced after the sudden loss of Rachel. At least he could console himself that William was alive. He listened to the news on the wireless with extra attentiveness, particularly when there were reports of bombing near London.

Hitler had by now invaded Norway and Denmark, and heavy units of the British fleet had been sent to help the invaded countries, but the war still left Little Weirwold unruffled except for those few who missed William. It was sad that he wasn't around to witness early spring. Already buttercups were appearing in the fields, and in the woods wet primroses and violets had burst through the soggy dark earth.

Tom waited patiently for a letter. After the first week when there was still no word from him he thought William was probably too busy to write, for he would probably have his hands full doing chores for his mother. He thought the same the second week, but by the third week he began to feel anxious. He himself had written four letters. He knew that Zach had sent several also, but there was no reply to any of them.

One night he awoke violently from a nightmare. In

the dream, he had been locked into a tiny space with no air inside. It was as though he was being buried alive. But it was the voice that had woken him. He thought he had heard William calling out to him for help. He woke with a jerk only to find Sammy standing by his bedside, panting. He staggered out of bed and fumbled his way towards the bedroom window. Carefully easing the blackout curtains to one side he peered out. It was still dark. He opened the door, walked across the hallway to the living room and looked at the clock. It was three A.M. Almost time for his fire duty anyway. He'd go and relieve Hubert Pullett early. He pulled his corduroys and thick jersey on over his pyjamas, got into his boots, and stepped outside into the damp night slinging his trench coat, cap and gas mask on as he walked. Sammy followed him dragging a bit of old blanket in his teeth.

The fire post was a makeshift platform on top of the village hall. A ridiculous piece of extravagance, Tom had thought, when it was being built. He climbed up the ladder that leaned onto it. Mr. Pullett was sitting with a blanket wrapped round him and was in the process of falling asleep in a chair. He woke up, pleased to see Tom so early. They chatted for a while until Mr. Pullett decided to leave for the warmth of his bed. Tom made himself as comfortable and as warm as was possible, and Sammy snuggled in between his legs.

As he stared at the sky he couldn't rid himself of the dream he had just had. If William was in need of help, surely he would write to him. He gazed out at the galaxy of stars and brooded. Two hours later the dawn injected its colors into the sky and Mrs. Butcher came and took his place.

On the way home he caught sight of Miss Thorne's

sister, May, on her ancient bicycle. She was delivering the mail. He ran after her.

"Nothing for you, I'm afraid," she said. "I'm sorry." She hesitated before moving off again.

"Mr. Oakley," she added anxiously, "I'm afraid I have a telegram. It's for Annie Hartridge."

He looked up, startled. The last telegram had brought the news of Michael Fletcher's death.

"I'm a little worried," she went on, "what with her baby due so soon. I'd like to wait till the midwife is visitin' before delivering it, but it's against regulations."

Tom frowned thoughtfully. "You seen Mrs. Fletcher?"

She shook her head. "Didn't like to disturb her."

"I'll go and see her now, suggest she might pop in to see her."

"Thanks."

He watched her wobble off and head towards the farming area on the south side of the village. Turning sharply back, he walked in the direction of the Fletchers' cottage.

Mrs. Fletcher had just seen her husband and Edward off to work. The kitchen door was still open, and the light from it was casting a pale glow onto the still-glistening garden. She was standing in the doorway.

"You ent on dooty, is you?" she asked, glancing guiltily at the light.

"No, I ent," said Tom. "I jes' wanted to have a private word, like."

"George and David are asleep. They won't be botherin' us. Come on in and have some tea. You's lookin' a little on the pale side."

He stepped into the cozy warmth of the kitchen. Sam padded after him and curled up on the floor in front of her stove.

She sat down at the table and poured out two cups of tea.

"Sit down," she said, sliding a cup across to him. "What can I do for you?"

Tom looked surprised.

"There is somethin' you wants me to do, ent there? Is it Will?"

Tom shook his head.

"Annie Hartridge has got a telegram."

Mrs. Fletcher put down her cup slowly. "David?" she asked.

"I don't know. I jes' thought with you havin' lost Michael and with her about to have her baby, she might need someone who could help, like."

"Of course," she said, and she stood up and hurriedly untied her apron.

"She ent got it yet," he added.

She rolled down her sleeves.

"I'd like to be there as soon as possible. In her state she might pass out or somethin'. I'll think of an excuse, like extra eggs from the Padfields, booties for the baby, that sort of thing."

Tom nodded. It sounded for the best. He watched her put her coat on.

"Them trains to London," he murmured.

"Yes?" she said, puzzled. "What about them?"

"They run on Fridees, don't they?"

"Yes. That's right."

"It's Fridee today, ent it?"

"Yis."

He stood up abruptly.

"I'm goin' to get on that train, Mrs. Fletcher, and what's more I'm goin' to get on it today."

———

Tom's journey to London was as bumpy and intermittent as William's had been. Dim blue lights lit the tightly packed carriages and the air was stifling. It was frustrating, too, not to be able to see the stations that they passed, but once it was evening it was too dangerous to attempt to peep through the blacks in spite of the faintness of the blue lights. Sammy, who had not only smuggled himself into the cart but had also jumped off it and followed Tom to the station, was now squashed onto his lap. A makeshift leash, made of rope, hung from between his teeth. Tom held him tightly even as he dozed on the long journey.

He had originally refused to allow Sammy to come with him but now he was glad of his company. It was going to be a lonely task searching for William.

It was nine o'clock when the train pulled into London. He clambered out with Sammy and stood on the platform feeling totally dazed. The noise was deafening. Hundreds of uniformed figures swirled around him shouting to each other. Another train pulled out, and a voice over a public address system was calling out platform numbers and destinations. It was a while before Tom could orient himself enough to hand his ticket in. He must have looked a strange sight, with his thick white hair and weather-beaten face, clad in an old cord cap, overcoat and country boots with Sammy barking nervously at his ankles. Peering through the hordes of young men, he finally spotted the ticket man. He slung the haversack that he had borrowed onto his back. It was filled with clothes and food for William, from people in the village.

He handed his ticket in. The man looked down at Sammy.

"Should 'ave a muzzle, that dog," he exclaimed.

Tom nodded, having no intention of ever getting one.

"Where you from?" the man continued. "You ain't a Londoner, that I know. On 'olidee, are yah?" and he gave a loud chuckle at the absurdity of his remark.

Tom looked at him blankly.

"Only a joke," muttered the man. "Ain't yah got no sense uv 'umor?"

"Where's Deptford?" asked Tom.

"Deppeteforrard?" imitated the man. "Never 'eard uv it. Say it agen!"

Tom repeated it and the man shrugged.

"Ern," he yelled to an A.R.P. warden who was passing. "You know where Deppeteforrard is?"

"Not 'eard uv it," said Ern. "And I knows most places rahnd London. Used to be a cabby. You got it writ dahn?"

Tom handed them the piece of paper with the address written on it.

"Oh, you mean Deptford!" they chorused.

Tom repeated their pronunciation of it. "Detferd," he said quietly to himself.

They waved their arms over to the left towards an archway and directed him towards a bus station. Tom thanked them and headed in the direction they had suggested. The two men watched him and Sammy walk away.

"You don't 'arf meet some queer 'uns 'ere," said the ticket man. "I 'ope 'e ain't a German spy!" and they gave a loud laugh.

Tom held on to Sammy's lead firmly, for in the unlit street he kept colliding into people. He finally got onto a bus that would take him part of the way to Deptford, but it was a painfully slow journey. He stared in amazement at the conductress in her manly uniform. She was a little irritated at first, and then realized that he was a stranger to the city.

"You one of 'em refugees?" she asked kindly.

"Noo," he replied. "I don't think so."

"Where you from, then?"

"Little Weirwold."

She didn't understand him. His accent was too thick for her.

"In the country, is it?" she shouted, thinking he might understand her better if she raised her voice.

He nodded.

"What brings you to London?"

"Come to see a little boy."

"Oh. Grandson, is 'e?"

Tom nodded. He knew it was a lie, but he didn't want to go into complicated explanations. Sammy sat obediently on his lap.

By the time Tom had changed buses and been directed and misdirected, it was midnight before he reached the area where Willie lived. Accustomed now to the darkness, he could make out only too clearly the awful living conditions. Small dilapidated tenements stood huddled together, all in desperate need of care and attention. So this was William's background, he thought.

Suddenly a loud siren wailed across the sky. He froze. What was he supposed to do? He had read about communal shelters in the newspapers and he knew that people often crowded into the tubes, but he had no idea where the nearest tube station was.

"Come on. Move on there," said a loud brusque voice. "Move on to the shelter."

A group of people brushed past him, grumbling and cursing.

"'Oo's got the cards?" yelled a woman in the darkness. "Alf, have you got me bleedin' cards?"

A young girl bumped into him.

"'Ere, mind where yer goin', Mister," she rebuked him sharply.

"Sorry," he muttered. He shouted after her, "Where's you goin'?" but she had run away.

He felt a hand on his arm. It was a warden, a breezy man not more than ten years younger than him.

"You seem a little lost, sir. Come wiv me."

Tom picked Sammy up in his arms and ran after him towards a long brick building with a large gray S painted above the door.

The warden, Tom discovered, was the caretaker of the local school. He and several other men had been elected to be wardens by the people in the area. He sat down by Tom.

"You know, dogs ain't allowed in shelters, sir."

Tom stood up to leave, but the warden touched him gently on the arm. "I think we can overlook that, though."

He gazed at Tom, puzzled.

"Where you from then? You look like a country man."

"I am," he answered. "I've come lookin' for a boy what stayed with me, like. Evacuee he was."

The warden looked astounded.

"I think you'd best head back home. We've hundreds of the blighters runnin' away. We send them back. Makes no difference. They just come runnin' back again. You're the first person I've met who's come lookin' for one."

A young girl peered cautiously over the edge of one of the hammocks that were slung from the ceiling. The warden caught her eye, and she lay back quickly and disappeared from sight.

"That's one," he said, indicating her swinging sleeping quarters. "Fifteen times she's run back here. She ses she'd rather be at home even if bombs do drop here than be miserable and safe in the country."

"He didn't run away," said Tom.

"Oh?"

"No. I had a letter from his mother sayin' she was ill, like, and could he come back for a while to help out. I ent heard nothin' since."

"How long has he bin gone?"

"Near a month."

"How long was he with you?"

"Near six months."

"Six months!"

Tom nodded.

"And he didn't run away!"

"No. We was . . . he was happy."

The warden rubbed his chin with his fingers and sighed. "Look 'ere," he said. "There's nothin' you can do, I don't think. Could be when he got home he forgot about you."

"P'raps. It's jes' that I'd like to see that the boy's well. Then I can rest peaceful, like."

"Blimey. I never met anyone who cared that much for them. I hear such stories about you country folk, not nice uns neither. No offense," he added, "but I can see some of you are a kind'earted lot. And," he went on, raising his voice, "some people, Helen Ford and brothers, is dahnright ungrateful."

The hammocks jiggled violently at this last remark.

"Maybe I can help you find this boy. What was yer name nah? Mister . . . ?"

"Oakley. Tom Oakley."

"Well, Mr. Oakley, you say he's from this area?"

Tom nodded and brought out the piece of paper from his pocket. The warden glanced briefly at it and looked up startled.

"Why, it's in this very road. I know number twelve. Willie Beech. That the boy?"

Tom's heart leaped. "You seen him then?"

"Not since last September. Saw a large party from the school leave for the station. That's the last I saw of him. Quiet boy. Didn't mix. No friends as such. Bullied and teased a lot by the kids. Sittin' target really. Sickly-lookin' boy. His mother thinks she's a cut above everyone. Don't fit in here at all. Never have. Overreligious type, Bible-thumpin', you know what I mean?"

Tom nodded.

"Still, it's part of me job to check who's here and who's not here, in case of bombin' and havin' to identify, and I ain't bin notified of him being back. I ain't seen much of her either." He glanced across the crowded shelter and waved to someone at the far end of it.

"Glad might know somethin'. Glad!" he yelled. "Glad!"

A fat woman who was sitting playing cards looked up. She smiled, exposing three teeth in a large expanse of grinning gum.

"Yeth, love," she lisped. "Wot ith it?"

"Is Mrs. Beech on night shift this week? She ain't 'ere."

"Is she ever!" retorted Glad. "Wot you wanna know fer."

"Man here looking for little Willie."

"Run away, has he? Didn't think he had it in him."

"No. Man ses Mrs. Beech wrote for him to come home."

At this Glad climbed over several sleeping bodies and lumbered towards them.

"Wot you on abaht? She told me he wuth stayin'. Said he wath wicked and wuth bein' sent to an home fer bad boys."

"Boy was never bad with me. That I can vouch for," said Tom.

" 'Oo are you then, sir?" Glad asked.

"Tom Oakley."

"Willie stayed wiv him for nearly six months." Glad shrugged.

"I ain't theen him thinth September."

"What about Mrs. Beech?" began Tom.

"She keeps herself to herself. Bit of a madam. Thinks she's a bleedin' saint if you'll excooth me languidge. She does night shifts so I don't never see her. I live next door, yer see. Mind you," she whispered, "I don't 'arf hear some funny noises. Very funny."

" 'Ow do you mean?" queried the warden.

"Bumps and whimpers."

"Bumps?"

"Yeh, like furnicher bein' moved arahnd."

"What's funny abaht that?"

"At three in the bleedin' mornin!! That's what's funny. She's probably dustin' her Bible."

The warden turned wearily.

"Looks like a dead end, don't it, Mr. Oakley?"

"I'd still like to see where he lives," said Tom.

"You cum wiv me, luv," said Glad. "You fond of that Willie, then?"

Tom nodded.

"Queer, that. You're the first person I know who is. I don't think his own muvver is even fond of him."

"Mebbe she'll see me," said Tom.

"Blimey, I forgot. She's gawn away. To the coast. For a Bible meetin' or somethin'. She told me last week. Dunno why. She don't usually condescend to even look at me."

"Why warn't I informed?" commented the warden.

"It's up to her, ain't it?"

The warden gave a despairing sigh. "Do you still want to see the place, Mr. Oakley?"

Tom nodded.

They had to wait a good two hours before they could leave. The small building grew foggy with tobacco smoke. A Women's Voluntary Services lady in green uniform visited them with tea and sticky buns, and a man called Jack unclipped a rather battered accordion and started playing it. The small group that Glad was part of was in the middle of singing. "We're Going to Hang Out the Washing on the Siegfried Line" when the All Clear was sounded, and they left it unfinished in their scramble to get out.

Tom was relieved to be outside again. His clothes smelled of stale tobacco and sweat. He breathed in the night air as if it was nectar. Glad was waiting for him. Together she and the warden accompanied him to Willie's home.

"She fancies 'erself, duth ahr Mrs. Beech," lisped Glad. "Sheeth got the downstairs and the upstairs room. She thumtimes rents her bedroom and thleeps downstairs—well, so she seth," and she winked and gave Tom a nudge.

They stood outside Number Twelve and peered in at the window. One of the newspapers had slid to one side. The interior seemed dark and uninhabited. The window still had brown sticky tape on it to protect the room from the blast of falling glass.

"Deserted," remarked the warden.

Meanwhile Tom's attention was drawn to Sammy, who had started to move in an agitated manner outside the window.

"What's up, boy?" he asked. "You smell somethin'?" He crouched down and stroked him. "What is it?"

Sammy began to whine and scratch frantically at the front door. He ran to Tom and, clinging to his trouser leg, pulled him towards it.

"No one in there, Rover," said the warden.

"Mebbe," said Tom. "But it ent like him to fuss over nothin'!" He jiggled the doorknob.

"You can't do that, sir. That's agin the lor."

"I think there's someone in there," said Tom urgently.

A policeman who had been attracted by the commotion joined them.

"This man reckons there might be someone in there," explained the warden. "I've looked inside, far as I can, and it looks empty to me."

The policeman pushed back his tin helmet. "What evidence do you have, sir?"

Tom pointed to Sammy, who had grown quite frantic. He began to bark loudly, still scratching feverishly at the locked door.

They all glanced at each other.

"I'd like to enter," suggested the warden anxiously. "I'm worried about the mother and boy who live in there."

They knocked on the door loudly, but there was no answer. Sammy leaped up and hurled himself at it.

"He can smell somethin', by all accounts," said the policeman.

After much deliberation they decided to break the door down. A small crowd began to gather round to see what was going on. Glad gave them a running commentary.

It wasn't a heavy door, and between Tom, the policeman and the warden, they broke the wood round the lock after only two attempts.

The door crashed open and they were greeted with a stench so vile as to almost set them reeling. It was as if an animal had died and was rotting somewhere. Sammy ran immediately to a tiny door below the stairway and barked loudly, scrabbling at it with his paws. The odor was at its strongest there. The warden lifted aside the latch and swung the door open. The smell was rank, so much so that the warden turned his face away quickly for a moment as if to retch. The policeman pulled his torch out of his pocket and shone it into the hole.

Rescue

—🌿 🌿—

The small alcove stank of stale urine and vomit. A thin emaciated boy with matted hair and skin like parchment was tied to a length of copper piping. He held a small bundle in his arms. His scrawny limbs were covered with sores and bruises and he sat in his own excrement. He shrank at the light from the torch and made husky gagging noises. The warden reached out and touched him and he let out a frightened whimper. An empty baby's bottle stood by his legs.

"You give me that baby, son," said the warden, but the boy tightened himself up, his eyes wide with fear. Sammy slipped in between the warden's legs and sat patiently waiting for his master's command. Tom turned to the policeman.

"I'd like to talk to the boy. 'E knows me, like."

The policeman nodded and left to call an ambulance and to disperse the crowd of neighbors who were now massed outside the front door.

Tom squatted down.

"It's Mister Tom," he said gently. "I was worried about you, so me and Sammy cum lookin' for you."

Will looked in his direction.

"He'll have to go to the hospital," said the warden. Will let out a cry.

"Don't worry, boy," said Tom reassuringly. "We'll stay with you. Now you jes' hang tight to that ole bundle and I'll untie you. This man's yer old school caretaker. He didn't know you was here and now he's goin' to help you git out. The light's on so's we can see the ropes more clear, like."

Very gently and laboriously he untied him. The warden, realizing that the boy looked calmer when the old man was by him, left him to it and watched.

Tom told him exactly what he was going to do. He knew that Will's limbs would be stiff and that they would be agony to move. He took hold of him firmly and maneuvered him gently towards him. It was difficult because Will clung so tightly to the bundle.

After Tom had managed to ease him out, he heard an ambulance drawing up outside and the sound of doors opening and slamming. The policeman crouched down beside him and handed him a blanket. Tom wrapped it round Will and the bundle and carried him to the ambulance.

"The dog's mine," he said firmly to one of the ambulance men who was about to push Sammy out. "And I'm traveling with the boy."

The warden climbed in after him and sat on the free stretcher bed in the back. The doors were shut behind them and the ambulance ground slowly forward.

"I'd like to git me hands on that woman," the warden growled furiously. "All pride and angel pie on the outside, and inside this," and he pointed to Will, who was now lying on a stretcher in the warmth of Tom's overcoat.

"She must be orf 'er nut!"

Tom glanced at him. "I 'spose you'll be lookin' for her," he commented.

"Try and stop me!" The warden's pride had been shaken badly. It was embarrassing to have that policeman think he didn't know his job.

"Thank you," said Tom quietly.

"What for, guv?"

"For listenin' and breakin' in."

"Any time."

He gazed down at Will's face. A tiny speck of color appeared in his jaundiced cheeks and he began to move his fingers. The warden looked intently at the bundle and then at Tom. Tom gave him a nod.

"Reckon we could find a blanket for the little un, like?" he asked.

The warden caught on immediately.

"I'm sure we could, Mr. Oakley," and he unfolded one of the blankets.

"William," whispered Tom. "Will."

He opened his eyes and looked up at him.

"Yes," he whispered.

"Can I has a look at the little un?"

Will nodded and relaxed his fingers a fraction. Tom drew the folds of the cold bundle to one side. The baby had been dead for some time. It was thin and tinged with a grayish hue. He glanced at the warden. They didn't need to say anything. The look told all.

"I've just warmed this blanket up for the little chap," said the warden.

"It's a her," Will croaked.

"Oh, girl, is it? Wot's her name, then?"

"I calls her Trudy."

"Trudy. That's nice," and he leaned towards him. "You feel this nice soft blanket, Willie."

"I ent." He faltered. "I ent . . ."

"You ain't what?" he asked.

"I ent Willie."

The warden looked concerned.

"Shock," he whispered. "Must have gawn orf his chump."

"No," explained Tom. "We never called him Willie."

"Oh," said the warden, still not quite understanding.

"Will," whispered Tom.

"Yeh."

"Well . . . Will," began the warden again. "How's abaht givin' ahr little Miss Trudy a blanket of her own, like yours."

Will nodded and relaxed his grip.

"Hurts," he gasped as he attempted to move his arms.

"Takes yer own time," urged Tom. Will smiled as he recognized the familiar saying. "And keep breathin'. Sammy'll warm them arms, won't you, boy?"

Sammy was curled up by Will's legs. He stood alertly to his feet. Slowly Tom pried open Will's stiff arms, and with the help of the warden they took the baby and wrapped it carefully in the blanket.

Sammy was placed on Will's lap. Will jerked involuntarily. He was very sore. All he wore were the undershirt and pants that Miss Thorne's sister, May, had given him for his birthday. They were now a filthy gray and yellow. His bare feet were mauve with the cold and his filthy clawlike toenails curled inwards. Tom squeezed the feet with his hands to try and work some warmth into them.

Will's stiff arms were now enfolding Sammy. Suddenly holding a warm body instead of the cold one he had just handed over made him aware that something was wrong with the baby. He glanced urgently across at the warden, who was holding her.

"It's all right, son," he said. "I got her."

"Hurts," he whispered. "My arms. They hurt."

"They will do for a bit,' said Tom. "You been holdin' 'em in the same position for a long time. They ent used to movin' yet."

The ambulance jerked to a halt and the doors were

flung open. Tom carried Will out, followed by Sammy and the warden. They pushed their way through two heavy doors, into a lobby. A woman with glasses sat behind a small glass window. She looked up at them briefly as they sat down on some chairs.

"I'm sorry," she said. "No dogs allowed in here."

"Ent there somewhere I can leave him?" inquired Tom.

"I'm afraid not. He'll have to go."

The warden stood up and exchanged a few words with her.

"I see," she said, looking at Tom and Will. "There are some railings at the side of the hospital. You could tie him to one of those. I'm sure no one would disturb him."

"Tie 'im!" exclaimed Tom.

"Afraid that's the best they can do, Mr. Oakley," said the warden.

A cleaner bustled past them. She stopped.

"Cheer up, luvs," she said with a jolly smile. "It ain't the end of the world. You'll be all right here. They looks after you real proper."

Will and Tom stared blankly at her as she disappeared jovially down the corridor, singing "Wish Me Luck as You Wave Me Good-Bye."

A young man in a white coat came flying out of one of the doors in the corridor, followed rapidly by a nurse, and walked towards the warden and Tom. The young man glanced at the bundle.

"Dead," he said abruptly.

"Dead," whimpered Will.

"Dead cold he means, don't you, sir," said the warden, winking urgently at the doctor and indicating the boy.

"Oh, yes," said the young man. He was exhausted

and hadn't realized that the boy and the baby were together. He knelt down by Will and drew aside the coat
and blankets. The nurse, a dark-haired fresh-faced
woman who didn't look more than nineteen, knelt down
beside him. The doctor mumbled something about lac-
erations and delousing. He looked up at Tom.

"You a relative?"

Tom shook his head.

The warden spoke up for him. He knew how strict
regulations were about not allowing visitors who weren't
relatives.

"The boy stayed wiv him for six months in the country.
He went back home to his mother, who said she was
ill. He ain't got no dad, you see, and this gentleman
heard no word so he comes miles to find him. Mother's
left the boy."

"Looks like he found you in the nick of time," said
the nurse, and she gave Will a warm smile.

The doctor stood up.

"Best take him to the children's ward and clean him
up. Bit late for stitches. He'd better have a tetanus jab."

"That an injection?" asked Tom anxiously.

"Yes. Nothing to worry about. It's in case of infec-
tion."

"Good clean air'll cure that," said Tom.

"Nurse," said the doctor, ignoring him, "take him
to children's."

Tom stood up with Will still in his arms.

"Dogs aren't allowed," said the nurse, glancing down
at Sammy, who still stood alertly by Tom's side.

"It's all right," piped up the warden. "I'll look after
him."

"I'll come with you," said Tom to the nurse.

"I'm afraid that's not allowed," she said.

"I ent leavin' the boy with a load of strangers."

She gave a sigh.

"You can come as far as the ward but no farther. You'll have me for the high jump, you will." Tom observed her briefly. Here was this well-spoken skimp of a girl telling him what to do.

Will looked terrified when he handed him over to her.

"I'll take care of him," she said gently. "I'll ask if you can see him in the morning."

"I'm stayin' 'ere, Will," he said. "I'll be in that big hallway where we was sittin' jes' now. I won't be far away, boy."

He watched her walk away with Will in her arms and then headed back towards the lobby.

"I gave the receptionist the details," said the warden. "I have to make a police report nah."

"Where's the baby?" asked Tom.

"One of the nurses took her orf to the morgue."

He glanced at Tom, who stood looking very stunned.

"Wot you need is a nice strong cuppa tea. A mate o' mine's got a post just rahnd the corner from 'ere. Comin'?"

Tom shook his head.

"I promised the boy I'd stay here."

" 'Ere, luv," the warden yelled at the bespectacled receptionist. She blinked in amazement at his familiarity. "We're just going round to Alf's. If there's any changes wiv the boy, let them know where Mr. Oakley is." He smiled at Tom. "Come on," he said. "It'll be all right. You only need stay for a few minutes."

They crossed the hospital courtyard and out through the large gateway. Just outside the railings on the corner was a small hut with walls made of sandbags and a corrugated tin roof. A sign with **WARDEN'S POST** written on it hung above it. Inside sat a balding middle-aged man with a thick black graying mustache.

" 'Allo, Sid!" he exclaimed when he saw the Deptford warden. "Wot brings you 'ere? Not a bomb casualty, that's for certain," and they chuckled. " 'Itler keeps threatenin' to devastate us, don't he, Sid," he continued. "But he can't git near us. Not wiv ahr boys up there to protect us," he said, waving a patriotic finger up at the roof of the tiny hut.

Tom remembered David Hartridge. Was it only yesterday that the telegram had arrived? It seemed like a month had passed since then. He had been reported missing, believed dead. Poor Annie.

"Come in and warm yerselves," said Alf. "I'll restew me brew."

Inside the hut was a makeshift brazier made out of a bucket with holes in it. The bucket had some kind of coke burning in it. It was stifling hot inside the hut. Tom squatted down on a tin drum while Sammy squeezed in between his legs.

"You ain't from rahnd 'ere," commented Alf.

"No," said Tom. "No, I ent." And so the story of Will's discovery was told yet again.

"Wot you goin' to do nah?" asked Sid.

"Take him back," remarked Tom. "To Little Weirwold."

"Don't think you can do that. I think they'll have to find 'is muvver first. Probably prison for her."

"And Will?" asked Tom.

" 'Ome. Children's 'ome, I s'pose."

"I'm takin' him back," said Tom firmly.

The warden glanced at Alf. They knew better. Tom drank his tea and returned to the hospital. He tied

Sammy to a railing at the side, opposite some tiny stone steps.

"I'll come and visit you soon, boy," he reassured him soothingly. "It's only temporary, like."

It was dawn by the time he had sat down in the lobby. Three ambulances had driven up with casualties and he had given the ambulance men and nurses a hand. A communal shelter had collapsed on fifty men, women and children. Tom helped load and unload the stretchers.

By the afternoon there was still no word of Will and no answer to Tom's repeated questioning. He continued to sit patiently in the lobby, alternately dozing and going out to see Sammy.

At last a fair-haired nurse came up to him.

"Are you Mr. Tom?" she asked.

"Yes," he said, standing abruptly. "How is he? Can I see him?"

"You're not a relative, are you?"

"No, but I'm pretty near—the boy lived with me, like. He ent got no father and his mother's deserted him."

"A psychiatrist has been to see him, Mr. Tom. He's from a special children's home and he's agreed that it's all right for you to see him."

"Sichitrus? 'Ow d'you mean?"

"A man who cares for sick minds."

"Oh yes. I read about them somewhere," and he grunted. "Nothin' sick about his mind, though."

"He's under deep psychological shock," said the nurse. "He keeps suddenly screaming out for no apparent reason. We've had to keep sedating him."

"Sedatin' him?"

"Putting him to sleep."

"Why?"

"To stop him from screaming."

"Mebbe he needs to."

"That's as may be, Mr. Tom, but we have to consider the other children in the ward."

Tom nodded. The sooner Will could get out into some wide-open fields, the better.

"When can I see him?"

"Now. Follow me."

They passed through the maze of corridors. Since Tom had helped with the emergency, he had begun to learn his way around. Two nurses nodded and smiled at him. They thought he was a volunteer helper.

The fair-haired nurse pushed aside the swing doors into the children's ward. Tom strode in and looked around. She pointed to a bed on his left. The first one by the door. Accessible. Easy to get to in an emergency—although why he felt that was important he had no idea.

Will was propped up by pillows. His hair had been shorn off completely, revealing an array of multicolored cuts and bruises around his bald skull. He was well scrubbed and smelled strongly of disinfectant. Sitting in a voluminous white hospital nightshirt, he appeared quite shrunken.

"Didn't recognize you with yer army cut," said Tom.

Will smiled weakly. His teeth were still the same yellowy-brown color.

"How you feelin'?"

"Stiff."

His lips were pale and cracked and it was obviously an effort to speak.

"I gits nightmares," he whispered. "And when I wakes up they stick a needle in me and then I can't move or speak." He fell back exhausted onto the pillows. "How long does I have to stay here?" he croaked.

"Not long, I shouldn't think. You look well patched up." He felt Will's thin fingers. They were cold. He gave them a blow and rubbed them between his hands. Picking up his haversack from the floor, he slung it onto the bed. "Got a new pair of gloves fer them hands," he said. "Had a feelin' you might be needin' them. You'll has to put on a bit more flesh though, else they'll slide off."

"Where's Sammy?"

"Outside. Regulations. Not allowed in. Case he brings in germs, I s'pose." He glanced around the ward. "Though I reckon there's more germs in this here hospital than most places." He gave a gruff laugh.

Will leaned awkwardly on one elbow.

"This bloke came to see me."

"Oh yes. Doctor, was 'e?"

"I dunno. He said he was from a home and that I'd be goin' there and I'd get better there." He clutched at Tom's arm. "Can't I come back with you?"

"Course you can. Don't know the law side, mind, but we'll git round it somehow."

"Mr. Tom," interrupted the fair-haired nurse from behind him. "I'm afraid you'll have to leave now."

Will hung tightly to Tom's sleeve.

"Don't go yet!" he urged. "Stay a bit more."

Tom sat closer to him on the bed.

"I'm sorry, Mr. Tom," said the nurse nervously. "But you must go now."

"The boy would like me to stay for a bit," he replied calmly.

"I'm sorry, it's against regulations."

"Whose regulations?" Tom said, turning to face her.

"Now come on, Mr. Tom, let's not have any trouble."

"What's going on, nurse?" boomed a loud noise at the end of the ward.

"Nothing, sister," said the nurse shakily.

The sister, a middle-aged woman with a loud step, walked firmly down the ward towards them.

"Time to go!" she said in a no-nonsense manner.

Tom stood up and leaned over Will's bed.

"Afraid I'll has to go, but I'll be in the hallway and I'll see you tomorrow."

Will clung to his arm with both hands now. He could barely sound the words. "Don't go," he pleaded. "Don't go!"

"Please leave, sir," said the sister sharply. "You're only upsetting the boy."

"I think it's your regulations what's upsettin' him, ma'am."

He turned to Will.

"Tomorrow'll come awful quick," he added comfortingly.

The sister stepped forward and firmly wrenched away Will's hands from Tom's arm.

"Now go, sir! Immediately!"

Tom reluctantly began to depart. Will pushed himself up and tried to get out of bed.

"Stay where you are. There's a good boy," singsonged the fair-haired nurse.

Will began to whimper and make grunting noises.

"Go!" shouted the sister. "Nurse! Sedation!"

Tom walked dejectedly through the swing doors and listened helplessly to Will's cries.

He stood for a moment and then turned to look through the window. The two nurses were holding Will facedown. Another nurse joined them and gave him an injection in his bottom. A few seconds later Will sank helplessly into the bed and the nurses let go of him.

"Mr. Tom, is it?" said a quiet-spoken voice behind him. Tom jumped and turned sharply. A man in his thirties wearing a gray suit had been standing behind him. He must have a soft step, thought Tom, who had heard no movement. The man was going bald and the hair that remained was of a thin texture. His skin was as white and shiny as that of a cloistered nun. He gave Tom a bland smile and held out his hand.

"I'm Mr. Stelton," he half whispered. "I expect William has told you about me."

Tom nodded.

The man observed Tom in a seemingly detached manner and then looked quickly away to gaze at a wall in the corridor. Neither of them spoke, and Tom had a feeling that the man had no intention of breaking the silence. He was leaving that to Tom. Tom was irritated by this, but he wanted to find out about Will.

"Yes," he said. "He told me you want to put him in a home."

"Ah," said Mr. Stelton quietly. "Did he?" and he gave another bland smile and gazed back at much the same place.

"Wall interestin', is it?" inquired Tom.

"You see yourself as a wall, do you?" the man commented, still staring at it.

"Stop shilly-shallying and tell me about the boy."

Mr. Stelton turned and faced Tom briefly.

"Of course," he said.

They found a few chairs in a corner and sat down. Tom couldn't help observing the quiet manner in which Mr. Stelton walked. It was a slow lope and his toes pointed slightly inwards. He sat next to Tom with his knees together and rubbed the tops of his thighs gently up and down as he spoke.

"I believe in a more modern approach, Mr. Tom," he said. "I don't use drugs."

"Oakley," corrected Tom. "Mister Tom's the boy's name for me."

"Ah," he said and gave a significant nod. "You don't wish me to call you by the boy's own name."

"About those drugs," interrupted Tom, before Mr. Stelton could gaze into space again. "I don't use them either."

"Of course not," and he gave another bland smile.

Tom wondered why Mr. Stelton spoke in such a subdued tone. Was he afraid of disturbing someone?

"I deal with disturbed children," he went on quietly. "And I work in conjunction with a home. There, children are well cared for and are given lots of attention. We feel . . ."

"We?" inquired Tom.

"Myself and the head of the school."

"Thought you said it were a home."

"It's also a school. We feel," he continued, "that he would benefit from treatment there."

"What sort of treatment?"

"Psychiatric treatment. Analysis. We want to encourage him to talk about his background and find out why he is the way he is."

"Thought that's pretty obvious," said Tom. "The boy ent had a lot of lovin'!"

"Ah," said Mr. Stelton quietly.

Not another silence, thought Tom. The idea of Will spending time talking to a man who semispoke, semiwalked and gazed in the distance whenever one made eye-to-eye contact did not appeal to Tom. As far as he was concerned, it would be enough to drive the sanest person mad.

"I'd like him back with me," said Tom firmly.

"Ah," sighed Mr. Stelton, taking several mental notes.

"And you can ah till the cows come home. That's what I want and that's what the boy wants."

This was followed by another silence while Mr. Stelton rubbed his thighs gently up and down.

"You're not a relative," he softly intoned.

"No," answered Tom. "But . . ." He stopped.

"Yes?" said Mr. Stelton looking vaguely interested for the first time.

"I'm fond of the boy."

"You're fond of the boy," and he gave a nod and turned to gaze away from Tom's penetrating green eyes. "You could visit me," he suggested, back to staring at the wall. "And William, while he's at the home. I'm sure if you are . . ." He paused, "If you mean what you say, you'll want the best for him. The staff at the home are younger than you and well trained." He stood up. "We're picking him up the day after tomorrow. Monday. If you would like to come with us you are welcome. We're not like a hospital. We encourage visitors. So long as they don't disturb the children," he added.

He gave Tom another neutral smile, shook hands and padded quietly away down the corridor.

Tom began to walk dejectedly towards the lobby.

"Give us a hand, will you?" asked one of the nurses as he passed her.

A large elderly man with a misshapen leg needed to be lifted onto a stretcher fixed to a trolley. Tom helped lift him.

"You Red Cross people are marvelous!" the nurse said, having recognized him as a helper from the shelter casualty emergency. "Are you here tonight as well?" Tom nodded. Why not? he thought. It would stop him from thinking about Will. He ran down the corridor to give a hand with some newly arrived casualties, and when at last the lobby was reasonably quiet, he stepped outside for some fresh air and paid a short visit to the railing, where Sammy was attached. He untied him and they sat on the stone steps.

"What we goin' to do, boy?" he murmured as he ruffled Sammy's chest. "We ent got much time." He stared out at the street beyond the railings. It was already beginning to get dark again. He rubbed his chin. Gray stubble had started to sprout where he hadn't shaved.

"Oh, Rachel," he said half aloud to the sky. "What would you do?" and he saw her, in his mind, swing round in her long dress and flash her dark eyes at him.

"Kidnap him," she said laughingly.

Tom gave a start. Rachel wouldn't have said that. On second thoughts, Rachel would. He rose slowly. "I'll jes' play it be ear," he muttered. "Mebbe if . . ."

His thoughts were interrupted by the sounds of several ambulances arriving. He tied Sammy back to the railings, ran briskly along the side of the building and round the corner to where the entrance doors swung and immediately began carrying people into the hospital.

Three hours later he was walking back down one of the stairways, carrying a blanket, when he realized that he was standing outside the children's ward. He peered quickly through the small window. The fair-haired nurse was still on duty. She was slumped asleep across a table with a small night light beside her.

Tom looked quickly around the corridor. There was

no one in sight. Before he allowed himself time to think, he crept into the ward and gently eased the swing doors to a close. Will was fast asleep, well knocked out by the drugs.

As Tom drew the sheets aside, one of the smaller children on the other side of the ward woke up and started coughing. The nurse opened her eyes and lifted her head. Tom hastily pulled the sheets back into place and crouched down on the floor. The nurse spoke to the child soothingly, gave her some medicine and tucked her in. She then returned to the table. She was trying to study for an exam on anatomy, but soon her eyelids grew heavy again and within minutes she had fallen asleep.

Tom whipped back the sheets, lifted Will out and wrapped the blanket he was carrying around him. He stuck one of the pillows down the bed and tucked the sheets round it. Not very convincing, but it was all he had time for. Holding Will firmly in his arms he stood up. If the nurse woke up now, he thought, he'd be in for it. One of the children turned over in his sleep and gave a little moan but the nurse went on sleeping, quite undisturbed. He glanced out the window. Very quickly, he swung the door open and walked firmly out and down the corridor. He knew that if he looked furtive he would give the game away. He met the nurse who had chatted to him over the elderly man. She smiled at him.

"It's all go, isn't it?" she said.

Tom nodded and headed for the lobby, where he had left his haversack. Two ambulances drew in, and in the general confusion that followed he picked up the haversack and strode towards the swing doors. He glanced quickly at the receptionist. To his relief, it was a different woman on duty. As soon as he was outside, and the drivers had turned their backs, he ran into the dark unlit courtyard, round the corner and down to where he had left Sammy.

Sammy leaped up excitedly and began to bark. "No!" whispered Tom urgently, placing a firm finger on his nose. "Down, boy. Quiet!"

He laid Will on the bottom step and feverishly undid the haversack. Quickly he put some warm underwear and socks on him.

"You keep guard, Sammy," he whispered, and he untied him and put the leash into his pocket. The next garments to go on Will were a brown patched pair of corduroy shorts, a gray flannel shirt, a navy roll-neck jersey and a green balaclava. The balaclava at least hid his bald head. Unfortunately he had no boots or overcoat for him. He hid the blanket in a dark corner and wrapped his own overcoat round Will. Slinging the haversack onto his back, he walked towards the open courtyard with Will in his arms, Sammy following. A firm step, he thought to himself as he strode across it. At any moment they might discover Will's absence. He continued out through the gates and down the street. Suddenly a voice called out sharply to him.

"Oy. Mister!"

He turned. It was Alf. He had forgotten about the Warden's Post. Drat it.

"You got the boy then?"

He nodded.

"Good on you. Takin' him back to the country?"

Tom nodded again, waved good-bye and strode firmly down the street, wanting desperately to run or look behind and not daring to do either.

After much climbing on and off buses the three of

them arrived at the large station. They spent the remainder of the night in a shelter nearby. There were no trains going to Weirwold the following morning, but there was one going two thirds of the way, to a village called Skyron. Tom hurriedly bought tickets, tied the leash round Sammy's neck and headed for the platform. His tickets were clipped by the same ticket man.

"Got yer grandson there?" he remarked cheekily. "Deep sleeper, ain't he? You'll spoil him carryin' him like that. I'd wake him up and make him walk, lazy tyke."

"He's ill," said Tom.

"Oh," said the ticket man, startled. "Not contagious, I hope."

"No."

The man handed the tickets back and Tom and Sammy ran along the platform. The train was due to leave within minutes.

"That dog should have a muzzle," yelled the ticket man after them.

They climbed into the train and sat by a window in an empty carriage. Not long now, thought Tom, and they would be out of London. A tapping on the window interrupted his thoughts. He looked up to find a policeman looking down at him through the glass. He pointed to Will. Tom quickly covered his stockinged feet with his coat.

"Air raid keep him up, eh?"

Tom nodded.

"Have a safe journey."

"Thank you."

At last the train drew out of the station. They were joined by an elderly woman who sat crocheting for most of the journey and who chatted about the weather and rationing and how she missed butter. She left them halfway to Skyron. For the rest of the journey, they had the carriage to themselves.

Skyron was a large village not much bigger than Weirwold. Tom walked through it and headed for the open road, where he began to hitch for a lift. They had three lifts—one in an army truck, one in a vet's broken-down old Morris, and one in a trailer. Tom walked the final five miles to Weirwold. It was a cool crisp day but the sky was clear and sunny. As soon as he saw the river, he felt overwhelmingly happy. How untouched and different it was from London. The water sparkled beneath the sun's keen gaze. He stood on the top of a hill and drank in all the fields that lay below. He now understood Will's bewilderment at suddenly confronting so much open space after his background in Deptford. He glanced down at Sammy, who had begun to limp slightly. His small tongue was hanging out of his mouth like a piece of old leather.

"Not long now, Sammy," he said encouragingly.

By the time they reached Weirwold he was carrying both Will and Sammy in his arms. He tramped over the old cobbled streets as twilight fell, on through the square, past the closed shops and towards the blacksmith's.

He knocked firmly at his door. A window opened from above.

"Mr. Oakley!" cried the brawny, dark-haired man. "You's back from London."

Mrs. Stoker, the blacksmith's wife, appeared at his side.

"Has you really been to London?" she asked in awe. He nodded.

"You look fair done fer," and she disappeared and reappeared at the front door.

"You must be starvin'," she said. "I'll make you a meal."

"That's very kind, Mrs. Stoker, but I want to start out for Little Weirwold soon," he replied.

"Put the boy by the fire," she said.

Tom placed him in an armchair by the hearth. Mr. Stoker eased the armchair nearer and pushed back the overcoat to allow the warmth of the flames to reach his limbs. As he did so he let out a gasp. Mrs. Stoker turned to look at him.

"Oh, my luv," she said. "He's in a bad way. Good job you went for him, Mr. Oakley."

By now the news had spread fast about his journey to London.

"Well, you keep that to yerself, mind," said Tom.

The Stokers decided not to ask any more questions. What you don't know you can't tell on, and that was that.

After a rest and some tea, Mrs. Stoker lent him some blankets for Will and gave him a bag filled with sandwiches.

It was dark by the time Dobbs was harnessed for the journey. Tom tucked Will up with Sammy in the cart and clambered up to his seat to take hold of the reins.

"Come on, me ole gal," he yelled in delight as Dobbs jogged forward. "Take us home."

Will awoke to the sound of Tom singing. He opened his eyes to discover a starry sky above him. Sammy was slumped in an exhausted stupor by his feet. Will pushed aside a few of the blankets and looked up to where Tom was sitting. He struggled to his knees, but his legs were too wobbly and he sank back into the pile of blankets.

"Mister Tom," he croaked. "Mister Tom."

Tom stopped the cart and turned round.

"Woken up, eh?"

Will blinked his eyes until Tom came clearly into focus.

"You ent dreamin'. Lie back boy. We ent long from home." He tucked the blankets round him again.

"But," stammered Will, "how did I git here?"

Tom shook the reins and Dobbs moved forward.

"I kidnapped you," he said over his shoulder, and then he suddenly realized the enormity of what he had done and he burst into laughter. "Yes, that's what I done, boy. I kidnapped you!"

Will lay back and fell asleep. He next woke to find himself being carried through the Littles' front door and into their sitting room with its large array of books and cozy armchairs. Tom put him down on the sofa by the fire and Mrs. Little called her husband. Dr. Little leaned over Will and with the gentlest of hands pushed his balaclava back and examined him.

"You seem pretty well patched up, Will."

Mrs. Little gave him some hot milk and toast, but he fell into another deep sleep before he had even attempted to touch it.

The Littles listened to Tom's story.

"I know I done wrong," said Tom. "But I couldn't let him be taken to a home."

"Country air," put in Mrs. Little. "Familiar surroundings. People who love him. Best thing for him."

Her husband looked at her over his ever-sliding spectacles.

"They're bound to track him down sooner or later."

"Nonsense," expostulated Mrs. Little huskily. "They're too busy to go chasing evacuees. They didn't even know he'd returned to London."

Dr. Little turned to face Tom.

"The sores will heal. They healed before. It's the wounds inside that will take the longest to heal."

"I know that," said Tom. "I'll give him me support when he needs."

"Me too!" cried a voice behind him.

They turned to find Zach standing at the doorway in his pyjamas. He ran across to the sofa and looked down at Will's inert body.

"I knew you'd bring him back," he said fiercely, tears in his eyes.

"You look tired, Tom," said Mrs. Little. "Sit down."

Tom thanked her and sank gratefully into an armchair.

Zach continued to gaze silently at Will.

"Mister Tom," said Zach earnestly, "if you need any help . . ." but it was useless continuing.

Tom was asleep.

Recovery
— ❧ ❧ —

Will felt himself being shaken violently into consciousness. He opened his eyes and peered around the darkened room. He could see no one, nor could he even see a window. He raised himself on his elbows and strained his eyes, searching for something recognizable and familiar. As he gazed at one of the walls, it lurched forward in his direction. He turned to look for the door so that he could leave, but found himself facing another wall. This too was moving towards him. He glanced quickly behind. A third wall was closing in on him, and as it leaned nearer, the ceiling shuddered and began to descend. He leaped out of bed and flung himself at one of the walls in a desperate attempt to find a doorknob. By the time he had slid his body along the fourth wall, he realized with horror that there was no door. He was trapped. He pressed himself against the walls to prevent them moving any closer but they only pushed him backwards. Terrified, he let out a scream, only to find himself surrounded by four tall figures dressed in white.

"If you scream," said one of them, "we shall put you to sleep forever."

"No!" he shrieked. "No! No!"

But the black airless tomb began to smother him and he screamed again.

"We warned you," said the four figures. "We warned you." He watched them, paralyzed, as they produced a long hypodermic needle.

"Turn over," they said. "Turn over, turn over, turn over."

He backed up against one of the walls. Two arms burst through the hard surface and gripped him from behind. Helpless, he watched the cold steel tip of the needle glinting as it traveled towards him. He struggled to break free but was forced down by a multitude of hands.

"No! No!" he cried. "Please. Let me be! Let me be!"

As the needle entered his right buttock he woke with a frightened start. He was in his bed in the attic bedroom. His pyjamas and sheets were sticking to his drenched skin, and blankets lay scattered about the floor. The blacks were up and a nightlight stood burning on his little side table. He heard footsteps coming up the steps. It was Tom. He hoisted himself up through the trapdoor and sat on Will's bed.

Will clung to him fiercely. Tom put his arms round his soaking body and held him firmly.

"You keep breathin', boy," he murmured. "Don't you go holdin' it in."

"They said they were going to put me to sleep if I screamed," gasped out Will.

"Who did?"

"The tall people in my dreams. I were frightened. I couldn't help screamin'. I had to."

"You scream as much as you likes. No one'll hear you except p'r'aps me and Sammy. You might reach the vicarage, but yous'll have to be pretty loud for that. No. You yell away. Give them ole bones in our front garden a good rattlin'!"

Will smiled weakly.

"Now, we'd best get you dried and warmed up."

He carried him down the ladder to the front room. Hanging in front of the stove were several sheets on a wooden clothes horse. Tom stripped Will, and after he had sponged and dried him, he put some clean pyjamas on him and wrapped him in a blanket. He left him with Sammy curled up in the large armchair.

By the time Tom had remade the bed, Will had fallen asleep. His small stubbled head lay flopped over one of the arms of the armchair. Tom picked him up and carried him back up the ladder. It was the fifth time that he had changed the sheets and had soothed Will after a horrific nightmare.

Will was relieved when daylight filtered into his room. He dreaded the terrors of night.

Zach meanwhile visited the cottage regularly, but Will was usually asleep when he called and Tom didn't want to disturb him. Day after day a tremendous fatigue swept through and drained Will's entire body. Eating took a supreme effort, and the smallest task, be it cleaning his teeth or holding a book, exhausted him into another deep sleep.

One night he was so feverish that Tom stayed by his bed keeping watch. Sammy had been left downstairs in the front room with the door closed firmly behind him.

Will moaned and cried out, pushing the blankets away from his legs. He arched his back and gritted his teeth like a baby having a hysterical tantrum, and with flailing limbs he appeared to be fighting some powerful force. The sweat trickled down him in never-ending streams. Tom felt quite helpless. There was nothing he could do except stay with Will and go with what was happening. He hugged him when he woke and encouraged him to talk about his nightmares as much as possible.

By four o'clock in the morning Will had soaked every sheet in the cottage and was now reduced to wearing yet another of Tom's shirts. He grew increasingly hotter until, at one point, Tom was sorely tempted to run over to the Littles' to fetch the doctor. He quickly dismissed the idea. He didn't dare leave in case Will should wake from one of his nightmares during his absence.

It was during one particular dream that Will suddenly froze on the bed. He spread his legs and arms outwards as if backing up against a wall, tipped his head back, and let out the wildest and most terrifying scream Tom had ever heard. It shook him to his very bowels. He couldn't remember how long the scream lasted. It sounded like a baby crying in despair, an old forgotten scream that must have been swallowed down years before.

He found himself being dragged back to the day when Rachel had given birth to their son. Tom had been a young man of twenty then and still very deeply in love. He remembered how he had paced the floor in the living room listening to her moans from the bedroom and then the sudden silence. He had turned to find the midwife standing at the door shaking her head sadly. He remembered how he had run across the hall and into their bedroom, how he had clasped Rachel's hand. She had smiled so tenderly at him. He had tried to ignore how thin and pallid she was and had glanced down at her side to where a tiny red-faced baby lay.

"Ent he beautiful," she had whispered, and he had nodded and watched helplessly as the old familiar color of scarlatina spread across both their faces.

"Yous'll have to git blue," she had whispered to him, for during her pregnancy he had brought her a new pot of paint for each month of her being with child.

The ninth was to be blue if she had given birth to a boy, primrose yellow if it had been a girl.

After they had died, he had bought the pot of blue paint and placed it in the black wooden box that he had made for her one Christmas, when he was eighteen. As he closed the lid, so he shut out not only the memory of her but also the company of anyone else who reminded him of her.

He glanced down at Will, who had suddenly become quiet, given a start and opened his eyes. His lips had turned blue. Tom raised him to a sitting position and stroked his back as if he was a baby with wind.

"Keep breathin', boy," he murmured. "Keep breathin'."

Will released his breath, and as he gulped in a fresh lungful of air he began to vomit violently.

It was after this incident that he began to sleep more easily. He had reached the climax of his nightmares and they no longer haunted him.

One morning, several days later, he awoke feeling refreshed.

A smell of bacon and eggs drifted between the floorboards, and although the blacks were up and his nightlight was still on, he could hear the sounds of birds and the old familiar whirring of a tractor in the distance.

"Mister Tom," he yelled. "Mister Tom."

In seconds Tom's head appeared through the hatchway and Sammy ran across the floor and jumped onto his bed.

"You's lookin' good," Tom remarked. "You got color in yer cheeks."

He walked over to the window and removed the blacks. Sunlight danced into the room. Tom propped the window up and extinguished the nightlight.

Will pushed his legs over to the side of his bed and stood up with a wobble, only to sit down suddenly again.

"They ent had much use," commented Tom, noticing the anxious frown on Will's face. "They'll git stronger. Remember . . ." but Will finished the sentence for him.

"Everythin' has its own time," and he laughed.

It was good to see Will smile again. It made Tom feel lively, rejuvenated.

"Breakfast in bed, sir?" he said cheerily. "I takes it yer hungry."

Will nodded and grinned.

Tom propped his pillows up and left him sitting happily with a book. Sammy snuggled in next to him. It was like the old days.

Downstairs, Tom began to prepare a royal breakfast. As he broke an egg into the frying pan he started singing. He too felt released. While he was singing he heard a tap at the window. He looked up to find Zach peering in.

"Come on in," he said.

"I say," blurted out Zach excitedly as he ran breathlessly into the room. "He's better, isn't he?"

Tom nodded.

"You can see him after he's eaten his breakfast."

"Oh gosh, I can't wait till then. He'll take an age with that lot," he said, indicating the toast and mushrooms, egg and bacon. "You know what he's like. He chews his food."

"That's usual, ent it?" remarked Tom in surprise.

"Oh no. I just give mine a few bites and swallow it, but he chews and chews. Couldn't I sort of drape myself inconspicuously on a chair while he's devouring that lot?"

"You inconspicuous?" commented Tom wryly. "You

jes' wait. You's waited long enough already. A few minutes won't make that much difference."

"That's what they say in novels," moaned Zach. "A
few minutes can be a jolly eternity," but his words were
lost on Tom, for he was halfway up the ladder.

Zach plunged his hands deep into the pockets of his
red corduroy shorts and stared out at the graveyard.
It was a glorious spring day. He had discarded his boots
and socks and had retrieved his battered sandals from
their winter hibernation. The only other garment he
wore was a white collarless man's cotton shirt with the
sleeves rolled up. It billowed out in voluminous folds
between his braces.

It was now the first week in May. The spring holidays
had ended and already the summer term had begun.
Now that Mrs. Hartridge had had her baby and was
no longer teaching, Mrs. Black had been splitting her
energies between the two classes.

"You want tea?" asked Tom on his return.

"Yes, please. How is he?" he added urgently.

"Hungry."

Zach took a large gulp from his tea and gave a yell
as it burned his lip.

"I know, you don't have to tell me," he said, catching
Tom's eye. "Look before you leap," and he blew on it
and sipped it hurriedly.

"Does he know I'm here?"

"No. I didn't want to disturb his breakfast."

"Oh, Mister Tom," Zach cried despondently, thrusting his cup dramatically onto the table.

"No offense to you," Tom added. "It's jes', I knows
how overexcited he gets."

After what seemed hours to Zach, Will called from
upstairs. Zach followed Tom into the hall.

"Wait," Tom whispered.

"I see. Then it'll be a surprise. I say, what a wizard . . ." but Tom was already through the hatchway.

He reappeared soon after.

"All right," he said. "You can come on up."

Zach waited impatiently for him to reach the bottom of the ladder, and then half running, half stumbling, he flung himself upwards.

Tom stood in the hallway listening to their yells of delight He cast his eyes upwards to an imaginary heaven.

"Couple of doughbags," he remarked.

Zach bounced at the end of Will's bed and hit his head on the rafter. A round pink lump appeared immediately at the side of his forehead. Sammy scrabbled over the bedcovers and smelled and nuzzled him all over.

"You're ever so bony," exclaimed Zach, "but you look much much better."

"Me legs are a bit wobbly."

"How romantic to be stuck in bed with a fever. Rather like Keats, or Elizabeth Barrett Browning or the Brontë sisters."

"Romantic?"

"Yes. I wonder if you'll be like Heidi's cousin, you know, the one in the wheelchair who has it pushed down the mountain and then she walks."

"Wheelchair?" said Will in alarm. "I ent that bad."

"Pity!"

They looked at each other and smiled broadly. The stubble round Will's head had grown past its prickly stage and had developed into a thin layer of sandy-colored fluff.

"I expect you're dying to know all the news," said

Zach, crossing his legs and making sure he was quite comfortable.

"You's goin' to tell it to me anyway," remarked Will.

"I say, you've lost your London accent. You've gone all yokel."

"Have I?"

"Miss Thorne will have the screaming abdabs when she hears you. She gives elocution lessons now, to the dramatics group."

Will pushed himself up excitedly. "Is she still doin' plays, like?"

"You bet, and she can't wait for you to be well. You're one of her prodigies. I'm as jealous as anything, of course," and he smote his chest and gazed up at the ceiling.

"What was it like? *Toad of Toad Hall?*"

"Oh, great fun. I was marvelous, of course. Missed you though terribly, and Carrie. She's still cramming madly for this wretched exam. She's even learning Latin and a bit of Greek from Mr. Peters. I'm sure she needn't. Folks round here already say she's a queer one. Oh, by the way," he added after a pause, "Mrs. Hartridge has had a baby girl."

"A baby," repeated Will, and he paled.

"I say, are you all right?"

"Yes," said Will quietly.

"You don't look it. Do you want me to call Mister Tom?"

"No. I'm all right."

"If you say so. The baby's called Peggy. Oh dear," he sighed. "I haven't cheered you up very much. You've been looking miserabler and miserabler ever since I came in."

Will smiled.

"Oh, I forgot," Zach said suddenly. "Lucy missed you terribly too. Mrs. Padfield told me she hasn't eaten properly in weeks. She's lost her pudding look, well, round her body. Her cheeks still seem just as enormous."

Will scowled.

"You don't like her very much, do you?"

"It ent that," said Will squirming. "It's jes', it's jes' . . . She's a girl."

"So are the twins."

"They're different. They ent, they ent . . ."

"Lovey dovey?"

"Yis. Lovely dovey," and he couldn't help but laugh at his own embarrassment.

"And," continued Zach, remembering something else, "Aunt Nance and Uncle Oz dragged out one of their children's old bicycles and I've been cleaning and derusting it and doing odd jobs so I can save up for two new inner tubes. The old ones are riddled with holes."

He sat back and puckered his brows in an effort to remember any other news. "Oh yes," he said. "There's talk of forming a Home Guard, same as Local Defense Volunteers only more official I think and, oh yes, there's two land army girls up at Hillbrook Farm and there's talk of the Grange being used as a maternity hospital."

"Hospital?" said Will, alarmed.

"Well, nursing home," said Zach, sensing that he had put his foot in it.

"What's that?"

"A place where women who can't be at home have their babies."

"Babies," said Will, feeling sick.

"Yes," said Zach, puzzled at his reaction.

"Don't they come from Jesus, like?"

"Of course not. Oh," he said, "you don't know."

"Know what?"

"About sex."

Will blushed scarlet. "I know it's somethin' dirty and you goes to hell for it."

"Rot!" exclaimed Zach. "We wouldn't be here if it wasn't for sex. It's what happens between men and women when they love each other."

"What, kissin' and touchin'?" said Will, feeling a little hot.

"Well, that's a good beginning."

"But kissin's a sin, ent it?"

"No. That's what you do when you love someone. Look, the woman has a seed inside her and a man has a seed inside him and when they reach one another they join up and the man gives the woman his seed. If the seed sticks to one of the woman's seeds it grows into an egg, and the egg grows into a baby inside the woman, and when the baby's grown enough and is ready to be born it shoots out of the mother."

"Are you sure?"

"Yes. My parents told me and they don't lie."

"Your parents told you!"

"Yes. Look, ask me any questions you want. I'll tell you all I know."

"Thanks."

"It isn't dirty," continued Zach, "unless you make it that way."

"Can't a lady have a baby on her own?"

"No. There has to be a man to give her his seed." He stood up abruptly. "I'm going to get Mister Tom. You look dreadful."

Tom popped his head through the hatchway.

"What was that about me, then?" he asked. He glanced at Will. "I think you'd best go home, Zach. Overdone it a bit."

"Yes, that's what I thought. Can I come again tomorrow?"

"Oh yes, please do," urged Will.

Tom sat at the end of the bed and waited till Zach's footsteps had disappeared out of hearing.

"Now then, what's up?"

Will looked startled.

"Best tell me."

"It's about Trudy."

"I think you know already," said Tom quietly.

"She's dead, ent she?"

He nodded.

"My fault," he choked out. "My fault. I killed her. I made her die."

"How?"

"She cried and cried and I nursed her, like. I held her real good. I rocked her. I gave her the milk in the bottle and then there wasn't no more."

"Ent your fault. The milk runnin' out."

"But I should have got out, like. I waited. I shouldn't have waited. I thought me mum'd be back any minute, only . . ." But he couldn't get the words out.

"Only she never did, that what yer sayin'?"

He nodded.

"Baby needs milk. You couldn't give her that. You was tied up."

"Zach said—" He blushed. "He said that a woman can't have a baby without a man. Is that true?"

"Yes."

"So me mum must have met with a man."

"Yes."

"She lied. Why did she lie? She said men and ladies goin' with each other were a sin."

Tom took out his pipe and began to stuff tobacco into it.

"I has a feelin' that your mother is very ill."

"She must have had Trudy growin' inside her, like. Mebbe that's what she meant when she said she were ill."

"There's another kind of sickness that some people has. It's a sort of sickness of the mind, usually an unhappy mind. Reckon yer mother is a bit like that."

"Mister Tom, I want to stay here. I don't want to go back to her, even if she says she's ill."

"You won't go back to her. Authorities wouldn't allow it."

"But why did you kidnap me then?"

"They were goin' to put you in a children's home. I wanted you back here."

"Why?"

"Why? Well . . ." In an embarrassed manner he puffed out a billow of smoke from his pipe. "Because I'm fond of you, boy. That's why. I missed you." He stood up. "And now I'll git out all the bits of paper I've bin savin' up for yer drawrin'. Then you can come downstairs and scrawl away."

Will watched him slowly descend the ladder. "Mister Tom," he said.

Tom raised his head back up through the hatchway. "Yes, boy."

"I love you." And instead of the cold feeling he had imagined would happen if he uttered those words, he felt a wave of warmth flooding into his stomach and through to his chest, and he beamed. Mister Tom's face became flushed. He cleared his throat.

"I love you too, boy," he grunted. "And now I'll git on with downstairs." And he disappeared quickly down the ladder.

As May flew into June Will steadily grew in strength. He remained indoors, happy just to draw and read. Zach, George and the twins and even Lucy came to visit him, but he tended to fall asleep midconversation and would wake to find that they had gone, leaving a little pile of fruit and comics beside him.

It was several weeks before he ventured as far as the tiny patch of front garden overlooking the graveyard. He and Tom would carry the large wooden table outside so that he could lay out his paints and brushes on it. The constant fresh air increased his appetite, and as he ate, so his energy returned.

Meanwhile, in London, Neville Chamberlain had resigned as Prime Minister and a plump, bald man of sixty-five had taken his place. His name was Winston Churchill.

Soon afterwards the inhabitants of Little Weirwold were shaken by the news of Dunkirk. The British Expeditionary Force had been driven back to the coast of France by the Germans, and thousands of troops, some very badly wounded, had to be evacuated by sea to Folkestone. Hundreds of ordinary people who had vessels risked their lives to help in the evacuation. Many were killed. "Sir" from the Grange, and his son Julian, had taken a motorboat. The Grange was now no longer to be a maternity hospital but a convalescent home for wounded and shell-shocked soldiers. One weekend, several truckloads of vacant-eyed, wounded young men in uniform rumbled their way through the village. The villagers cheered and threw garlands of flowers at them and handed them homemade cakes, bread and eggs as they passed. Some of the youths managed numb smiles, but most of them were too dazed to know what was happening.

On the last Saturday in June, Will made up his mind to do something that he had been putting off for some time. He had finished his cottage chores and was sitting outside reading. Tom had left a shopping list for him on the table. He was helping over at Hillbrook Farm, as were George and Ginnie. Carrie was at the vicarage with the vicar, studying Latin.

Will closed his book, picked up the list from the table and headed for the shop. On his way back he called in at the Littles'. If Zach wasn't doing anything, maybe they could go off somewhere. Then he could postpone his venture again.

He found Zach covered with oil and surrounded by soiled rags and small tools. Propped upside down on its handlebars was an old bicycle.

"I've nearly got it working, you know. This is the first mechanical thing I've ever done in my whole life. I'm determined to complete something once and for all."

They chatted briefly and Will returned home. He left a short note saying where he had gone and headed in the direction of Annie Hartridge's cottage. An hour later he was still staring intently at her front door.

After much deliberation he crossed the rough narrow lane, knocked three times and stood back nervously. It was a blistering hot day and his shirt clung to his body. He shook it to fan some cool air inside. No one answered the door. Perhaps she wasn't in. He felt relieved. He could come back another day. He took hold of the smooth brass knocker and tapped it again. There was still no answer. He was about to leave when Mrs. Hartridge's head suddenly appeared around the corner. He jumped.

"I thought I heard someone," she said. "I'm in the back garden. Come round. I heard you were back," she added gently. "This is a surprise."

On the grass in the back garden was a large tartan rug. She told him to sit down and make himself comfortable while she made him a glass of homemade lemonade. He watched her go into the cottage and remained standing. He glanced furtively round the garden, taking in the vegetable patch, the herb garden under the kitchen window, the tall trees that stood by the lane; and then he gave a small gasp, for standing in the shadow of the trees was a baby carriage.

He stared numbly at it, not daring to breathe for fear he might disturb whatever lay there. Annie Hartridge stood at the sink looking out of the window. She was about to lean out and ask him whether he would like honey in his lemonade, but when she saw the look on his face she kept silent. News always spread like wildfire round the village, and she knew some of what he had been through.

Will, meanwhile, was making slow, steady progress toward the carriage. It shuddered slightly and two small chubby legs rose into the air. He moved closer until he was standing beside it. There, lying under the protective shade of a hood, was the tiniest of babies. She had dark wispy hair and round brown marble eyes. She waved one of her hands absently and looked up startled as one of the fringes at the edge of the hood flickered.

Annie Hartridge let him stand quietly for some time before breaking the silence.

"Lemonade and ginger cake coming up," she said brightly. Will turned round feeling self-conscious at being caught staring at the baby.

"She's rather beautiful, isn't she?" Annie remarked, strolling towards the carriage and lifting her out. She gazed into the baby's eyes and kissed her cheeks.

"I'll let you have a little romp on the grass, my love," and she laid her face down onto the rug. "There you are, my precious."

Will sat beside her with his lemonade and watched her, fascinated at the enormous power the tiny, helpless being held over him.

He stayed in the garden till dusk talking with Mrs. Hartridge about books and ideas for obtaining paper and where you could buy the cheapest paint. He didn't mention Mr. Hartridge and she didn't talk about his mother or Trudy. Sometimes in the middle of a conversation they would stop suddenly and look at each other with understanding.

In Will's eyes she was more beautiful than ever. A little on the thin side now, but her eyes were still as large and blue, her hair still as golden and her voice was just as melodious, if not more so. He watched her hold the baby in the air and bring her down to her face, where she blew raspberries into her tummy. Sometimes she would just gaze at her and look happy and sad all in one moment.

They were in the middle of a conversation when Will heard a knock at the front door. Annie stood up with Peggy still in her arms. "Here," she said, handing her over to Will. "Hold her while I answer the door."

She walked briskly away not daring to glance back

at him. She had no idea whether she was doing the right thing or not. Instinctively she wanted Will to know what it was like to hold a warm, live child.

Will sat stunned, clutching the tiny infant in his arms. He felt tense and awkward. The baby blew a bubble, which burst and dissolved into a long dribble. It dangled down the side of her chin and headed towards her flimsy cotton dress. She felt soft and had an extraordinarily pleasant smell, thought Will. He began to relax a little and the baby puckered up her mouth and made a small gurgling sound, then for no reason at all screwed her eyes up and began to cry.

Will glanced frantically round for Mrs. Hartridge. He rocked Peggy and held her close to him, but she continued to cry. He stood up with her still in his arms, searching for a bottle.

Mrs. Hartridge opened the back door and crossed the garden. She took Peggy in her arms and smiled.

"I know what you want, my love," she murmured, and sitting down in a canvas chair, she unbuttoned the front of her floral blouse and placed one of her breasts in the baby's mouth.

Will was too shocked to avert his gaze. He felt that he should shut his eyes or excuse himself, but his feet remained rooted to the spot and soon he forgot his embarrassment and became mesmerized by the slow rhythmic sucking of the baby. He watched her small arms lying outstretched while her fingers curved inwards and outwards contentedly. A pinkish flush spread across her cheeks.

When the baby had taken her fill, Mrs. Hartridge buttoned up her blouse and looked at him.

"Mister Tom's waiting for you out front."

Will thanked her for the lemonade and ran to join

Mr. Tom. He was sitting on the grass with Sammy, staring at the long thin rows of pink-tipped clouds in the distance.

As they walked home Will felt suddenly lighter. Tom had been right. He couldn't have given Trudy what she had needed. It wasn't his fault that she had died. He was still saddened by her death, but the awful responsibility that had weighed so heavily on him had now lifted. He thrust his hands into his pockets and walked with a brisker step.

When he and Tom arrived at the cottage, they found Zach waiting for them in the front garden, with the old bicycle.

"I've fixed it. I've actually fixed it," he announced proudly. "I say, Mister Tom," he added, giving a broad grin, "how far is it to the sea?"

The Sea, the Sea, the Sea!

❧ ❧

Zach opened his mouth and began singing the same old rousing song again.

"At Playarel in Brittany, down by the Breton Sea,
If a man would go a-fishing,
Then let him come with me-ee,
For the fish lie out in the distance there
Deep in the Breton Sea-ee-ee
Deep in the Breton Sea."

He had sung it so many times that Tom and Will knew it almost by heart.

"And green is the boat," they sang,

"And red is the sail
That leans to the sunlit breeze,
And music sings at a rippling keel—
What can a man more please?
It is sweet to go to the fishing grounds
In the soft green Breton Sea."

It was August. The sun shone in a clear, uncluttered azure sky and Zach, Tom and Will sat on the rough plank seat of the cart while Tom held the reins. They were into the third day of their travels on the road. The coolness of the early morning had worn off and another blisteringly hot day had begun. Zach and Will peeled their shirts off and threw them together with their socks and sandals into the back of the cart. He and Zach sat barefooted, their braces dangling at their sides and their lean sunburned legs swinging gently and

rhythmically from side to side as the cart jogged on-
wards.

"Shouldn't be far now," murmured Tom as he shook
the reins.

He left Dobbs and the cart at a farm. In exchange
for her help in harvesting, the farmer would take care
of her. They unloaded the cart, in which Sammy, two
bicycles and several panniers lay heaped together. Tom
and Zach wheeled the bicycles out onto the road while
Will carried the panniers.

Zach had painted his machine. Its frame was now a
pillar-box red and the mudguards were yellow. He hung
two of the panniers onto a small frame attached to the
back wheel. Tom's bicycle was black in color, but it was
just as conspicuous as Zach's, for it was a tandem. Will
couldn't ride a bicycle, so being a second rider was the
next-best thing.

A wicker basket was strapped to the front handlebars.
Tom checked the tires and, like Zach, tied the panniers
securely over the back wheel. He climbed onto the tandem and held it steady while Will planted Sammy in
the basket and then hauled himself onto the back seat.
Zach was already astride his bike, his foot resting on a
pedal.

"Let's go!" cried Tom, and he gave the tandem a
sharp push forward.

"Wizzo!" yelled Zach.

They cycled steadily and rhythmically on, past fields
of fresh swaying corn and lush green trees. Cream and
amber butterflies flew intermittently from behind the
hedgerows, and strange, exotic smells hit their noses.
They wheeled the bicycles up a very steep hill and stood
at the top breathless at the climb. There at last, vast
and calm below them, lay the sea.

Flinging their bicycles into the hedgerows they leaped and pranced about waving their arms in the air and yelling at the tops of their voices, and when suddenly Will and Zach realized that Tom was dancing too, they clutched their stomachs and laughed hysterically till the tears rolled down their cheeks.

After recovering, they gulped down some overheated lemonade, clambered back onto their bicycles and eased them gently down the hill, half mesmerized by the immense expanse of blue that sparkled below them. Sammy continued to lie slumped and boiling under an old piece of tarpaulin that was fixed over the basket. As soon as he felt a flicker of breeze he hung his head over the edge, his tongue dangling in anticipation of a cool and shady spot.

Although there were no signposts to welcome them, Tom felt sure the fishing village they rode into was the place. It was called Salmouth. They weren't the only holiday makers but, as the roads to Salmouth were very narrow, most of the people who ventured there were cyclists like themselves or ramblers. Tom walked from cottage door to cottage door asking if anyone would take them, including a dog, for bed, breakfast and an evening meal for a fortnight. After several refusals they chanced upon a middle-aged widow called Mrs. Clarence. She was delighted to have them stay with her. Her four sons had been drafted and she lived alone with a dog called Rumple. Unlike Sammy, Rumple was ancient and spent his days lying lazily cushioned in layers of his own wrinkled fat.

Tom and Zach wheeled the bicycle and tandem along a tiny stone pathway at the side of Mrs. Clarence's cottage, towards her neat and well-stocked garden. Will untied the panniers and together they carried them in.

"You jes' go for a walk," announced Mrs. Clarence cheerfully. "It'll give me a chance to sort your rooms out."

They happily agreed to this suggestion and strolled leisurely down the tiny main street in the direction of a small harbor. Three tiny cobbled alleyways sloped gently down towards it. At the corner of one stood an old weather-beaten pub called the Captain Morgan. A wind-battered sign with a picture of some old sea dog on it hung outside.

"By George, I say," whispered Zach, clutching Will's arm in excitement, "I wonder if there are any smugglers or pirates round here."

Tom and Sammy had walked on down the lane and were standing at a tiny landing dock. Will and Zach joined them.

They passed a fishmonger's, where clusters of crawling crabs and lobsters, inert cockles and shellfish, were placed in the front window on display. A heavy odor of fresh fish emanated from the doorway.

A few yards down was a shop filled with what Zach called "sea things," from fishing tackle and compasses to longjohns and thick navy-oiled jerseys. Zach stared wistfully through the glass and sighed.

"Oh to be a pirate!" and he began to murmur something about "Drake being in his hammock" and "Captain art thou sleepin' thar below."

Will was drawn like a magnet towards the small dock. He stood on the ancient wooden quay and gazed in wonder at the sea. The waves lapped gently against the timbers below him. He had imagined that the sea would terrify and engulf him, but instead he felt surprisingly calm. It seemed as if his mind had suddenly opened and all his worries, painful memories and fears were flooding to the surface and drifting away. Sammy barked at the sea gulls that caw-cawed and swooped above his head, but Will was quite deaf to his yelps.

Around the jetty itself were groups of men in fishing boats, long high-masted wooden vessels with wet nets hanging over their sides. Left of the jetty, a mile away, lay a sheltered bay. A handful of small anchored sailing boats bobbed on the surface. Will plunged his hands into his pockets. He felt overwhelmingly happy at the thought of spending a fortnight in Salmouth. Fourteen whole days. He could sit by the quay and sketch to his heart's content and there was so much to see, new shapes to draw, new colors to store into his memory. There were some things though, that he could never capture, things like smells and feelings and sensations of touch. They were "now" things to enjoy only for a moment.

"Are you coming, Will?" yelled Zach.

He turned quickly.

"We's goin' further along towards that long V," said Tom, pointing to the estuary. "You want to stay here or come along?"

"I'm coming," he replied, walking towards them.

They turned up a second alleyway and pressed their noses against the dirty glass of an old secondhand bookshop. It was a treasure house for all three of them. If it hadn't been for Sammy tugging at Tom's corduroys they might have disappeared into the shop and stayed there for the remainder of the afternoon.

"That's a rainy-day shop," commented Tom.

The nearest beach was a mixture of sand and pebbles. They sat on it and gazed out at the bay.

Three or four families and a few couples were sitting on deck chairs or swimming in the sea. Tom had previously read in the newspapers that most of the beaches in England were heavily populated. Salmouth, to his delight, was relatively quiet.

By the time they returned to Mrs. Clarence's, they were ravenous.

"I've took your bags to your rooms," she said. "I've put you two boys together in the back room, and Mr. Oakley," she added, "you're in the front bedroom next to mine."

Tom thanked her and they all sat down to a meal of fried mackerel, freshly picked broad beans, potatoes in their jackets, and slices of fried zucchini. Tom offered Mrs. Clarence his ration of sugar and butter and anything else she might need.

Zach had eaten fish many times. He had spent several summers by the sea when his parents were doing summer seasons, but it was the first time he had ever had a companion of his own age to share those summer joys. Most of the time he used to wander alone, chatting to people, but his odd appearance and forthright ways seemed to annoy them and they tended to ignore him. With Will, he felt that he could do and be anything and anybody and Will would still like him.

Will was eating fish for the first time. Mrs. Clarence showed him how to gently make an incision, fold the fleshy parts to either side and carefully pull out, intact, the long skeleton.

After the fish meal, they had baked apple with honey poured over it. Mrs. Clarence had been talking so much that she had forgotten that they were in the oven and they had burst into oddly shaped foaming heaps. She apologized profusely but Tom, Will and Zach said that they preferred them exploded.

During the meal Tom observed Zach and Will. Will's

skin, which had gone through various stages of pink on the journey, was now approaching a bronze hue. A profusion of freckles covered his entire face.

"I say," exclaimed Zach, also noticing the new phenomenon, "you've got hundreds of freckles."

"Have I?" remarked Will in surprise.

"Yes. They must have been lurking under your skin for years and years and years."

Will glanced down at his arms. His shirt sleeves were rolled up to above his elbows.

"I've got lots on me arms too," he commented. "How strange."

Zach licked his mouth. "My mouth tastes salty, does yours?"

Will licked his lips and nodded.

"Mine too," added Tom.

"I'm going to rename this village Salt-on-the-Mouth," said Zach, sitting back and looking very pleased with himself.

"I like that," said Will, smiling.

The sea air caused Zach and Will to feel sleepy and, as they were excited about sharing a room, they went to bed quite willingly, leaving Tom and Mrs Clarence to listen to *Henry Hall's Guest Night* on the wireless. While she knitted and talked, Sammy tried vainly to stir some life into Rumple, who now occupied the best position by the hearth.

Upstairs Zach and Will undressed and put their pyjama trousers on. Their beds stood on either side of a bay window that overlooked the sea. There were two window frames with thin strips of painted white wood that crisscrossed across the glass. Each window had a latch that pushed it outwards. Both were now flung open, for Mrs. Clarence had said that as long as they kept the lights off, they needn't have the blacks up. Zach and Will leaned out and allowed the cool night air to brush their faces. A full harvest moon hung in a clear navy sky. Waves slapped against the shore below the tiny back garden.

Downstairs Tom sat reading, when he wasn't interrupted by Mrs. Clarence. She was a shy woman and her shyness manifested itself in great bursts of incessant chatter.

Mrs. Clarence didn't understand the relationship of the two boys to Tom. "Is Zach a friend of your son's?" she asked.

Tom looked up from his book, surprised.

"My son?" he asked.

"Will. He's very like you. Has your ways."

"Evacuee," he began, but he didn't get any further. She took it that Zach was the only evacuee.

"How kind of you, Mr. Oakley, to take an evacuee on holiday," and she couldn't praise him enough.

The praise made Tom feel awkward, so rather than mention that Will was also an evacuee, he said nothing, hoping that the matter would be dropped. He went up the stairway to Zach and Will's room and found them still leaning out of the window staring at the sea. He tucked them both into bed, ruffled their hair and closed the door behind them.

Zach lay on his back, his head leaning on his hands, his elbows up.

"I say," he said, "isn't this the most wondrous, scrumptious, exciting thing that's ever happened in the whole wide world?"

"Yeh," agreed Will.

They lay in silence in the semidarkness, the moon

shining its beams across the whitewashed floorboards.

"Ent it a fine sound?" whispered Will, staring happily up at the ceiling.

"What?" asked Zach sleepily.

"The waves."

Zach turned over and gave a grunt. Will was sitting cross-legged on the windowsill with a sketch pad on his knees. He glanced down at Zach's brown face and wiry black hair lying against the crisp white pillowcase and returned to his drawing. Zach gave another grunt, opened his eyes and looked over at Will's bed. Seeing the empty sheets, he rolled out of bed quickly and then caught sight of Will on the windowsill.

"How long have you been up?"

Will shrugged.

"About an hour, I s'pose."

"Why didn't you wake me?"

"Thought mebbe you wanted to lie in."

Zach leaned on the windowsill next to Will's legs. A slight mist hung over the sea.

"I say, it's going to be a wizzo day. A real scorcher."

He glanced at Will's drawing, which consisted of two gulls hovering above a tranquil sea.

Will sighed. "I wish I could get the sun shinin' on the waves, sort of sparklin' like." He leaned back against the wall.

"Oh Will," retorted Zach. "It's smashing. If I drew that, it would be just one long wiggly line in the middle of the page, a couple of silly clouds above it and a few wavy lines below."

Will gave a laugh.

Mrs. Clarence knocked on their door.

"Breakfast in five minutes, boys," she sang.

"Rightio," yelled Zach.

Will climbed down and put his sketch pad on the small white wooden table under the sill.

It was the beginning of another of Zach's "glorious" days. Tom had also risen early, and had already been out with Sammy for a walk along the beach.

The three of them all sat down to a generous breakfast and then set off immediately with a picnic lunch to the beach. They walked for a mile along the coast towards some cliffs and climbed up a rough pathway that had been hacked out of the grass and bracken. Once they reached the top they went on walking until they came to a small opening in a clump of gorse. They scrambled down another rough pathway and came to a sheltered and sandy cove. The cliffs curved round on either side of them like the arms of an enormous armchair. Zach and Will peeled off their clothes down to their underpants while Sammy dug into the sand, sending cascades of it into a pile behind them. Tom rolled his trouser legs and shirt sleeves up and put a four-knotted handkerchief on his head.

Zach and Will walked down towards the sea. Will stood at the edge while Zach splashed and yelled about the coolness of the water. He shrank back as an icy spray cascaded over him.

"Come on," yelled Zach, who was treading water. "There are warm bits if you keep moving about."

Will nodded mournfully. He waded in as far as his ankles and allowed the water to swirl around his feet.

Tom sat on the shore and watched. Will turned and gave him a casual glance. He wanted Mister Tom to be near him and at the same time he didn't want to appear a coward. Tom wanted to help but didn't want to mollycoddle him. The glance from Will moved him into action.

"Come on, Samuel," he said, eyeing the hot furry heap that was now sheltering in a hole. "Come and have a bit of salt water, boy," and with that he picked him up and carried him in his arms to the water's edge.

Once Will saw Sammy barking at the sea, chasing it and being caught by it, some of his fear disappeared, for Sammy was very funny. Tom paddled in after him.

"Come on, Will," he said encouragingly. "Take some handfuls and splash some around you. You can git used to it then. I'll catch you if you fall."

Will slowly walked in as far as his waist, and with the help of Zach and Tom he was soon splashing around quite pleasurably. Tom hadn't swum for at least twenty years, and then that was only in the river in Little Weirwold. By the time all three of them had sat down to their picnic lunch, he had decided to buy three swimsuits. After they had eaten and had had a gentle snooze in a shady part of the cliffs, they ventured into the sea again. Will learned to float quite quickly, to the envy of Zach. Zach could do breaststroke, crawl and backstroke, but had never managed to float. The thought of lying still unnerved him. He always liked to be on the move. But for Will it felt wonderful to be still. First he would lie and screw his eyes up, peeping through the lids at the dazzling bright sky above him, and see how long he could count without sinking. By the end of the afternoon he began to forget, and once he almost fell asleep.

The first and second day passed very swiftly and so too did the days that followed. Most of the time was spent in the sea, the three of them swimming in their new woolly swimsuits, or playing cricket on the beach, or building sandcastles and collecting shells.

One day they walked along the cliffs and round the bay to a mansion. Another day Will spent down by the harbor sketching boats while Zach went off on a cycling trek and Tom took Mrs. Clarence for a ride on the back of his tandem.

At the end of ten days Will had learned to do the breaststroke and Zach could count up to ten while floating.

During their stay, the news bulletins on the wireless had begun to grow ominous, so much so that one evening a worried Zach sneaked out of bed to listen to the eight-o'clock news. Besides his mother now being an ambulance driver, his father was also with the Auxiliary Fire Service.

The locals in Salt-on-the-Mouth were convinced that the recent heavy bombing attacks on the large towns were a prelude to a large-scale invasion. Seventeen parachutes had been discovered in the Midlands, there had been raids on Southampton and the R.A.F. brought down an average of sixty planes a day besides carrying out heavy raids on Germany. Then came the stunning news of a bomb raid on Croydon in which three hundred factory workers were killed. Tom had been tempted to return immediately to Little Weirwold, for he had felt, for some strange reason, that Zach and Will would be safer there. Mrs. Clarence, however, was so insistent that they stay that he had decided that they would spend the remaining three days as planned.

The weather continued to be almost tropically hot, and they felt sorry for anyone who had to work in a city with no sea breezes to cool them. On their last Saturday, as they cycled back from a day of swimming, they were startled by the news headlines on a large placard leaning outside the newstand. It read South West London Blitzed, Malden Badly Hit. The shop was sold out of newspapers. With paper rationing, copies of newspapers were at a premium, and the few that there were had automatically been given to the locals. Luckily, Mrs. Clarence had a copy and Zach pored anxiously over the contents. The newspapers reported that the sirens had not been sounded and this had resulted in many deaths.

"S'pose you'll be wanting to know how your parents are," remarked Tom.

Zach nodded. He had written to them nearly every day, so that they knew of his holiday address, but he had had no word from them. Normally an absence of letters didn't worry him. His parents were often so tied up in the last-minute chaos of technical and dress rehearsals that they had barely time to eat or sleep, let alone write a letter, but once a show was on, if he was living apart from them, he would usually receive a bumper bonus letter to make up for it. However, with the news of London being bombed, their silence caused him great anxiety.

"We'll find a telephone and contact the Littles," suggested Tom. "Happen they might 'uv left a message, like."

"Thanks awfully," said Zach.

"You goin' to phone before or after supper?" asked Mrs. Clarence.

Zach looked visibly pale even under his almost-black tan.

"Now," said Tom.

When they returned Zach was back to his happy self. His parents had left messages with the Littles to say that they were well and safe and that they were sorry they hadn't written but that casualties were so heavy that their time was filled giving help.

The following day was Sunday and was their last day in Salt-on-the-Mouth. Tom and Will went to the village church while Zach found a sheltered spot by the sea. Although it wasn't his Sabbath, he gripped his little round cap into his heathery hair and swayed gently to and fro saying the few Hebrew prayers that he remembered. It comforted him to sing the strange guttural sounds. It was like uttering a magical language that would make everything all right. His parents had taught him that whoever or whatever God was, he, she or it could probably understand silent thoughts; but it made Zach feel better to voice his feelings aloud.

That day Mrs. Clarence cooked them a special Sunday lunch. They had roast chicken, roast potatoes and vegetables followed by ice cream. Mrs. Clarence had made it herself with the help of a cool corner in the fishmonger's so that although the ice cream tasted of vanilla, it smelled of mackerel.

In the afternoon Tom, Will and Zach took a last cycle round the village along the bumpy lanes that lay inland from the cliff tops. They wheeled the bicycle and tandem along the beach and, as dusk approached and a pink-and-orange haze stretched itself across the sky, they sat and watched the sun slowly disappear.

After supper Zach and Will took a stroll down to the tiny quay. It was a clear night and the sea was bathed in moonlight. They spoke in low voices. They were sorry to leave Salt-on-the-Mouth, and yet at the same time they were looking forward to seeing George and the twins again. Will had three sketch pads full of drawings from the holiday, but he felt that he had only just begun. Zach had started yet another epic poem about a brutal band of smugglers, but he had talked so much about it that his energy for the topic was exhausted by the time he had written the third verse. They talked quietly about ideas for plays in the autumn term. Zach talked about his ambitions. He wanted to be a worldwide entertainer. Will's ambitions were a little more homebound. He just wanted to draw and be in the next autumn play. They gazed silently out at the sea and walked leisurely back to the cottage. Tom was sitting talking to Mrs. Clarence by the fire. A curly two-week-old white beard now surrounded his chin. Will and Zach joined them, and after chatting for a while they drifted upstairs to bed.

The next morning they stood outside the cottage with their panniers strapped to their bicycle frames and said their last farewells. Mrs. Clarence felt sad at their leaving. She had enjoyed their company. As they pushed the bicycle and tandem forwards, she watched them slowly ascend the hill till they finally disappeared over its brow.

The first day, after they collected Dobbs and the cart, was another fine one, but on the Tuesday it rained and they had to sit in sou'westers and gabardine capes. They sheltered for a while underneath an archway of trees to have a picnic, for although they were on their way home, the return journey was still a part of their holiday. By Wednesday it looked as though autumn had begun. The fields, trees and flowers still appeared summery, but a cold gray sky hung above them and a blustery wind hindered their progress.

By the time they had arrived in Little Weirwold and had watered and fed Dobbs, it was nearly dusk. On the table in the living room of the cottage was an assortment of welcome-home goodies from the twins and George. Mrs. Fletcher had delivered groceries and had left a large saucepan of vegetable soup on the well-stoked stove.

The goodies consisted of flowers and a bowl of blackberries from the twins and a home-grown squash and cabbage from George. There were also several welcome-home cards. Zach sat and had some bread and soup with them and then left for the Littles'.

He wheeled his bicycle through Dobbs's field and along the tiny arched lane, and leaned it against the Littles' hedge. He was just struggling with the gate when an urgent voice came suddenly out of the darkness. He was so startled that he physically jumped.

"Sorry!" said the voice. "I didn't mean to scare you, like."

Zach peered over the hedge.

"Carrie!" he cried in amazement. "What are you doing here?"

She helped him wrench open the gate and waited till he had wheeled his bicycle through.

"You look like a black man," she remarked.

He grinned. "Marvelous for *Othello*, eh?"

"What are you on about?" she said, feeling quite exasperated, for she had been waiting for his arrival for a good three hours.

"The passionate Moor," explained Zach. "You know, Shakespeare."

"Oh, Shakespeare!" groaned Carrie. "You know, I ent read him yet."

"Yet! You mean you might actually be tempted to?"

"Yes. Oh, Zach." She clutched his arm and stared fearfully into his eyes.

"What?" he said. "What's wrong?"

"I've passed the exam. I got a scholarship. I'm to be a high-school girl."

Spooky Cott

𝒴 𝒴

On August 31st, the last Saturday before they returned
to school, Zach, Will, George and the twins sat on an
old dead branch beneath the beech trees behind Blake's
field. They had all decided to go to Spooky Cott.

Will folded their map up and slid it into his pocket.
Between them they carried flashlights, string, a penknife
and an old rope. Will and Zach watched the others crawl
along the field to the edge and then they followed suit
in the opposite direction. Instead of going by the road,
where they might be seen, they crawled parallel to it
on the other side of the hedge. After a while they hit
the woods. They rose and ran quietly and swiftly from
tree to tree, but they needn't have bothered, for there
was nobody human around—only the odd squirrel collecting nuts for its winter hibernation. Soon they heard
the soft swishing sound of the river and they slid down
its muddy bank. They stood still for a moment and drank
in its peacefulness. Will was just about to start drawing
the basic outline of a water vole on the back of the
map when Zach spoke.

"I say, we'd better get a move on. The others will
be there ages before us. George will be hooting away
and think we've been savaged to pieces."

They climbed up the bank towards the trees. A scatter-
ing of clouds had blotted out the sun and a wind began
to rattle through the branches. As they reached the high
hedges that surrounded the cottage, the sky became
gray.

"Hope it don't rain," said Will, peering upwards. "Be a shame to have to go back again. Still, we could always shelter in Spooky Cott."

Zach gave a nervous shudder.

"You cold?" asked Will.

"Er . . . a little."

Just then, three distant hoots came drifting across to them from the other side of the woods.

"I'll give the signal for 'let's git nearer,' " said Will, and before Zach could prevent him, Will had barked three times and followed it by two howls.

By now the sky had grown darker and the wind was rustling venomously through the leaves.

"What's that?" cried Zach in alarm.

"Only some twigs breakin'," answered Will.

Suddenly from beyond the high hedgerow came a sound that caused Zach's scalp to tingle to its very roots.

"Cor!" whispered Will excitedly.

The sound was high-pitched and seemed to come from the cottage. It soared and dipped, sending an eerie chill through the undergrowth surrounding it.

They froze, hardly daring to breathe, and all Zach's joky images of ghosts rapidly came flooding to the surface. He began to feel a little sick.

"I think we'd better signal that we're all right," suggested Will and he gave two long mournful howls. Zach felt even worse. It wasn't long before a rather shaky "let's get out of here" signal came soaring back from the other side of the hedge.

"Doughbags," said Will. "Jes' as it's gittin' excitin'." Without consulting Zach he gave the "we're all right" and the "let's get closer" signal.

The high wail from the cottage floated through the air again and was followed immediately by a "we're off" signal from George and a great crackling of twigs and shaking of bushes. Will was mesmerized by the sound. "It's like what Mister Tom sometimes plays on the organ," he whispered. He turned to Zach. "Are you still game?"

Zach nodded, knowing well that each nod was a lie. He would have dearly loved to run back to the village with the others, but he couldn't let Will down.

"Good," said Will, grinning, and he edged his way through the dense hedge, followed at a safe distance by Zach.

The closer they came to the cottage, the louder the wail grew.

I'm sure my hair will turn white, thought Zach as they climbed out of the wild hedgerow and stood waist deep in grass and dandelions.

Will tugged at Zach's sleeve. "Look," he whispered. "The door's open. The music's coming from inside."

Pots of red geraniums stood starkly on the two windowsills. They looked odd against the neglected background of the cottage with its dusty windows and rain-washed wooden door. Will walked slowly forwards and stood in the middle of the tangled garden opposite it. It looked dark inside the cottage. Zach crouched in the grass.

"I think you ought to take cover," he whispered urgently, but Will stood like one in a hypnotic trance. The music seemed to touch some painful and tender place inside him and it flooded his limbs with a strange buzzing sensation. Then it stopped, and all he could hear was a repetitive swishing sound followed by a tapping and a click.

"You can come in if you like," boomed a man's voice from the darkness.

Will jumped and Zach screamed and fell over backwards.

The tapping grew louder and a young man in his
mid-twenties with brown wavy hair, blue eyes and a mustache appeared at the doorway. He wore a pale-blue
open-necked shirt and gray flannels, and his face looked
in need of a good shave. His left trouser leg was pinned
up to his thigh and he supported himself on a crutch.
They glanced down at the empty space beneath it and
then looked quickly up at his face. One of his ears was
missing. He observed them looking him over.

"Not a pretty sight, eh!" he said at last.

Will and Zach were too surprised to speak.

"Sorry if I scared you," said the man. "I thought you
must have seen me through the window." He smiled.
"On second thoughts I don't suppose anyone could see
anything through those windows. Must be at least ten
years' dust on them."

Zach still sat immobile with only his brown face visible
above the grass. The man looked at Will.

"You like music?"

Will nodded.

"Mister Tom plays some on the organ, like," he said
quietly. "I lives with him."

"You local then?"

"No."

"Evacuee?"

"Yeh."

"Where from?"

"Deptford."

"If there's any left of it. I used to live in London,
till nine months ago. No reason to go back now," he
added grimly.

"Is you from the Grange hospital?"

The man nodded and held out his hand. "Geoffrey Sanderton's my name."

Will stepped forward and shook it. "I'm Will."

"And I'm Zacharias Wrench," said Zach, stumbling to his feet.

"Ah, he has a voice," said Geoffrey.

A strong blast of wind shook the trees. He stared up at them.

"Too light to put the blackouts up, too dark inside to paint. Damned nuisance really."

"Paint?" asked Will, wide-eyed.

"Yes," he said. "I can offer you tea, bread and jam. That suit you? You can either sit out here or come inside."

"I'd like to come in," blurted out Will. "I mean, if that's all right, like."

"I'll sit on the step," said Zach.

Will followed Geoffrey into the front room. At one end was a long, raised fireplace with a fire already laid but unlit in the grate. He glanced briefly around. Apart from some bits and pieces from the Grange, the room was almost devoid of any furniture. Will's attention, however, was caught by the piles of paper and bits of canvas scattered about the floor and a tall wooden easel. A picture of half a landscape, painted in oils, was resting on it.

"Are you a painter, mister?" he asked, following him into the kitchen. The kitchen was empty but for one shelf of food, a few cups and several pots of paint.

"An artist, you mean? Yes. I had my first exhibition in London just before I was called up."

"Were you at Dunkirk?"

"Yes."

"Cor. Good job you didn't lose your arms, eh, mister? Lucky, eh?"

"Lucky?" he repeated with bitterness. He didn't think so. His fiancée had been blown out of his arms by a bomb. He had lost two of his closest friends, and his parents had been found dead under a pile of rubble. His leg and ear had been blown off and he had had a nervous breakdown. Hardly lucky.

"Yeh," said Will. "You can still draw, like."

"You draw?" asked Geoffrey.

"Yeh."

"What, at school?"

"And in me free time."

"Do you?" said Geoffrey in surprise. He was about to change the subject from habit, for in the past amateur artists would invariably ask him to give his opinions on their work, and he found it all very embarrassing. He hesitated for a moment and then picked up a piece of paper and a stubby pencil. He handed them to Will.

"Show me."

"Show you?" said Will in alarm. "But . . . but you're so good."

"And you're not?"

"He's marvelous," said Zach, who had by now plucked up enough courage to leave the doorway and enter. Will blushed.

"I'll draw outside," and with that he pushed Zach aside and went and sat on the steps.

Zach and Geoffrey talked intermittently in the kitchen while they put some jam on pieces of dry bread. Zach carried a tray with the bread, a pot of tea and cups on it towards the steps. Geoffrey followed and stood at the doorway. Will could feel his ears burning as he approached and his hand began to tremble. He had drawn a rough sketch of Sammy by the oak tree. Geoffrey peered down at it.

"How old are you?"

"I'm ten next week."

He gazed quietly down at Will's sketch and after a short silence said, "You have a gift, Will."

Will's heart soared. He felt excited and frightened all in one moment.

"Who teaches you art?"

"I used to have Mrs. Hartridge but she's left. She's got a baby, see. There's only Mrs. Black now, but sometimes Miss Thorne helps out."

"And now there's a load more evacuees," joined in Zach, "and if they don't bring teachers with them I don't know who we'll have."

"Short of teachers, are they?" said Geoffrey, and he slowly maneuvered himself down to the steps and sat between them. It felt strange to Will to have someone sit next to him with a space where a leg should be.

"Yes," replied Zach.

They picked up the slices of bread and jam and began eating.

"I'll see if I can teach at your school," said Geoffrey at last, and as he spoke he felt happier than he had felt for a long time. "I don't know how one goes about it, but once I decide to do a thing I usually end up doing it." He placed a hand on Will's. "Would you like extra lessons of your own?"

Will thought his heart would explode through his chest. He nodded and was quite unable to stop himself from smiling broadly.

"Wizzo," yelled Zach. "I told you one day you'd be famous. We can both be famous together."

"Oh yes," said Geoffrey wryly. "And what are you going to be famous at?"

"I'm going to entertain the world," he announced grandly, and then he blushed at his own arrogance.

"You'll have to work very hard and make a great many sacrifices to achieve that."

"I don't want to be famous," said Will. "I jes' wants to draw and paint. But I want to draw real good, like."

"Are you willing to work at it?"

"Oh yes," said Will quite simply.

Geoffrey glanced up at the sky. "I'll put the blackouts up and light the fire."

"I'll help," offered Will.

"Me, too," said Zach.

Between them, the fire was soon licking its way up the chimney, sending a warm glow around the candle-lit cluttered room. Geoffrey handed Will a record in a cardboard cover. There was a picture of a dog in the middle with **His Master's Voice** written on it. In the corner near the fire was a gramophone. Geoffrey wound the handle, slid a little round metal tray to one side, took out a needle and changed it for one which was fixed to the end of the curved arm. He took the record out of its sleeve, held it by the edges, put it on the turntable and pushed a small metal disc to one side. After the record had begun to rotate he lifted the arm and gently lowered the needle onto the edge of the record. It gave a few crackles and then burst into music.

"That was the Brahms violin concerto you heard in the garden," said Geoffrey.

Zach stood at Will's side. "And to think I was scared out of my wits by that!"

It was then that they told Geoffrey the cottage's nickname and how the other three had run away.

"I wondered why no one ever disturbed me here," he said. "I was really quite relieved. I needed to be alone for a while. I've even been having my food delivered to me from the Grange so that I didn't have to go into the village."

"Oh," said Will, a little perturbed.

"Would you rather we left?" added Zach.

"No. I think it's about time I came out of hermitage."

He placed the needle back on the beginning of the record so that they could listen to it again, without talking. They sat cross-legged by the fire, watching tiny pieces of wood being sucked up the chimney while the flames crackled and spat in the grate. When the music had ended Zach and Will stood up to leave. They said their good-byes, and after scrambling back through the hedgerow they headed towards the woods. They ran down the road and hung outside the front gate of the graveyard talking.

"I say," said Zach, turning round. "There's a car outside the church. Wonder whose that is."

Will shrugged. "Someone lookin' for Mr. Peters mebbe," he said, and he swung open the gate.

Zach cut across the graveyard and climbed over the wall. "See you tomorrow," he yelled.

Will ran up the path, pushed open the front door and slammed it behind him. He couldn't wait to tell Mister Tom about Geoffrey and the art lessons. He flung open the door, his cheeks burning, his heart soaring, only to be brought to a sudden halt.

Sitting in the room with Mister Tom were a policeman from Weirwold, the warden from Deptford, a middle-aged man in a pullover and corduroys, and a woman in a green hat and coat.

"This the boy?" asked the policeman.

The warden stared at Will's brown freckled face and thick shiny sun-bleached hair. The boy he was looking at stood straight and had muscles on his legs. He wasn't the thin weedy Willie he knew.

Tom stood by the range, holding Sammy in check.

"You're Mr. Oakley, ain't you?"

Tom nodded.

"I know you look a bit different wiv a beard, but I recognize you all right." He turned back to Will. "But this ain't Willie Beech, is it?"

"William," corrected Will.

"Oh, cheeky now, is he?"

The woman touched the warden's arm. She was in her thirties, a fresh-complexioned lady with light brown hair and soft hazel eyes.

"I'm afraid we've brought you some rather bad news, William," she said. "It concerns your mother."

He looked at her, startled.

"She wants me back?"

"No."

He smiled with relief. She paused.

"William." She hesitated. "I'm afraid your mother is dead. She committed suicide."

He looked blankly at her. "I don't get you."

"She killed herself."

Will gazed at her in stunned disbelief.

"Killed herself? But . . . but why?"

"I don't know. I suppose she just didn't want to live anymore."

How could anyone not want to live, thought Will, when there were so many things to live for? There were rainy nights and wind and the slap of the sea and the moon. There were books to read and pictures to paint and music.

"I'm from a children's home in Sussex," she explained. "It's an orphanage and it's right out in the country. There are lots of children there and we usually find foster parents to take them into their homes, young parents with children of their own." And she smiled.

"What the lady is saying," said the policeman, "is that she's willin' to have you at the home."

Will thrust his hands deep into his pockets and looked her straight in the eye.

"No," he said, somewhat shakily, "I'm not willin'. This is my home and I'm stayin' here."

"Now now, son," said the warden. "That ain't the way to talk. You don't have much choice in the matter. Your Mr. Oakley has not been keepin' to the lor. Kidnappin's a serious offense."

Will took a deep breath.

"When you kidnap someone you usually want a ransom. There ent no one in the world who'd pay a ransom for me"—and he glanced at Tom—"except Mister Tom perhaps, and he's the one that's supposed to have kidnapped me. Well, I reckon I weren't kidnapped. I reckon I was rescued."

"Oh you do, do you?" said the Warden.

"Yes," reiterated Will, "I do."

And then, as if he was no longer in the room, the policeman, the warden and the woman began to discuss him. Will and Tom just looked at each other, and all the while the middle-aged man in the pullover and corduroys sat by the stove smoking a pipe and silently observed them.

"Will," said the policeman, "we'd like you to go up

to your room for a while until we make up our minds."

Will glanced at Tom. Tom nodded and handed Sammy over to him.

"Here, boy," he said gently. "Let him keep you company, like."

Will trailed mournfully to the door and whirled round in a great surge of anger.

"I won't go with you," he stated firmly. "Even if you tie me up and put me in prison, I'll run away and come back here." With that he slammed the door behind him and stood in the hallway trembling. Clutching Sammy in his arms, he clambered up the ladder to his room. He sat on his bed in the dark feeling both furious and helpless.

"I won't go," he whispered to Sammy. "I won't go. I'll run away. Yeh! That's what I'll do. I can't go to Zach's, though," he muttered. "That's the first place they'd think of lookin', nor the twins, nor George. I've got to find someone else who'd hide me. Someone they won't think of." He racked his brain frantically, going methodically through the people in the village.

"Of course!" he cried. "That's who! Lucy! She'd hide me. She'd hide me fer blimmin' years. She thinks the sunlight shines out me bootlaces."

He could visualize her, all adoring, smuggling cups of tea and bread and dripping, to the hayloft in the Padfields' barn.

"Sammy," he said urgently, "I'll have to leave you here, boy."

Slowly he eased open the trapdoor, only to catch sight of the policeman and the warden in the hall.

"Dash it!" he muttered, closing the trap. "Too late!"

He clenched his fists angrily and braced himself for their approach. He was ready to fight them now. He needn't have bothered, for he could hear them at the front door chatting quite amicably. He pressed his ear to the floor but all he could make out was something about them coming back with the papers.

The front door slammed and he heard Tom coming up the ladder.

"They's gone," he said, lifting up the trapdoor. "You can come down now."

He climbed down the steps with Sammy, who leaped immediately out of his arms and ran into the front room to bark at the strangers. Will scowled and perched himself on the stool by the stove.

"I ent goin' to apologize, like," he muttered.

Tom sat in the armchair. "I'm sorry about yer mother."

Will forgot his anger for a moment and caught Tom's eye.

"I dunno why she did it," he said, feeling totally bewildered. "Was it because of me and Trudy?"

"Partly," said Tom, picking up his pipe and stuffing it with tobacco. "But it weren't your fault. She was ill. She couldn't cope, see."

"What's goin' to happen to me, then?"

Tom looked up at him quickly.

"I'm adoptin' you."

"Wot!" exclaimed Will.

"You ent got no other relations, boy. The authorities have checked up on that, so I'm adoptin' you. That man in the pullover and cordeeroys, he were one of them psychiatrists. He were a bit different from that other one. Had a sense of humor. Anyway, he said that this were obviously the best place for you and any fool could see that and the others agreed. They's bringin' official forms and the like and are writin' reports on me. If all goes well, and I don't see how it can't, you'll be my son."

"Your son!" cried Will jumping off the stool. "You mean, you'll be my father, like?"

Tom nodded.

"I s'pose I will."

In an instant it suddenly dawned on him that Will would be growing up with him. With a great yell of joy he leaped up from the armchair.

Will threw his arms around him and together they danced and cavorted across the room shouting and yelling, while Sammy whirled around their ankles chasing his tail and barking in lunatic fashion.

Back to School

On Thursday morning Will rose earlier than usual. He met Zach outside the Littles' and together they headed for the twins' cottage. Ginnie answered the door in her nightdress and dressing gown. George was already in the kitchen looking very sleepy eyed.

"Come on, Carrie," called out Mrs. Thatcher up the stairs. "Or you'll be late."

Zach stood at the foot of the narrow stairway.

"I say," he exclaimed as she appeared on the tiny landing. "You look magnificent."

She glanced shyly at him and came down the stairs. She was wearing a navy jumper, a cream-coloured blouse and a navy tie with a wide green and narrow red stripe. On her feet were fawn woolen socks and a pair of brown lace-up shoes.

"It feels ever so strange wearing a tie," she remarked, tugging at it. "Dad showed me how to do it, like."

Her father came out of the kitchen and gazed proudly at her. Mrs. Thatcher was still none too keen on Carrie going to the high school, but Mr. Thatcher was backing her all the way and had even done some extra laboring so that she could have a new uniform.

"She's worked hard for it," he had said. "She ent goin' to start with no hand-me-downs. She's goin' to start proper."

They heard a car drawing up outside.

Carrie blushed with excitement.

"That'll be Mr. Fergus," she exclaimed.

Her mother handed her a wide-brimmed felt hat to put on and a rather large navy blazer with narrow green braiding around it. Her ginger hair, which was still fought into two plaits, stood out starkly against the navy. She picked up a shiny leather satchel which was empty save for her lunch. The straps and buckles jangled in their newness.

"Don't expect too much on yer first day," commented her father.

"Good luck," said Zach warmly. "I'll see you when you come back."

"You look real fine," added Will. "Real fine."

Carrie smiled nervously and ran outside to where the car was waiting. She opened the door and sat next to Mr. Fergus, leaving the others standing outside the cottage, where they waved to her until the car had driven out of sight.

Ginnie gave a shiver.

"You'd best get dressed," said her mother. She turned to the boys. "You wouldn't say no to tea and some bread and drippin', would you?"

They grinned and followed her into the kitchen. Mr. Thatcher was closing his lunch tin and filling up a small tin jug with tea.

After they had eaten, Will and Zach left together and headed for the woods. There was still plenty of time before school started. The early-morning air was clear and crisp and all the fields and hedgerows were covered with a layer of sparkling dew. The sun filtered through the trees so that Will and Zach were constantly moving into patches of gloom and out into sudden patches of sunlight. They reached the small river and listened to it gently rippling past them.

Zach leaned on one leg, as was his habit, and with

his hands deep in his pockets he stared anxiously into the water.

"I think war has started properly now," he muttered.

"But the Nazis won't bomb here," replied Will. "Will they? Mister Tom says he doesn't think they'd bother."

Zach gave a sigh.

"It's my parents *I'm* worried about. I know they're busy, but I wish they'd write or phone more often so I'd know they're all right. Last night, on the wireless, they said there was more heavy bombing."

"Couldn't they stay here?"

Zach shook his head.

"Father says if he can't fight for England he wants to help entertain the fighters and help protect the families that are left. That's why he joined the A.F.S."

"A.F.S.?"

"Auxiliary Fire Service. Mother feels the same." He slammed a fist into the open palm of his hand. "I wish I could visit them just to see if they're safe."

"There might be a letter waiting fer you now," said Will encouragingly.

"I doubt it."

They stared up through the colorfully clad branches. The sun spread through them like a warm X ray lighting the thin skeletal lines in each leaf.

Will and Zach chatted quietly, absorbing the peace of the river, and then turned back to the village.

They dropped by at the Littles' to see if there had been any post but there was none. Zach walked towards the graveyard cottage with Will and they took Sammy out for a romp in the fields. By the time school had started, it felt late enough to be the afternoon.

To their surprise and delight, sitting next to Miss Thorne at the front of the class was Geoffrey Sanderton.

"Mr. Sanderton and I have decided to choose a nature project," began Miss Thorne. "This means that we shall be going on expeditions which you will plan. We would also like some of you to write and illustrate a nature diary."

Zach looked a little disappointed.

"In addition to the project we shall be reading some of the nature poets—William Wordsworth, for example, and some of Shakespeare's sonnets."

At this Zach beamed.

"I thought it would be rather a good idea," added Geoffrey, "that, as we have to be careful with the amount of paint we use, we could create pictures using different-colored leaves and bark and anything interesting that you can find, and it might be fun too if we made up short poems to go with them."

"Perhaps an epic saga based on some expedition," said Miss Thorne, gazing directly at Zach. "And George," she remarked, looking up at him, "you will be in charge of some of the nature trails we shall take. Now are there any . . ."

She was interrupted by a knock at the door. Geoffrey opened it. Zach looked towards the hallway and was surprised to see Aunt Nance. Miss Thorne disappeared into the hallway with her and returned shortly. She glanced at Zach.

"You're to go home," she said gently.

Zach felt very hot and a little sick. He rose quietly from his desk and left the classroom. Will listened to his footsteps fade away down the hallway. He glanced up at Miss Thorne, who caught his eye and quickly turned away.

"Right," she said briskly, facing the class. "Let's see

how your spelling has deteriorated over the summer holidays."

The remainder of the morning was taken up with arithmetic, sharing out books and planning the first "expedition," but Will's heart was elsewhere. As soon as it was lunch he ran to the Littles' and knocked on the back door.

"Come in, Will," said Mrs. Little, opening it. "Zach will be pleased to see you. He's upstairs packing."

"Packing?" gasped Will. "Why? What's wrong?"

"His father has been badly injured. One of the large warehouses by the docks caught fire and he was buried under fallen timber for several hours. He's in a hospital in London."

Will ran upstairs and found Zach kneeling over a small, battered case. He was holding a photograph of his father. He looked up at Will. His eyes were pink and swollen.

"I'm catching the Friday train to London," he said, his voice quivering. "Mother doesn't want me to, but I begged her to let me. I have to see him in case . . ." and he became hoarse and stifled a sob. "In case I never see him again."

Will squatted down beside him.

"I want you to take care of this," Zach said, handing him his old tattered copy of Shakespeare's works. "It was my great-grandfather's."

"Oh, Zach," protested Will, but Zach's pained expression prevented him from refusing. He took the book and smoothed the leather covers with his hand.

"I'll look after it real fine."

They spent a miserable afternoon together. Ginnie and George called round after lunch and Carrie rushed in later, for a few brief moments before having to fly home to do her homework. It was a wretched time for Zach, as he wanted to leave immediately. All the waiting only increased his feelings of frustration and helplessness.

The Littles drove him to the station in Weirwold the following morning. His mother had said that whatever happened he was to stay in London only for the weekend. She didn't want him to be injured as well, and she knew that his father would have felt the same way.

The day after Zach's sudden departure was Will's tenth birthday, Saturday, September 7th, 1940.

Will spent the morning at the Hartridges' and Padfields' cottages. In the afternoon he and Tom decorated the living room. Mrs. Fletcher and Mrs. Thatcher arrived armed with home-baked cakes and biscuits while Aunt Nance brought homemade ginger beer and a parcel that Zach had left for him. By late afternoon the cottage was filled with children, with Tom, Ginnie and George leading the games. The high spot of the party, however, was when everyone swarmed round the cottage screaming hysterically and hiding from Tom, who was chasing them and pretending to be a monster at the same time. They played musical chairs and pass the parcel, ate doughnuts with their hands tied behind their backs, passed oranges to each other under their chins and, of course, ate.

Will left Zach's parcel unopened until the last person had gone home and he and Tom had sat down to relax with a cup of tea. The table was already littered with books, candy and pots of paint. He picked up Zach's parcel and began to unwrap it.

Inside was part one of an epic adventure called *The Villainous Doctor Horror*. At the bottom was a little postscript. It read "P.S. Part two will be written on my return."

In addition to the poem were two new paintbrushes, a secondhand book on painters, and a lopsided sketch of Will in an artist's beret and smock. It showed him standing at an easel. The canvas on the easel was empty but Will himself was covered with paint.

"I shall put that on my wall," said Will half to himself and half to Tom.

At eight o'clock they listened intently to the news on the wireless.

It was reported that flares had been dropped all over London and hundreds of German planes had been spotted. Spitfires and Hurricanes had soared up into the skies to fight them. It was one of the longest massed raids that London was experiencing. While the news was being read, heavy bombing was still continuing.

"Hope Zach's all right," said Will, frowning.

Tom puffed at his pipe. "He's so skinny, a bomb would probably skip past him."

"I hope so."

The next day, for the first time in weeks, it rained. Will woke to the sound of it scuttling down the roof and bouncing off his open window. He washed and dressed quickly. Tom was already in the church organizing extra seating arrangements, for it was to be a national day of prayer.

At ten A.M. the villagers were shocked by a special news bulletin on the wireless.

"It is estimated," said the announcer, "that four hundred people at least were killed in the first few hours of air attacks. Fourteen hundred are believed to be seriously injured. London's Dockland is on fire and many homes in the East End have been blitzed to the ground."

The Littles still hadn't heard from Zach or his mother, and Will grew steadily more anxious. He woke in the early hours of Monday morning from a nightmare of amputation units, people with their heads blown off, vans with DEAD ONLY written on them and disfigured bloodstained people wandering and screaming through dense rubble.

He and Tom switched on the wireless for any early-morning news flashes. According to recent reports there had been continual bombing throughout the night, and fires were burning all over London. Becton gasworks had been hit. Moorgate lay in smoky ruins. Balham had been badly smashed. Bombs had fallen on one of the platforms on Victoria Station and on the outskirts of Windsor Castle. The news was devastating.

Will hurried on to school and spent the morning outside, gardening. He joined George, Ginnie, Lucy and Grace on a blackberrying expedition in the afternoon, and returned at dusk, flushed and happily tired, only to hear that Dover was being bombed.

The following morning he awoke to the sounds of voices downstairs. It was odd to have visitors so early unless, of course, he had overslept. He rose quickly and clattered down the ladder. As he approached the front room, he recognized the voices—they were the Littles'. His heart gave a lift. Perhaps they had news of Zach. He strode in excitedly and they turned to face him. Dr. Little looked grave and Aunt Nance had been crying. They didn't need to say anything. He knew Zach was dead. In one black moment he felt his legs buckling up underneath him and he collapsed into unconsciousness.

Grieving
— ❧ ❧ —

In the weeks that followed the news of Zach's death, Will survived each day in a zombielike daze. Outwardly he went on as normal, helping Tom, and catching up with schoolwork. Inwardly he felt too numb even to cry.

He avoided the Littles' cottage as much as possible and chose to walk to the school or shop by the church and cottages. At school, finding it painful to sit next to an empty chair, he would scatter papers untidily over the two desks in an effort to hide Zach's absence.

Miss Thorne asked him to be in the Christmas play and, although he agreed and took part in rehearsals, the whole procedure felt very unreal to him. Miss Thorne was pleased with him but he felt as if his body and voice were totally expressionless.

Even in drawing and painting classes he would sit and look blankly at the empty page in front of him, devoid of ideas. His private classes with Geoffrey Sanderton were just as bad.

"I ent got anythin' left inside me," he would say repeatedly, for he felt that half of himself had been cut away, that life without Zach was only half a life and even that half was empty.

Most of the time Geoffrey set him still-life pictures to draw, so that for several hours Will could forget the dull pain that gnawed his insides and concentrate on the shapes in a bowl of fruit, the color of a flower or the shades of light that fell on a bottle and boot. But always, when he left Spooky Cott, the same dead feeling sank into him and all his activities seemed meaningless.

Four months passed. Christmas saw heavy rationing but Will didn't notice, for it still seemed a very rich one to him. He and Tom made toys with scraps of wood and paints, and Ginnie and George came round to help.

Since September and the continual blitzing of London that followed, the number of evacuees that came flooding into the village grew weekly. Many had no homes in London to return to. At Christmas several parents came to Little Weirwold to share in the festivities with their children. Tom and Will decided to make toys for those who had lost parents and for the many who were so poor that they wouldn't have had presents anyway. Will welcomed the opportunity of doing anything that would take his mind off Zach. He still tended not to talk very much, and apart from when he was rehearsing, he would withdraw into his numb little shell. Tom continued as normal, waiting for the moment when Will would finally accept and mourn his friend's death.

Carrie had completed her first term at the high school. She arrived home long after dark, and after tea she would immediately begin her homework, then go to bed, rising early in the morning to learn Latin declensions or French verbs before leaving again for school. The weekends and Christmas holidays were the only times anyone saw very much of her. She missed Zach dreadfully, for he was one of the few people with whom she didn't feel such an odd fish. She didn't dare let her parents know of the unpleasanter aspects of high-school life, as her mother still didn't approve of her going and her father had worked so hard for her uniform and sports clothes. For that she would be eternally grateful, for it made some of her difficulties easier to bear. Her main embarrassment was her accent. Most of the girls in the school spoke a different kind of English, a posh B.B.C. English like Zach. Their parents paid fees whereas she was a poor scholarship girl, with an accent that many of the girls either ridiculed or could not understand. Ginnie had said that she was beginning to talk more la-di-da and her mother was constantly telling her not to let "that school" go to her head. She didn't put on a different way of talking intentionally, it was just that all day she was mixing with teachers and girls who spoke differently from the people in Little Weirwold. She was beginning to feel that she fitted into neither Little Weirwold nor the girls' high. She was grateful that there was so much schoolwork for her to do, and her loneliness acted as an incentive to work harder.

She called in on Will several times, but as soon as she mentioned Zach he would always abruptly change the subject. This added to her loneliness, for she dearly wanted to talk about him to someone.

One chill afternoon in January, however, an unforeseen event caused Will finally to accept Zach's death.

It was a bitter raw day and, although Will was wearing a heavy overcoat, scarf and balaclava, the frost penetrated into his very bones. He let the graveyard gate clang noisily behind him and set off towards Spooky Cott, taking as usual the route around the fields on the Grange side. He always avoided retracing the way he and Zach had taken on their last morning together.

It seemed as if the ground itself had frozen. The hard furrows in the fields were as immobile as waves of corrugated iron, and the few surviving tufts of grass that remained crackled as his boots hit the hoarfrost that coated them. Eventually he came to the gap in the hedge, which served as Geoffrey Sanderton's gate. He crunched his way up the tangled garden and knocked on the door.

He glanced round at the trees, which were now quite naked and thin, and blew into his hands, stamping his feet into some semblance of life. He was just thinking how vulnerable the trees appeared with Geoffrey opened the door.

"Hello," he said cheerily. "I've just put the kettle on. Sling your coat on an armchair and make yourself warm."

Will gladly divested himself of his heavy winter garments and curled himself up at the foot of an armchair by the hearth.

"Get those fingers loosened up first," yelled Geoffrey from the kitchen. "Don't go sticking them straight out in front of the fire."

But Will didn't need telling. He remembered last winter, when he had held his frozen hands above the stove and how painful the sudden transition from cold to hot had been. Geoffrey came hobbling in, carrying a large pot of tea. Since having a wooden leg he had dispensed with his crutches completely and now used a magnificent ebony walking stick that Emilia Thorne had given him. It was silver topped, with strange ornate designs carved around the knob.

The cottage had changed radically since Will's first visit. Geoffrey and Emilia Thorne had taken an instant liking to each other, and between the two of them they had cleaned and painted the walls, adding shelves, bits of furniture and potted plants on the way.

"What have you brought me to see?" asked Geoffrey, as they sat down by the fire.

Will glanced shamefacedly down at the rug. He undid a cardboard folder and produced a drawing of a chewed-up bone in one of Tom's slippers. Geoffrey examined it intently. Will avoided his eyes.

After they had drunk their tea Geoffrey put the teapot on the mantelpiece above the fire. Beside it, he placed a photograph of two young men with their arms around each other. They seemed to be laughing a great deal. In front of the teapot he laid his pipe.

"Those are your subjects for this afternoon."

Will recognized one of the young men as Geoffrey.

"Who's the other man?" he asked. "Is he your brother?"

"Best friend," he replied. "Killed in action. Very talented. A brilliant sculptor."

"Oh," said Will quietly.

"That's his pipe, actually."

"You use his pipe?"

"Yes. I know he would have wanted me to have it. It makes him still a little alive for me whenever I smoke it. Do you understand?"

Will didn't, nor did he wish to. It was bad enough possessing Zach's old Shakespeare. He had wrapped it up and given it to Tom to put away in his cupboard together with the cartoon picture that Zach had drawn of him.

He sat down immediately to work. Usually he could immerse himself totally in the objects he was drawing, but every time he caught sight of the laughing young man in the photograph, and the pipe, it disturbed him. They no longer seemed inanimate objects. They were alive. He began to wonder if the two men had even drunk tea together out of the same teapot.

He attempted to draw steadily but found his hand trembling. Suddenly he saw Zach on his colorful bicycle, singing and lifting his arms high into the air yelling, "Look, no hands," and falling straight into a hedge, and he remembered his scratched face grinning up at him. He sat for three hours at the drawing and spent most of the time gazing morbidly through the window watching the sky grow darker. Geoffrey put the blacks up and lit the gas lamp.

"Time to stop," he said, and he peered over Will's shoulder.

"I'm sorry," mumbled Will. "I don't seem to be able to . . ." His voice trailed into silence.

"Sit down by the fire and I'll toast us some muffins."

Will cheered up a little at this. He curled up in the armchair.

While Will was gazing dreamily into the fire he heard a click. Geoffrey had opened the gramophone and was winding it up.

"What are you doing?"

"Putting on some music."

The record made its swishing sound as the needle circled around its dark edge, and then the music started. It was the same that he and Zach had listened to, when they had sat amongst the chaos and candles, the day they had first come to the cottage.

Will wanted Geoffrey to take it off. But he couldn't bear to speak or look at him lest he break down, so he returned to staring at the fire. As he did so he suddenly felt that it was not just he who was gazing into the flames—it was both he and Zach. He could feel Zach sitting beside him, bursting with excitement and desperately wanting to move with the music, while he was happy just to listen. It was an unnerving feeling. He caught sight of the photograph on the mantelpiece and it reminded him of a snapshot that Mrs. Clarence had taken of him and Zach in Salt-on-the-Mouth.

As soon as the record had come to an end and the

needle swung indolently and repeatedly in the center of it, he pushed himself firmly to his feet and grabbed his balaclava and coat.

"I must leave, get back," he choked out hoarsely.

Geoffrey nodded and showed him to the door. He squeezed Will's shoulder gently.

"Better to accept than pretend that he never existed," he said quietly.

Will didn't want to hear. His eyes were blurred and his body hurt all over. He stumbled into the darkness, and instead of leaving through the gap in the hedge he found himself free of it and headed blindly in the direction of the woods and river.

Tripping and falling over the roots of trees, he scratched his face against unseen branches. A disturbed owl screeched loudly and flew above his head, but he hardly heard it. At last he reached the river. He stood by it staring at its glassy surface, his chest and shoulders pounding, his gut aching. He felt again Zach's presence next to him, felt him staring up at the starry night and coming out with some strange fragment of poetry.

"No, no," he whispered, shaking his head wildly. "No, no. You're not here. You'll *never* be here." With one angry sob he picked up a dead branch and struck it against a tree trunk until it shattered. Wildly he picked up any other branches he could find and smashed them, hurling the broken bits into the river, not caring if he hurt any animals that might be hibernating nearby, for he felt so racked with pain that he no longer cared about anything else but the tight knot that seemed to pierce the very center of him. He was angry that Zach had died. Angry with him for going away and leaving him.

With an almighty force of venom he tore one tiny

rotting tree up by its roots and pushed it to the ground. Catching his breath for a moment, he stood up stiffly and looked up through the branches of the trees.

"I hate you, God. I hate you. You hear me? I hate you. I hate you. I hate you."

He stood yelling and screaming at the sky until he sank exhausted and sobbing on to the ground.

He had no idea how long he had lain there asleep. It felt like a year. Slowly he crawled to his feet, rigid and shivering. He hauled himself up the bank and stumbled through the woods.

Tom was waiting for him by the gate. He was about to give Will another five minutes before heading out towards Spooky Cott when he heard light footsteps coming along the road. He peered through the darkness and caught sight of a blond tuft of hair sticking out of Will's balaclava. His face was covered with earth and tearstains and his lips and eyelids were swollen and puffy.

"Come on in," he said, breaking the silence, and he put an arm round Will's shoulders as they walked along the pathway to the cottage. Just as he was opening the front door Will turned quickly.

"I'm sorry, Dad," he said. "I didn't think you'd be worried, like. I had to be on me own, see. I had to. I forgot about you. I didn't think. Sorry."

"You're home now," said Tom. "You look fair whacked. You'd best get washed and go to bed."

It wasn't until Will was asleep and Tom was lying in his own bed that he allowed the full impact of Will's words to sink in.

"He called me Dad," he whispered croakily into the darkness. "He called me Dad." And, although he felt overwhelmed with happiness, the tears ran silently down his face.

"Will!" cried Aunt Nance, opening the back door. She was speechless for a moment. "Come in! Come in!"

Will stepped into the kitchen.

"Mulled wine?" she began, and then stopped herself. Mulled wine was Zach's nickname for hot black-currant juice.

"Yeh. Please," answered Will, and he sat down and watched her making it.

"We've missed you coming round," she said, handing it to him and joining him at the table. She lit half a cigarette lovingly as if it was the last one left in Great Britain, took a deep drag and began coughing violently.

"I've left Zach's room as it was," she said, recovering.

Will nodded and blew into his drink.

"Dr. Little and myself, we didn't want to touch anything until you'd been, until you wanted us to. All right?"

Will looked up and smiled. "Yeh."

"Good," and she sat back, feeling relieved.

"Can I ride his bike?"

Mrs. Little wasn't quite sure if she had heard correctly. "What?" she queried. "What did you say?"

"Can I ride his bike?"

"Zach's?"

"Yes."

"If you want." She stared at him for a moment. "You'll probably have to lower the seat."

"Yeh. I know."

"I didn't know you could ride."

"I can't. Not yet. But I will."

"It's in the Anderson. It'll probably need oiling and pumping up."

"Has you got any oil?"

"Yes. And there's a pump attached to it."

She rose from the table and opened a door leading to a pantry. In a large box below the bottom shelf was a collection of tools and string. She bent over it, moving the bits and pieces from one side to another.

"Ah," she cried, waving a spanner in the air. "I'll lower the seat for you."

"No," said Will, rising to his feet. "I want to do it meself."

"Are you sure?"

"Yeh."

"I tell you what, you do the dirty work and I'll hold the bike steady for you."

He was about to refuse but changed his mind.

"Rightio," he said and then blushed, for that was one of Zach's expressions.

They dragged the bicycle out of the shelter and wiped the moistness off with an old dry rag, oiled it and reset the back wheel, as it was leaning heavily against the frame. The chain, which was loose, hung impotently against the pedals. Will took hold of it and placed it firmly and gently back in place. One of the inner tubes had a hole in it. With the help of Aunt Nance and Zach's puncture kit, he patched it up. He wiped the mudguards and scraped the rust away from around the handlebars. It was a strange feeling working on the bicycle, like touching a part of Zach.

He wheeled it round the cottage and through the long, overgrown grass. He was just struggling with the gate when Mrs. Little came running after him, carrying a small canvas shoulder bag of Zach's.

"I've made you a few jelly sandwiches," she gasped breathlessly, her thin chest heaving, "and there's a bottle of ginger beer inside."

He gazed at the bag uncertainly. "Thanks," he said at last.

Taking the bag, he put it over his head so that it hung loosely and securely across his back. Mrs. Little pulled at the gate to let him out and watched him wheel the bicycle down the lane.

As Will approached the cottages he could feel his ears burning. He turned left and avoided looking around lest anyone notice him. He was playing truant from school, a thing he had never done in his life. Unnoticed by him, Emilia Thorne was standing by the school window and she observed him, saying nothing.

Will continued until he was well out of sight of the cottages, and when he had found a reasonably smooth stretch of road he swung his leg over the saddle and sat still for a moment. He placed the toe of his boot on one of the pedals. Gritting his teeth and taking a deep breath, he pushed it down and wobbled forward. The bicycle curved and swooped into a nearby hedge. He picked himself up and climbed back onto the seat. Again the bicycle skidded over to one side, so that he grazed his knees on the rough road. Undaunted, he clambered back on again; and each time he swerved and fell, he only grew more determined.

In spite of the hoarfrost that covered the hedgerows and surrounding fields, learning to ride was hot work, and soon his overcoat was left dangling from the branch of a nearby tree.

At times he managed to keep the bicycle balanced for a few yards, only to swerve into another clump of brambles or icy nettles. He could hear his dad's words over and over again inside his head. "Takes yer time, everythin' 'as its own time." But whether it was because it was Zach's bicycle or because the colors were so intense, he felt frustrated and impatient. He wanted to learn now. When at last he managed to ride it for a reasonable distance, he rewarded himself with Aunt Nance's black-currant-jelly sandwiches and the ginger beer. Perspiration trickled down his face and into his shirt and jersey. Soon the crisp January air was freezing it into a cold clammy sweat. He hung the bag on a branch and pushed the bicycle forward. The break had been a good idea, for when he set off again it seemed easier, far less of a struggle.

Soon he began to grow confident. He put his coat back on, leaving it undone, and slung the bag over his head and shoulder. He understood now why Zach loved riding so much. There was a marvelous feeling of freedom once you'd got the hang of it.

As he rode, his coat flapping behind him, the crisp wind cooling his face, he suddenly felt that Zach was no longer beside him, he was inside him and very much alive. The numbness in his body had dissolved into exhilaration.

"Yippee. Callooh! Callay!" he yelled.

The bicycle shuddered over the small rough road, jangling his bones in such a way that he wanted to laugh.

"Wizzo," he cried, steering the bright machine with a new dexterity round a corner. He stopped abruptly. A steep hill had conquered his unused bicycle legs. He wheeled it up to the brow. It was wonderful to stand at the top with the bicycle leaning gently against his body. He looked down at the wide stretch of fields and woods and tiny icy streams. The sky was pale and cloudless. A small patch of sunlight was working its way through the woodland's dark branches. He breathed in deeply. "Zach isn't dead," he murmured. "Not really. Not the inside of Zach." And he gazed happily down at the fields. "No one can take memories away, and I can talk to him whenever I want."

He watched the sun gradually sinking into the roots of the trees.

"Now, Zach," he said out loud. "What shall I do now?"

"I should turn slowly and leisurely back," he replied to himself, "and pop in to see Annie Hartridge."

"What a good idea," said Will.

"And oh, I say," continued the imaginary Zach. "Jolly well done. Learning to ride my bike." And Will patted himself on the back.

He turned the bicycle and cycled back down the hill, controlling the fast decline with his brakes. It was even more pleasurable to ride after his little sojourn on the hill. He was more relaxed, more at peace with himself.

He was winding his way round a corner when he caught sight of Annie Hartridge's cottage. He wheeled the bicycle to her front door and leaned it against the wall.

"I'll knock," said "Zach," and he took hold of the brass knocker and banged it vigorously against the door.

Annie opened it, holding a telegram in her hands. She was crying.

"Oh hello, Will," she said, half laughing. "Come in, do come in." She closed the door behind him. "I've just had the most wonderful news. Mr. Hartridge is alive. He's in a prisoner-of-war camp in Germany. We can write to each other and I can send him Red Cross parcels, food parcels. Oh Will!" she cried. "I'm so happy. I can't believe it. I want to write to him right now."

She looked at Will's grubby face and followed his body down to his feet.

"What have you been doing? You're covered with grazes and scratches."

"I've been learning to ride Zach's bike," he said absently. Annie was speechless for a moment.

"Did you manage to stay on it?" she said at last.

"Eventually," he answered, plunging his hands into his shorts pocket and leaning on one leg.

"Why, you . . ." but she stopped. She was about to say that he looked and sounded a little like Zach. He had an extrovert air about him that was unusual in Will.

During the weeks that followed the bicycle-riding incident everyone noticed a dramatic change in Will, especially Emilia Thorne. She had decided to do her own version of Peter Pan. She cast Will to play Peter Pan, but to her surprise he stood up in the hall and in front of everyone said, "I'd like to play Captain Hook. May I?"

Miss Thorne had been a little taken aback. Captain Hook was a comic, flamboyant role.

"Let's try you out," she said, after recovering her breath.

Will surprised her and everyone in rehearsals. Unbeknownst to the others, while working on his lines up in his room he would place a cushion in front of himself and say, "Zach, how do you think I should say this line?" or "How do you think Hook's feelin' in this bit, when the crocodile appears for the third time?"

Then he would sit on the cushion and not only answer his questions as Zach but even deliver the lines as him.

The play was a great success. Will had people laughing helplessly at his angry Hook outbursts of temper and his cowardly flights from the crocodile. It was so obvious that the audience loved Will that when several of the children pushed him forward to take a separate bow, the hall erupted into cheers.

Tom was terribly proud of him, but then he had been for a long time. He met him outside the tiny back door which led to the communal dressing room behind the stage, and they walked home chatting in animated tones all the way back to their graveyard cottage.

As Will lay back in his bed that night he felt a little sad, in spite of all the applause. He was sad that Zach hadn't been there to share it. He realized now that the Zach he had been talking to for the last weeks was a person created from his own imagination and a handful of memories. It was just that the Zach part of himself, the outgoing, cheeky part of himself, had been buried inside him, and it was his friendship with Zach that had brought those qualities to the surface.

He snuggled down deep into the blankets and was just about to fall asleep when he gave a sudden start.

I'm not half a person anymore, he thought. I'm a whole one. I *can* live without Zach even though I still miss him.

He turned over and listened to the wind howling through the graveyard. He was warm and happy. He sighed. It was good to be alive.

Postscript

—— 🌿 🌿 ——

Squatting down with a trowel in his hand, Will surveyed what was now the garden. Since the Dig for Victory campaign, he and Tom had pulled up all the flowers and had been planting vegetables in every available space. It was a shame really. The flowers had looked so colorful. All that remained now were neat brown rows with tufts of greenery sticking out of them.

He pushed the sleeves of his jersey up. He was wearing Zach's old red one with the hundred darns. Sticking the trowel firmly into the earth, he began to dig a small trench. As he loosened the earth, several startled worms slithered away. He watched their gleaming bodies heading for the cabbage patch.

Will sat back on his heels and took a handful of seeds from a paper bag. Picking them tenderly one by one, he placed them in the trench. He was so absorbed in his task that he was oblivious to footsteps approaching the gate. He heard it clanging as it bounced to a close and looked up. It was Carrie. She was running down the pathway, her face flushed.

"Did you get them?" she panted.

He nodded. "They's in my room. You want them now?"

She glanced down at his earth-stained hands. "I could go and get them myself. You going to be long with that?"

"Just got two more rows. Then I'm finished."

"Can we go down the river?"

Will looked surprised. "Ent you got no more chores?"

She shook her head and grinned. "I climbed out the window. It was the only way. As soon as I finish one job she finds me another one. If she sees me with so much as my fingers on a book she jes' gets hoppin' mad."

"I thought she was better now."

"She is, but she still thinks readin' is being idle."

She squatted down beside him and stared intently into his eyes.

"If I don't read a book soon I think I'll explode."

Will laughed. "Well, don't do it over me plantin'."

"Have you another trowel? I could give you a hand, then we could clear off quick. If she finds me here I'll have to go back home."

"No, I don't. Look, you go up to my room. If she comes round she'll see I'm on me own. We can go up to the river on the tandem. I'll lower the other seat."

Carrie's eyes sparkled. "Wizard!" and she sprang to her feet and made towards the cottage. "Oh," she cried despondently, swinging round. "How can I ride, wearing this?" and she tugged at the pale green woolen dress she was wearing. "Won't the crossbar make it go up?"

Will frowned for an instant and then hit on an idea.

"You can wear a pair of my shorts!"

Carrie looked doubtful. Will was a head smaller than her.

"Or Zach's, they'd fit you."

"I daren't," she said, feeling quite excited at the prospect. She'd been asking her mother for ages if she could wear shorts, but had been told that she'd turn into a boy if she did and no man would want to marry her. Her father had said it was all right by him, but he had already let her have her own way about the high school and didn't want to cause any more friction.

"Why not?" said Will.

"You don't think I'll turn into a boy if I wear them?"

Will looked up at her. Her hair stuck out in little wispy curls round her forehead and ears. Two pale-green oval eyes stared down at him above permanently freckled cheeks.

"Carrie, you don't look anythin' like a boy and who cares if you do?"

"Yes. Anyway," she said, suddenly feeling appalled at the thought, "I don't want to get married. Imagine having to do housework all the time, every day. Yuk!"And with that she turned and ran into the cottage.

Will found her sprawled across his bed engrossed in a book. She jumped, raised her eyes guiltily and slammed the covers automatically to a close. She laughed.

"I thought you were Mum!"

Will strode across to a box in the corner where several of Zach's old clothes were folded neatly inside. He lifted up a pair of red corduroy shorts with patches on the seat and found a green pair underneath that were less threadbare.

"Catch," he said, throwing them at her and flinging a pair of braces onto the bed.

"I'll have to wear a shirt," she added, joining him at the box. She found a white baggy cotton one and pulled it out.

"You better wear this, too," and he picked up Zach's Joseph jersey.

"Oh, I couldn't."

"Why not?"

"Well, it's special, isn't it?"

"Zach would be jolly pleased if you wore it. You know he would."

She nodded and felt tears coming to her eyes. Will looked concerned.

"It's all right," she said hastily. "I'm not going to blubber." She picked up the shorts and put them on. "They fit almost perfect." She tugged at the waist. "They're a bit baggy here, but the braces'll keep them up." She unbuttoned her dress, stepped out of it and slipped her petticoat off over her head. Will buttoned the braces onto the shorts. He was surprised to see two tiny swollen lumps protruding gently outwards from underneath her undershirt. He wanted to reach out and touch her arms but stepped back quickly.

"There," he said, and he found himself laughing excitedly for no reason whatever.

Carrie pulled the shirt over her head and tucked it into the shorts, raising the braces up over her shoulders. Lifting up her arms and legs, she cavorted around the room.

"They feel so comfortable," she said, bouncing on the end of the bed.

Will produced four books from out of his haversack.

"That's where they were!" she cried.

"I couldn't get *We Didn't Mean to Go to Sea*, but I've got it reserved for you. So I got you this one instead."

She took it from his hands.

"*At the Back of the North Wind* by George MacDonald. Never heard of it." She flicked over the pages and began reading chapter one. "It looks all right. You got the others, did you?"

"Yeh. Here," he replied, handing them to her. "*A Little Princess, David Copperfield* and *Black Beauty*."

"Wizzo!"

"Don't start readin' them now or we'll never get down to the river."

Carrie looked disappointed.

"Well, bring one and I'll take my sketch pad." He emptied the haversack and shoved the pad and a piece of tarpaulin in. Carrie was chewing over which book to take. She chose *At the Back of the North Wind.* She put Zach's Joseph jersey on and Will slung the haversack onto his back.

"I'll go down first. See if the coast is clear," he whispered.

Carrie felt a sudden urge to giggle. She placed her hand firmly over her mouth and crouched over the open trapdoor, while Will slipped quickly down the steps and out the back door. He reappeared soon after.

"Drat it!" he murmured. "I'll need you to hold the bike steady while I lower the seat."

Carrie crept down and followed him out into the back garden. She held the tandem firmly while Will twiddled away with the spanner. She began to grow anxious and her forehead felt hot. It would be rotten if her mother caught her now.

"There," he said, surveying the seat. He put the spanner in the saddlebag. "Now let's wheel her."

They pushed the tandem out through the back gate and turned right twice so that they were beside the graveyard wall. Will grinned back at Carrie, who was by the rear seat. He motioned her to the ground. Crouching down, they maneuvered themselves unseen to any possible eyes towards the open road. He beckoned her up.

"Get on quick," he urged.

"If anyone sees me now," she giggled, "it'll be all

over the village in no time," and she flung her leg over the bar and sat down, her feet comfortably resting on the pedals. Will followed suit and pushed off.

They cycled on, seeing no one, until they reached Annie Hartridge's cottage. She was in the front garden with the baby. She stared at Carrie in amazement and they left her openmouthed as they sped, shrieking with laughter, up the road.

They stopped by a hedge near the woods and pushed the bike through a gap and down a small slope.

"We can leave it here," said Will, leaning it up against a large oak. "No one'll see it."

They ran silently and swiftly in and out through the trees, hiding behind them in case anyone else was in the woods. When they finally reached the river they burst into hysterical laughter.

"You should have seen her face," spluttered Carrie.

Will immediately held his haversack as if it was a baby and did an imitation of Annie Hartridge watching them cycle by. Carrie clutched at her stomach and laughed helplessly.

"No, stop it!" she cried. "I'll wet my pants if you don't."

"You mean Zach's pants," he added.

"Please, please . . ." she begged, and she crossed her legs and tried to think of disasters in an effort to control herself. Will collapsed onto the ground and leaned against a tree. He stared across at the river, panting. Carrie calmed down and joined him.

"Here," he said, pulling the raggedy tarpaulin from his haversack, "you sit on this." He spread it out at the foot of the tree.

"Where are you going?" she asked when Will left her sitting on it.

"Only over here. I'm going to draw you."

She picked up her book and propped it up open on her bent knees. Raising her eyes for a moment, she gazed at the bubbling spring river and glanced at Will. He was sitting cross-legged on his haversack several yards away, his sketch pad already open. He looked up and smiled.

"Don't it make you feel strange, me wearing Zach's clothes?"

He shook his head. "I'm wearing one of his jerseys."

"Yes, I know, but . . ." Her voice drifted away. "I've never worn a dead person's clothes before. I should feel horrid, shouldn't I? But I don't. I feel good." She sighed and let her body sink into the tree trunk. "I wish the holidays could be like this all the time," she murmured. "Mum's been so horrid."

"Is she the same with Ginnie?"

"Ginnie likes housework! She doesn't complain. She says the more she learns now, the better wife she'll be when she's older. Anyway, Mum gives me extra to make up for the term. She says learnin' and doing homework isn't work. And she says I'm getting stuck up. Do you think I am?"

"No."

She stared back at the river. Will put down his sketch pad.

"Are you still unhappy at the high?"

"It's gettin' better now. I came fifth in the end-of-term tests."

"I know. You told me."

"Did I?"

He nodded.

"It's jes' that it's important. They were really shocked. They think because I talk countrified I must be stupid.

Did I tell you, one of the girls came up and started talking to me real friendly, like, on the last day of term."

"No."

"Yes. She said I weren't to take any notice of the other girls. That I was a lot cleverer than most of them."

Will stared at her.

"What's the matter?"

"You talk different now."

Carrie looked crestfallen.

"You sound a bit like Zach."

Her face brightened. "That's all right, then."

"Are you going to read your book? I want to draw."

She nodded and happily sank herself into chapter one.

Will began sketching her face. The he sketched her body, her foot, her hands holding the book, her knee; and as he did so he was filled with an intense joy. Carrie was lost in a *North Wind* world, eagerly devouring each page. Neither of them noticed the time passing until they discovered that they were screwing their eyes up in order to see.

"Crumbs," said Carrie, startled. "I'd better get home."

Will packed up the haversack and they ran through the woods and up the slope towards the tandem. They squeezed it through the hedge and clambered back onto it. The blackouts were already up on Annie Hartridge's windows. They sped past and dismounted at the graveyard wall. Crawling swiftly beside it, they turned the corner and ran with the bike along the road and through the gate. Will opened the back door and peered in.

"Run," he whispered urgently to Carrie, and he beckoned her in and cautiously closed the door behind them. He heard Sammy barking in the living room.

"Drat!" he murmured.

Carrie scrambled up the steps and flung herself through the open trapdoor, Will following close behind.

He found her fumbling in the half light for her dress. She tore off Zach's clothes and danced around in her undershirt and pants, too absorbed in getting into her petticoat and dress to feel embarrassed. Will felt surprised that he wasn't embarrassed either. They climbed down the ladder and tiptoed quickly out through the back door into the garden.

"Made it," she said.

"You forgot the other books," said Will, noticing that she still had only the one she was reading.

"I'll sneak the others in one by one. I'll stuff this one down my knickers in case I'm caught. I don't know when I'll see you next. I'll probably be kept in for a week now," she added grimly. "Still," she said, smiling, "it was worth it."

Will walked with her as far as Dobbs's field. They stood quietly for a moment and drank in the evening.

"Looks like it's going to be a good spring," said Carrie, breaking the silence, and she pointed to a cluster of small swollen buds on the branches of a nearby tree hanging silhouetted against the sky.

"Do you think," said Will, gazing over the wall at the oak tree, "do you think you can die of happiness?"

Carrie looked at him, puzzled.

"It's jes' that I feel as if I'm going to burst, and that if I did, there'd be bits of me all over this field."

She laughed, and after they had parted at the gate by the arched lane Will returned to the cottage. He pumped water into a large tin jug and carried it past the long, deserted Anderson and through the back door into the hallway. As he hung his cap up he became conscious that his peg felt lower than usual.

"I used to stretch up to that," he muttered to himself.

He picked up the jug of water and carried it into the living room. Sammy leaped around his ankles, vying for attention. Will put the jug on the floor and squatted down to stroke him.

"How strange," he thought out loud, looking at Sammy's face, "to think that I was once terrified of you."

Tom was sitting in the armchair looking at the wireless program in the newspaper. The kettle was steaming on the stove. Will picked it up with a cloth and poured a little into a teapot. After he had swirled it around to warm up the pot, he poured it away and added some tea and more water. He allowed it to stew for a while before pouring it into two cups. Sammy flopped down by the pouffe and Will plonked himself down beside him.

"Anythin' good on?"

Tom folded up the paper.

"Not really. It's all music for the Forces." And he picked up his pipe from the little table and began stuffing it with tobacco.

As with the sudden discovery of the lowness of his peg, Will noticed now how old and vulnerable Tom looked. It unnerved him at first, for he had always thought of him as being strong. He watched him puffing away at his pipe, poking the newly lit tobacco down with the end of a match.

Will swallowed a few mouthfuls of tea and put some fresh coke on the stove fire. As he observed it tumbling and falling between the wood and hot coke, it occurred to him that strength was quite different from toughness, and that being vulnerable wasn't the same as being weak.

He looked up at Tom and leaned forward in his direction.

"Dad," he ventured.

"Yes," answered Tom, putting down his library book. "What is it?"

"Dad," repeated Will, in a surprised tone, "I'm growing!"